The Ends

The Ends

TOM SHAKESPEARE

Farrago

First published in 2025 by Farrago, an imprint of Duckworth Books Ltd
1 Golden Court, Richmond, TW9 1EU, United Kingdom

www.farragobooks.com

Copyright © Tom Shakespeare, 2025

The right of Tom Shakespeare to be identified as the author
of this Work has been asserted by him in accordance
with the Copyright, Designs & Patents Act 1988.

All rights reserved. No part of this publication may be reproduced,
stored in a retrieval system, or transmitted, in any form or by
any means electronic, mechanical, photocopying, recording or
otherwise, without the prior permission of the publisher.

This book is a work of fiction. Names, characters, businesses,
organizations, places and events other than those clearly in the
public domain, are either the product of the author's imagination
or are used fictitiously. Any resemblance to actual persons,
living or dead, events or locales is entirely coincidental.

A catalogue record for this book is available from the British Library

Printed and bound in Great Britain by Clays Ltd, Elcograf S.p.A.

The authorised representative in the EEA is Easy Access
System Europe, Mustamäe tee 50, 10621 Tallinn, Estonia.

Paperback ISBN: 9781788425124
eISBN: 9781788425131

To Ruby, Sylvie, Sadie and Isla, who are never at sea.

'When beholding the tranquil beauty and brilliancy of the ocean's skin, one forgets the tiger heart that pants beneath it.'

Herman Melville

Dramatis personae

Fred Twistleton: a lawyer and author; also, a wheelchair user. Now co-CEO of Big Green Campaigning Machine, a London-based NGO; partner of Nel.

Nel Nichols: an ecologist, co-CEO of The Big Green Campaigning Machine; partner of Fred.

Hugh Appleton: a carpenter, schoolfriend of Fred; partner of Polly.

Polly Appleton: a social worker, college friend of Fred; partner of Hugh.

Bella Patterson: a retired nurse, maternal aunt of Fred; partner of Donna.

Donna Mitchell: a retired psychiatrist; partner of Bella.

Marvin G. Ridley: an American tourist.

Fleur Kidist Kristiansen: chief scientist aboard MV *Queen Ingegerd*.

Cyril Earther: ecologist, campaigner, journalist, author, yogi.

Lubna Khan: dancer, campaigner.

Heather Crisp: war crisis reporter, world editor on World News cable TV channel.

Paul Toal: UK police officer.

Walter Andersson: captain of MV *Queen Ingegerd*.

Helga Halvorsen: sailor aboard MV *Queen Ingegerd*.

Prologue

It was a bright night in April, somewhere off the coast of Norway. Polly couldn't sleep in the tiny cabin. Her head was still full of casework conundrums, and she got out of bed in the early hours. It was not easy to switch off from social work, even when you went on holiday. Some people had more than their fair share of problems, and it felt like you were society's safety net.

Polly swung her legs over the side of the bunk bed, let herself down to the floor, put on her socks, went for a wee, added trousers over the top of her pyjamas, put on a thermal vest and, on second thoughts, a thick sweater. As a final touch, she grabbed her waterproof coat and woolly hat, and thankfully remembered the key card before quietly leaving the bedroom. Polly Appleton could bustle for England. The engine throbbed on through the night, like the snores of an overindulged spaniel. Or was that her husband Hugh, who still seemed to be sleeping soundly – and noisily – on his bottom bunk? How did he manage to have a life with nothing to be anxious about?

Scorning the lift, Polly ran up the stairs to the door which led to the observation deck. Quietly, she opened it, and went outside, closing it with a reassuring clunk behind her. But it wasn't windy, and because it was April, it was getting to be grey rather than pitch-black in the early hours. The endless polar night was giving way to the endless polar daylight. Soon, the snow and ice would be melting across the Arctic. The weather was crisply cold, calm and clear, and the winter storms were almost forgotten. Polly felt rather hot in her carefully layered clothes.

To the starboard side of the ship, she could make out the lights of Norway, and its agreeably rugged coast. Offshore, they had passed many little rocky islands with tiny houses, each one with its boat moored. It was extraordinarily romantic, she thought, although she shivered at the thought of how isolated you could be. But that was how they preferred it around here, each in their *hytte*, as she had learned to call them, with their boat for escape, or else fishing.

To port, there was the ocean, stretching towards Iceland, and eventually Greenland. Weren't the Faeroes somewhere on the way? To the North, there was only the Pole, with Svalbard en route. The occasional bird still tracked the ship, but otherwise they were all alone, ignoring the few isolated oil rigs. Seeing a bird, Polly thought of her husband, imagined how excited he might be, and snapped a photograph on her phone. It was definitely not a gull, and it was flapping huge wings.

Maybe it was an albatross? Polly was still woefully ignorant about birds, but Hugh, always happy to give a lecture at a moment's notice, had no hesitation in teaching her what she was looking at, and what she was looking for. It was all about the jizz, apparently, which sounded rude, but was just that intuitive feel in the mind of the birder about what the bird could be. Had he been there, Hugh would no doubt have pointed out that the Arctic Ocean was the only ocean which contained no albatross. He might also have said that if it was an albatross, its wings would not be flapping. Additionally, he might have been unable to resist pointing out that an albatross weighed as much as a small dog, a fact which presumably had escaped the poet Coleridge when he'd hung one around the Ancient Mariner's neck.

The bird at which Polly was casting aspersions was a sea eagle. As she watched, it performed its star turn by plunging into the Arctic waters to catch a fish, like an urban driver pouncing on a vacant parking space. Polly shivered. The sea looked very cold.

Her daughter Freya, now nearly ten, had instructed her mother never to walk widdershins (something Polly blamed on the excess of storytellers in North London), so Polly carefully walked clockwise around the observation deck another ten times. She was not a step-counter; she felt steps were things you took, not did. She was now getting bored as well as sleepy. She felt that gazing at different patches of sea was an acquired taste, unless you were a bird, or possibly a fish. Didn't adolescent orcas find the sea rather boring, which was why they attacked yachts? Thankfully, this was not her problem. Her bunk below deck was feeling like an increasingly alluring prospect. By now, she considered, she was probably tired enough to fall asleep. Polly waved at a couple of passengers who were also wandering about – most likely North Americans, on a different time zone, rather than social workers – and started down the stairs.

When she had descended as far as their deck, she opened the door onto the corridor. Their cabin was near the lift. In the low light, Polly was about to use her card to open the door. But suddenly, she stopped and squinted down the corridor, in the gloom. Thinking she must be seeing things, she rubbed her eyes and looked again. What on earth was that? Whatever it was, it saw her staring, turned tail and fled. Pulse racing, hardly believing her eyes, Polly chased after it, shocked into action. When she got to the end of the corridor, where you had to turn right and right again, there was no sign of it. She looked both ways. Definitely not in sight. Had it gone into one of the cabins? It seemed incredible that it could have.

Maybe she was hallucinating? Was she asleep right now? It felt like a particularly vivid dream. She certainly needed her sleep, insomnia fighting its usual battle with exhaustion. She walked slowly back to their cabin, replaying what she had seen. Would she have forgotten what had happened by morning? Should she wake Hugh? She decided it could wait. Nothing could be done about it now. Her husband would never believe her when she told him. But she did not imagine stuff. Well, except for the worst. But that was a social-work thing.

Polly wrote on a piece of paper 'polar bear': she was 95 per cent certain she had seen it, and 100 per cent certain of what it was. That may sound terrifyingly impossible, she thought, but the numbers were on her side. Actual and live? She didn't know and couldn't think. Those things were savage. If live, definitely dangerous. Look what they did to the poor seals. Either way, a mystery. On the ship. On their deck. She should do something about it. But polar bears surely didn't need social workers. Therefore, not her problem. Safely back in her bunk bed, she fell asleep, dreaming of a world full of Glacier Mints and albatrosses.

Chapter 1

The previous December, London

The workers at The Big Green Campaigning Machine, the environmental pressure group, had downed tools. They weren't going on strike: Fred Twistleton and Nel Nichols were joint CEOs and, so far, the crew they led had been happily busy. Of course, no one had any actual *tools*, such as hammers and saws and other things that might be used for carpentry or metal work. They all lived in the brave new world of emails, websites and online meetings. Fred's friend Hugh would have called it skeuomorphism: using out-of-date language even when you were using new technologies.

The venture was somewhat new for Fred, who had started out as a solicitor in Norwich. He had met Nel – his partner both in business and in life – in Suffolk, where she was working for a local landowner as his chief pig-wrangler and resident scientist, and they had realised they had gone to the same college. The bond they formed led to a venture which had taken them to London; the scientific facts were plain and urgent. Fred's legal expertise and Nel's biologist credentials had appealed to an old university friend, who wanted to plough some of his hedge-fund wealth into Green causes. Which is why, a couple of years on from Fred's fortieth birthday, they found themselves as joint CEOs of an environmental pressure group, with Nel taking up the post of chief scientific officer, thanks to her expertise in zoology and ethology. Fred was putting his legal training to good work as chief legal officer, not that writing had been entirely put behind him. Fred had just published his first novel, which had apparently suggested even better things to come, and he still wanted to write fiction, but he knew he wouldn't make more than pocket money from that for a while, if ever. It would help if he could remember how he'd managed to be funny first time round, he thought. Write what you know, everyone said. Maybe there were jokes to be had out of rehabilitation?

The staff had tidied their messy office after lunch, because surely the fight for an unpolluted environment begins at home (or at least in the office close to home)? Wastepaper and takeaway containers had all been placed in the recycling. Washable reusable coffee cups had been dutifully cleaned. The dozen staff were gathering in the office kitchen for Friday drinks: the tradition that had been begun by Fred and Nel to give thanks to everyone, promote employee morale and start the weekend a bit early. This Friday in December, they had brought out half a case of sparkling white, because it was Christmas. Nel had already had her lift, by discovering the wine was biodynamic.

The week had not been easy. The land was stuffed with more enemies than a new development with flats: local authorities, water companies, developers, polluters. Now the staff needed reasons to be cheerful. Even the most right-on of campaigners needed to turn off occasionally. Consequently, the washing-up had been done, bottles had been noisily uncorked, and toasts made to the successes of recent battles and the downfall of all those enemies.

'So, where are you going for your jollies next year?' asked Damien, the Scouser who kept their technology going.

'Svalbard,' said Nel.

'Where?' asked Jo, one of the scientists. 'Is that in the Balkans?'

'It's the new name for Spitsbergen,' offered Fred helpfully. 'Which literally means "pointy mountains",' he added. 'In Norwegian.'

'Still a bit lost,' admitted Abigail, the community organiser they had recently recruited. 'Aren't all mountains pointy? Anyway, my geography's crap beyond Calais.'

'It's in the far North of Norway,' said Nel. 'Beyond the Arctic Circle. Halfway to the North Pole.'

Abigail shivered.

'Think of a tropical cruise,' suggested Fred. 'And then turn the thermostat way down.'

'Chilled, but not in a good way? Is this Nel's idea?' asked Damien, smiling at his bosses.

'Apparently, it has been known to get above 70°C in July, thanks to the climate emergency. Average of -25°C in the winter,' said Fred. 'Probably, in April it will be only a bit below freezing. Barely worse than the Lakes.'

'Only rather more spectacular,' said Nel. 'A perfect place to spend my fortieth birthday. Barely any humans. Nothing but the occasional polar bear, walrus or whale…'

'And of course birds,' added Fred, thinking of his friend Hugh, who was joining them on the trip and was a birdwatching enthusiast.

'What's the difference between Spitsbergen and Svalbard?' asked Nandini, who did their media relations. 'And are there really armoured polar bears?'

'The archipelago is called Svalbard, and Spitsbergen is the largest island,' said Nel. 'Svalbard means "cold shore", which is an understatement. The polar bears are endangered not armoured, sadly. You can't believe all you read in Philip Pullman!'

'Sounds like the ends of the earth!' said Damien. 'And there am I, going to Broadstairs to paddle with the bairns.'

'*Ultima Thule*,' said Joan, who was very much a literary type.

'What does that actually mean?' asked Abigail, who wasn't.

'I think it refers to the Northernmost inhabited island,' said Jo.

'Which is quite literally where we're going,' said Fred. 'For nine whole days.'

'It is very much the ends of the earth,' said Nel. 'We'll see glaciers that might not be there when your grandkids become adults, Damien. Seven national parks and twenty-three nature reserves. There's going to be a lot of science.' She felt like a tour guide.

'I'd rather see New York. A nine-day cruise could get you there and back,' said Sally. She was still envious that Fred had gone to the last UN General Assembly in New York. He'd combined it with a holiday and gone across by liner.

His excuse was that his friends would no longer talk to him if he flew.

'But where's the science in that?' asked Nel.

'Last chance to see, and all that,' said Fred. 'Or the first chance, when it comes to the Northwest Passage. Worth paying extra for.'

'Possibly the end of the Earth, as far as the human species goes…' added Nel. She didn't elaborate, but everyone knew what she meant. The co-workers had gone on outings to the local cinema to see every available apocalyptic movie, from *The Day After Tomorrow* to *Don't Look Up* and, most recently, *Breathe.* Seeing the worst that could happen somehow made their daily struggles seem more important and relevant. Nevertheless, Nel mentioning the end of the Earth somewhat put a dampener on the party. It's hard to see the cheery side of mass-extinction events, although Hollywood has done its best. In this office they enjoyed gallows humour, but they preferred battles they could win. Off-screen, the jury was out as to whether the climate was still a winnable catastrophe.

'Certainly, last chance to see your thirties,' said Sally, gloomily, downing her drink. It was bad enough to think of your own looming fourth decade, without thinking about the coming apocalypse as well. It was like the heat death of the universe: even though she'd not be there when it happened, it was still a cause of existential despair.

'We'll raise a glass to you,' said Damien, relieved to have got back onto solid ground.

'And we won't let you escape a party when you return,' said Sally.

'Damn!' said Nel. 'There was I, hoping I had got away with it.'

The co-workers broke into alcohol-fuelled chatter.

'Come on!' said Fred to Nel, slinging his bag across the back of his wheelchair. 'If we're going to be on time for supper with Hugh and Polly, we'd better leave now.'

The office was behind King's Cross, and their friends lived in Hackney. Their rendezvous was at a Peruvian eatery in Islington that their friend Alberto had spoken highly of.

'What about the mess?' said Nel.

'We'll clear it all up,' said Damien, hearing her. 'As long as we can count it as overtime?'

Everyone laughed. It was a workplace that was as friendly as it was dedicated. The world might be a bin-fire, but they were determined to enjoy it while it lasted.

Chapter 2

Kennington, the year before the cruise

The Arctic cruise had neither been an obvious option, nor the preferred choice. Following his own memorable fortieth birthday at Threepwood Hall, Fred had wanted to organise a big celebration for his partner, Nel, when it was her turn.

'Time for us to make a fuss of you!' he'd said.

'Certainly not,' she'd replied. 'The very word "fuss" sends a shiver down my spine.'

'A celebration dinner?'

'Why would you celebrate turning forty?'

'What about a quiet dinner for a few friends somewhere special?' said Fred.

'There you go again, that word "special",' said Nel. 'As you yourself have pointed out more than once, "special" normally means "rubbish".'

'Well, we've got to do something,' said her partner, increasingly desperate. 'It's a memorable birthday. Surely you can't just ignore it. Don't you want to mark it properly?'

'Look, I've got a pension now, and we've got a mortgage,' said Nel. 'Isn't that quite memorable enough? I don't need any more evidence that I'm middle-aged, let alone proper.'

'There must be something you've always wanted to do,' said Fred, who wasn't about to give up that easily. 'See the Pyramids or the Taj Mahal, or climb Machu Picchu? Or maybe, as you're a naturalist, you would prefer the rainforests of Costa Rica or the foothills of the Himalayas, or snorkelling the Great Barrier Reef?'

'I don't think all of those options are wheelchair-accessible and I don't want to go solo,' said Nel. 'Although, it's true, I would like to see the Reef before the warming ocean kills all the coral.'

'Then why don't we take the trip of a lifetime to Australia? I am sure I could snorkel. All the physios who worked with me during rehab seem to have emigrated to Sydney. I can't think why...'

'The climate?' said Nel

'That and the gay scene,' said Fred.

'But it would involve a long-haul flight – exactly what I've pledged not to do,' said Nel.

Fred could see her point. In their vocal campaigns against human-caused climate change, a public commitment not to take flights had been de rigueur. It would be hypocritical to go back on your word. Just because most public figures had all the consistency of pebbledash didn't mean you couldn't do better yourself. Though, he would be sad never to see his Antipodean friends again. Maybe the COP would be there one year, he thought, and that might be a reasonable excuse. Or he could go by merchant ship, if he ever had a couple of months to spare. Perhaps he could write another book. A long one, this time.

'Blue is more my colour than red,' said Nel. 'Heat always brings me out in a rash. I'd rather go somewhere cold.'

'That still leaves a lot of options,' said Fred. 'Antarctica, for example?'

'Fond though I am of penguins—'

'They mate for life, apparently.'

'As I was saying, much as I like penguins, I think it is just too far. It comes under the "no long flights" rule.'

'Iceland?'

'Possibly... Although, Björk's not my cup of tea. And doesn't Yoko Ono hang out there?'

'What about the Arctic? That's not too far, and I think you're unlikely to encounter pop stars.'

'Well...' began Nel. 'I wouldn't put it past them, and there's barely any of it left...'

'Then better to go now,' said Fred. 'Before it's all gone! Or Bono turns up.'

'It's not long-haul, if we were to fly to Oslo or Bergen, or even Newfoundland,' mused Nel.

'Northern Lights, midnight sun... icebergs...' said Fred. 'Lots of options.'

'True. And reindeer...'

'With red noses... And polar bears...' said Fred, delightedly. 'Leave it to me, I'll do some research.'

'Find us something we can afford,' said Nel. 'We have so many outgoings these days, with the effort of keeping the start-up going. I never realised how much more expensive London would be than Norfolk!'

'Blame the cost-of-living crisis,' said Fred, who felt he had done his bit by shopping in Lidl rather than Waitrose. 'But the sort of trip you'd prefer doesn't come cheap.'

Nel waved an energy bill that had been sitting on the kitchen table. They had begun wearing sweaters over their pyjamas and sharing bathwater.

'I get it,' said Fred. 'A birthday on a budget. No pushing the boat out.'

'No posh dinners,' said Nel. 'No fancy-dress contests. And no toasts.'

'We do have to have at least one toast,' said Fred. 'Please let me cheer you on?'

'I suppose four decades is a milestone,' she admitted.

'It's either this, or marriage, or kids,' teased Fred, half-seriously.

'Milestone, not millstone! I've already told you I'm allergic to marriage,' said Nel. 'Even to you,' she added, as he winced, not for the first time.

'But you're great with kids?' he said hopefully.

'Other people's,' she said firmly. 'The last thing the planet needs is more humans. Our species is prolifically profligate,' she said carefully. It was quite a tongue-twister but it would make a great soundbite.

'I quite fancy making our own little human,' said Fred wistfully. 'We've now had loads of practice—'

'The good thing about going away is that we're likely to be on our own,' said Nel, quickly changing the subject. 'Really, the last thing I want is to be the centre of attention.'

'A few friends?'

'One or two,' said Nel. 'No more! I know you and your ideas.'

'Just a couple of friends,' promised Fred. 'More of a gathering than a party. Surely Hugh and Polly have to be there?'

'No question,' said Nel, who felt they were almost part of the family. Certainly, all the family she needed.

With that, the conversation ended. Fred, glad to have won two concessions, felt positively gruntled. He was concerned that Nel might have become a workaholic. She had no problem thinking globally, but when it came to acting locally, she was like a gerbil on a treadmill. Or was it a hamster? He knew one of them was chasing its tail. Which Nel certainly was. She needed to take a break. That meant taking a holiday. Which was where he came in. Plus, of course, a small celebratory gathering... All of which was worth blowing some savings on.

Fred's dreams that night were filled with delicious icebergs. He had heard that there had been icebergs bigger than Belgium. But how did they set about measuring icebergs? He'd read that nine-tenths were below the waterline, but how did they know? Something to do with specific gravity of fresh as opposed to salt water? It was certainly a relief for the world of symbolism...

Chapter 3

Kennington, April, the day of the cruise

Fred packed chaotically, throwing things onto the spare bed as if he wanted to get rid of them. Medications, guidebook, coat, passport, boots, catheters, sweater, waterproof trousers, washbag. Faced with a worrying luggage Cheviot, he thought for a moment about wearing everything to save carrying it, but then realised that would make him too warm on the British leg of the journey. At the last minute, he remembered the Norwegian prices and added a bottle of whisky, along with a bottle of fizz that he thought would be perfect to toast Nel's birthday. Now the bag clinked as well as being rather heavy. No matter: the heavy clinking was only temporary, and he could strap it all onto his wheelchair.

Fred was not an anxious person, but for a while now something had been worrying him, even waking him in the early hours. The worst thing was that he didn't know what it was. He had begun to feel as if he was on his marks, waiting for the starting pistol to be fired, but nobody else was ready for the race. Given that he couldn't even walk, this was a concern.

It was only when he got to Fenchurch Street station that he identified what the problem might be. He had never been there before, except on a Monopoly board. He tried to forget those early humiliations. He had never been a good capitalist, perhaps because his elder brother Roddy had always been the banker and rather pedantic about the rules. Roddy had learned at an early age the enjoyment that could be derived from ordering other people about. Inevitably, he had become a politician in later life. Fred's playing piece had always been the dog, because that's what he'd always wanted.

Fred had arrived early, as advised, to ensure that the assistance people were ready with the ramp for the train. As he waited with the woman with the ramp, queries were flung at her, no doubt because she was wearing the railway uniform. Irritated, he turned away, both to signal that he was above such things, and also to look about him anxiously for Nel. She had yet again been delayed by a work emergency, but then she was as customarily late as he was early. Last year, they had missed their train to Paris for a Valentine's Day celebration. It had been his last-minute treat; she had forgotten Valentine's Day completely. Of course. He half-worried that she wouldn't come at all, so unenthusiastic had she been about her birthday celebration. Or perhaps she had got carried away at work and forgotten.

Fred became aware of a baby staring at him, as he waited on the platform. Like him, the infant had a woolly hat and was carried along on four wheels. They had a lot in common, although he thought it unlikely that the baby had a bottle of whisky about their person. He winked at the child, who continued to stare at him.

'Say hello,' said the baby's mummy.

'Hello,' said Fred obediently.

'Not you!' The mum giggled.

'Sorry,' said Fred, also laughing.

The baby broke into a smile. He seemed to be the sort of person who was delighted by everything, and who had already realised that what the world needed right now was laughing at.

Fred smiled back. He approved of this demeanour.

At this point, Nel came rushing up to him, dragging her bag on wheels behind her. She did look as if she had decided to wear everything, and was rather hot and a little bothered as a result. Fred just hoped she could now put work behind her for a few days and relax. She looked around, saw the baby and sighed.

'I see you've made a friend,' she said.

'He has an admirable attitude,' said Fred. He saluted the baby solemnly, and they boarded the train.

After the short train journey – followed by a ride on a bus on which the ramp, for once, worked – they arrived at Tilbury, and found their ship, not quite as tall as the others, but imposing on the skyline. Fred thought they should both really have duffel bags and crew cuts. Nel looked at their cruise liner as if it were a prison ship. She sighed, handed Fred her bag to carry on his lap and gave him a discreet push as they boarded the vessel, up what he felt he should call 'the gangplank', except it might make them seem like pirates – though, thankfully, there wasn't a bandana in sight. Sea shanties were now regrettably popular, but any outbreaks today would be frowned upon. Fred was momentarily hidden behind their bags, so it just looked as if Nel had a lot of luggage.

In public, Fred was allergic to people pushing or even touching his wheelchair. It felt like an invasion of privacy and a challenge to his independence. The last thing he wanted was to appear pathetic or become a parcel. Only Nel could offer help, and then only subtly. Her wordless acceptance of his need for dignity and autonomy was one of the things he loved about her. Her discreet push was second to none.

They were greeted at the top of the gangplank by two crew members, smartly dressed in dark blue uniforms with matching blue woolly hats. Peering around the bags heaped on his lap, Fred wasn't sure whether they reminded him more of Jumblies or the crew of the Starship Enterprise. He just hoped the ship was more seaworthy than a sieve, and that they would boldly go. At least the crew didn't seem about to burst into song.

The ship was full of bustling sailors and anxious passengers. The latter were mostly middle-aged Europeans – although Fred and Nel heard the occasional North American twang – presumably because young people could not have afforded the prices or were unaccountably uninterested in sea birds. They dropped their bags in what looked like an agreeably accessible double room. It could have been accommodation in a budget hotel, right down to the bottles of shampoo and shower gel in the wheel-in shower. Even the towels were in reach. Fred slid the fizz gently into their fridge, and followed Nel to see what else was going on. He declined an offer of help from a smiling American guest, who politely raised his hat in salute, and went on his way.

The cruise was starting from Tilbury, and then heading 'North', a word which was a recurrent feature of this holiday.

On the return journey, they would fly back from Spitsbergen's Longyearbyen Airport to Oslo, and then onward to London. Nel would rather have avoided flights entirely, but work called, and voicemail wasn't an option.

Now aboard the ship, Fred was pleasantly surprised to find that the rest of their party was already *in situ*. Hugh's punctuality had vastly improved since his marriage, and Fred had not yet readjusted his expectations. Previously, Hugh's lateness had been measured in days, not hours. He had lived in a van, where his main occupation had been playing his fiddle. But, newly married to Polly, he was a changed man, in terms of wardrobe as well as timekeeping.

Hugh was nearly as keen on science as Nel, especially when it had feathers. Fred had known Hugh since their school days, and he had met Polly at college. After Fred's fortieth, Hugh had gone to live in his van in Polly's drive, and had graduated first to her sofa and then to her bed – hence, the improvements to his wardrobe and his punctuality. He had made shelves for Polly, and for her daughter Freya an ever-evolving bed (Tardis! Bond villain's lair! Pirate ship! Home office!). Just as Polly's friends had begun to graduate from flat-pack furniture, or planks and breeze blocks in some cases, Hugh was on hand, able to offer kitchen shelves and bookshelves in any design they chose (anarchy symbol! Feminist symbol! Labrys!). North London may have had fewer birds, but it compensated with more carpentry customers. 'Reclaimed timber and ancient skills' is what it said on the marketing leaflets that Polly had made up. With his new family, and their new dog, Fenner, in tow, Hugh was able to get away to Norfolk, Somerset, and wherever else there was wildlife and a place to park the camper van. But he worried that the North London demand for shelving had now been filled, and the old van seemed to drink petrol.

'Feasts were very much more moveable when you were a grumpy bachelor,' said Fred, looking around the ship's saloon. 'But where's Freya? Is she already off exploring?'

'She's not on the voyage,' said Hugh. 'Thankfully.'

'She's staying behind with her friend Wildeve,' said Polly. 'Her mum Lisa is one of my mates. They drove us to Tilbury and waved us off.'

'Sick of your stepdaughter already?' said Nel. 'Tsk tsk!'

'Not at all!' said Hugh, defensively.

'She has become rather hard work in the last few months,' said Polly, coming to her husband's rescue. 'She's now nearly ten-going-on-sixteen, and moody as hell. Hugh perseveres, taking her to Woodcraft Folk.'

'We're worried she may have entered the tunnel of adolescence,' said Hugh. She's desperate for a smartphone of her own.'

'Or indeed, anything with a screen,' said Polly. 'It's a big relief that she's off with Wildeve and her mother.'

'That's such a Hackney name!' said Nel.

'It's from Thomas Hardy, *The Return of the Native*,' said Hugh.

'I'm not saying it's not cool,' said Nel. 'Just unusual.'

Polly shrugged. As she had learned when she called her daughter Freya, even the most unusual name could mysteriously become ubiquitous. Prospective parents were as vulnerable to fashion as anyone else.

'And we're off!' said Hugh, feeling the vibrations change under his feet, as the Norwegian cruise ship left its mooring at Tilbury Cruise Terminal.

'Shall we have a celebratory glass of fizz?' said Nel. 'Come to our cabin after the briefing, if the idea of a chilled bottle of English sparkling wine drunk out of a tooth-glass excites you. Better still, bring your own tooth-glasses!'

*

At the introductory briefing, sat in rows in the canteen, as if back at college, they were told about different parts of the vessel, including the Science Centre. They were more interested in gazing through the windows at the lonely sea and the sky. The speaker was the captain, a Viking bear of a man with a nautical beard. He beamed at them benignly. Although his uniform carried the embroidered label *W. Andersson* on his chest, and several yellow stripes on his epaulettes, he had a woolly blue hat like the rest of his crew. Captain Andersson was apparently a Swedish exile. He explained very seriously that he was allergic to meatballs, but the birthday party wasn't sure whether this might be what passed for wit in Norway. The humour was so dry that you thought a hosepipe ban was on the cards.

'Perhaps he doesn't like ABBA,' suggested Fred. It was a mystery they wanted to solve.

Captain Andersson explained their route.

'We sail down the Thames and up the North Sea, until we hit the coast of Norway. Not literally,' he added. 'Then we head up the coast, stopping once to explore a fjord, and then spend a few hours refuelling once we reach Tromsø. After that, it's due North to our destination, Svalbard.'

He firmly informed all the passengers that because it was spring, they were not very likely to spot the Northern

Lights, but that would not stop them optimistically pacing the outside of the top deck at midnight.

He introduced the ship's cat, Ingrid Traustason, who frowned at them from the table. Most of the passengers smiled. Those with cat allergies frowned back. Apparently, every ship had to have its cat, not least because of the mice (rodents, not computer peripherals). Mice were a pest at sea: they could gnaw through rope, electrical wiring and soft furnishing. Ingrid was male, the son of an Icelandic tom. Originally, the kitten was believed to be a female, hence the name. As he grew up, it was hard to ignore his masculinity, but it was too late to call him anything different, so Ingrid he remained. He had the liberty of the ship and might be found sleeping in the most improbable places: he was locked up only when in port. Captain Andersson said that Ingrid was better at predicting bad weather than the barometer.

The adventurers were then introduced to a young Norwegian woman called Sailor Halvorsen, who briefed them about health and safety regulations on board. Fred thought Sailor Halvorsen looked far too healthy for her own good. He half-listened as she explained the fire procedures and the location of the lifeboats. It was a good way of putting a dampener on things.

'I just hope they keep their eyes peeled for icebergs,' said Polly.

'I've never understood that expression,' ruminated Hugh.

'Icebergs?' said Polly, confused.

'No, eyes peeled,' said Hugh. 'Why would your eyes have a peel in the first place? What sort of peel? Wouldn't it hurt?'

Fred sighed. Not for the first time, he felt his friend might be being a bit too literal.

Sailor Halvorsen had moved on to the topic of polar bears. If spotted on their excursions ashore, the basic idea was to run like hell, polar bears being the sort of unusually fierce creatures who didn't usually receive many party invitations. In the unlikely event that they came across a bear who really insisted on hanging out with them, they would be in good hands, as each group going ashore would include a crew member armed with a rifle. If the worst came to the worst, a good tactic was to hide in a snow hole or cave. If you were out of sight of the polar bear, there was a reasonable chance that the animal would just lumber past you. Alternatively, of course, they might find you and savage you to death, which was generally best avoided. Or you might be killed in an avalanche, or frozen to death. More Norwegian humour, at which the birthday party smiled politely. Nobody expected to get up close and personal with a polar bear, though a few passengers were carrying telephoto lenses in case of a distant sighting.

*

The partygoers gathered in the room which Fred and Nel were to occupy for the next nine days. The different decks looked very similar, which Hugh could see might become a problem. But the ominous throbbing of the ship's engines increased as you got deeper, and cheaper.

Although Fred and Nel's room was very accessible, with no bunks, it had two single beds.

'They obviously think you can't have sex if you're in a wheelchair,' said Fred, pushing the two narrow beds together to increase the available floor space (and his chances of a cuddle with his partner).

'Of course you can...' said Polly, who had heard this one before.

'...you just have to put the brakes on!' Fred and Polly said in unison. Nel rolled her eyes as she popped the cork on the bottle of fizz.

'Cheers!' she said a moment later, as the four friends toasted Nel's birthday and clinked tooth-glasses with her.

'Here's your card,' said Hugh, handing over an envelope to Nel.

'Life really does begin,' Polly assured her. 'It's not just a cliché.'

'I seem to be in exactly the right place,' said Nel. Previously, she had been a dead-end naturalist in rural Suffolk, patronised by a sleazy millionaire. Campaigning to change the world certainly felt more like her style. She just wished it wanted to be changed.

'A job that suits you, a mortgage in Kennington and a partner! Anyone would think you'd sold out!' said Polly.

'If we're talking about joining the establishment, Mrs Appleton, I'll just point out that I was not the one who got married!' retorted Nel. Fred thought that this might make him Nichols-less, but felt it was a weak joke and best not spoken aloud.

'If you had a surname like Nobbs, then you would understand the sheer relief of adopting a different name,' said Polly. 'And as you know, I only answer to Ms.'

'Once a social worker, always a social worker,' said Fred.

A bequest from Fred's late dad had given them the deposit to buy their flat in Kennington, about which he still felt guilty, knowing that so many others faced a housing crisis. With their NGO, they were fighting a string of local battles: over-pollution in rivers, endangered sites of special scientific interest, and dodgy planning permits. The Big Green Campaigning Machine had gained some early wins and was widely respected. As long as it continued to be bankrolled by hedge-fund wealth, thought Fred, they were safe, although sadly the same could not yet be said for the British countryside. A 1980s popstar would come in useful for both.

Meanwhile, Fred's fellow lawyers were working to make global agreements worth more than the paper they were printed on, which is what he really wanted to be doing. But local action was what it was all about. While Fred might get occasionally frustrated with Home Counties planning regulations, Nel was happy with her work, and even published papers from time to time.

'How are Roddy and Heather?' asked Polly. Fred's brother, Roddy Twistleton, had become a Labour MP, thanks to his dazzling by-election victory in Stoke Central after the previous Tory incumbent was exposed as a serial sexual predator. Having done his bit to rebuild the Red Wall, Roddy had been rapidly promoted (whether beyond his competence remained to be seen).

'New Labour's answer to the Macbeths?' said Nel. 'He's now Shadow Secretary of State for Energy, and she's the world editor on some cable TV channel.'

'Is she still poisoning kittens?' asked Polly.

'I think you're being unfair,' said Fred. 'But she does report from crisis to crisis.'

'Every time there's a disaster, Heather is there... Suspicious, I'd say,' said Polly. The fact that Hugh stayed silent showed what a lot of tact he'd learned in two years.

'Have you heard the gossip about Charlotte?' asked Fred over his tooth-mug of sparkling wine.

Not to be outdone, Roddy's ex-wife, Charlotte Howells, had become a presenter on a digital radio station, where she was known as 'Charlie'; she had changed her wardrobe and become a gym regular. No doubt it was sheer relief to have dodged the bullet of becoming a politician's wife and spending weekends in Stoke-on-Trent.

'Well, I've heard that God has become rather more permissive,' said Polly.

'She met a thirty-something web developer in her gym,' said Fred. 'Her sons are horrified. They call her The Cougar.'

'Good for her!' said Polly.

Chapter 4

Twenty minutes and a bottle of rather fine English sparkling wine later, Nel and Fred were parting somewhat raucously from their friends. Lunchtime drinking on an empty stomach was the problem, thought Fred. Hugh excused himself, wanting to find some birds to watch, and Polly felt she should send an email to her daughter. Nel was just content to have marked the moment in style. That was quite enough partying for her.

Walking out onto the rear deck, Nel and Fred gazed back at Essex as they sailed away through the Thames Estuary. Goodbye to Plague Island, thought Nel. Bye-bye, Little England, thought Fred. They held hands and felt satisfied with life, as only two people who have found their person and their path can do. A passing fellow passenger obligingly took their photo, and their smiles for the phone camera were completely genuine.

'The high seas without a sea shanty in sight,' said Fred. 'A quiet life on the ocean wave.'

While Nel felt that communal singing had its place, she agreed that the peace was very welcome.

'And aren't you glad we took this trip?' said Fred, who was delighted by their much-needed and fully accessible holiday. They gazed wordlessly over the waves for a few minutes. The sea was agreeably flat. While the swell was gently rolling, the ship wasn't. Fred's and Nel's minds were as empty as anyone could wish for. In Fred's case, this was not wished for, because he needed ideas for his new book. Contrary to what certain newspapers announced every day, inflatable boatloads of migrants were nowhere to be seen. He felt that there was quite enough fiction written about migration.

'Fred!' shrieked an older woman out of the blue, destroying a calm which was on the verge of meditative with a storm of noisy excitement.

'Yoo-hoo!' bellowed a second woman, who also plainly knew Fred. Their identical headbands, flushed faces and determined expressions suggested that they had been speed-walking around the ship.

Nel sighed. She was much less sociable than her partner, or maybe it was that he had little choice in the matter. It was always the same, wherever they went. People everywhere remembered him. She imagined that they could have been deep in the Amazonian rainforest and still someone would have greeted Fred like a long-lost brother. The wheelchair made him memorable, as well as approachable. In fact, he could have coped with being less approachable, but total strangers persisted in talking to him. He had learned that he was far more likely to get help if he was friendly, and so he smiled at everyone, just in case.

The two older women approaching them were equally memorable in appearance. One was tall and slender with straight hair, and the other was short and well-built with curly hair, much like a matching pepper-and-salt set might be, if it was beaming and slightly out of breath. They wore yellow tracksuits, with black headbands and black trainers, which made them look a little like bumblebees. Or wasps, if you were being cruel – or they were.

'Aunty Bella!' responded Fred, in shock, addressing the taller woman. 'And Aunt Donna!' he added, seeing her shorter, rounder partner standing just behind her. 'What a lovely surprise!' he said, not entirely candidly. 'Whatever are you doing here?'

'We're doing our steps,' said Donna. 'How else do you fill retirement?'

'We might ask exactly the same thing of you,' said her companion, looking at them frankly. She was known throughout North Yorkshire for her boundless curiosity.

'We're celebrating a fortieth birthday,' said Fred, by way of explanation. 'We wanted a quiet place to mark it.' He emphasised the 'quiet'. He felt embarrassed that this special time with Nel was being invaded by a pair of slightly disreputable relatives.

'You reckoned without Grassington's finest!' said Donna, triumphantly. Fred winced. Quiet to Donna was like friendliness on X, formerly Twitter: it broke out from time to time, but never lasted long.

'We don't go anywhere without the Scrabble set,' said Bella, beaming at her nephew through her statement spectacles. 'We'll play anyone,' she added. The statement her spectacles were making was clearly: 'Life begins at retirement.' It was her own time now, and she was barely quieter than her partner.

'That sounds noisy already,' said Fred. 'Could we have a gentle game one evening?' he suggested weakly. It was a nine-day cruise, and he didn't see how he could avoid them for the full voyage.

'I'd also enjoy that,' said Nel, smiling at their new companions.

'Oh, where are my manners?' said Fred, realising how rude he had been. 'You've met my partner Nel, but it was only briefly. It's her landmark birthday we're celebrating. You remember Aunty Bella and Aunt Donna?' he said, by way of introduction. 'Together they're lethal,' he added to Nel under his breath.

'Happy birthday, dear!' said Aunty Bella to Nel. 'It's good to see you again.'

'We are relieved that any woman has managed to make an honest man of Fred!' said Aunt Donna, nudging him. He went scarlet and looked at the deck.

'It's great to meet you too,' said Nel, who had heard all the stories. 'But this woman is not about to marry Fred, or anyone else.'

Many partners might have buckled, but Nel was made of sterner stuff. She had grown up with two brothers, with groan being the operative word. A pair of beaming aunts was a big improvement on Fred's older sibling Roddy, the only other family member who loomed large in his life.

'Well, we'd better keep doing our steps,' said Aunty Bella, pacing on the spot.

'We'll see you at supper, then,' said Fred, smiling politely. He then took Nel by the hand and they speedily departed in the opposite direction.

'They're lovely. But if I didn't know you better, I'd say you just did a runner,' said Nel, when they were safely back in their cabin.

'Let's just say, it's best that they don't know where our cabin is... You might remember, Bella was my mother's younger sister,' explained Fred. 'She was a nurse. Donna was a doctor. They met at St George's, but they ended up working in North Yorkshire. At one time they had a house that was falling into the sea. Before you express sympathy, they chose it for precisely that reason. That's what they're like: a disaster waiting to happen.'

'Both sisters married doctors?' said Nel. 'Another GP?'

'No, Bella was a mental health nurse, and Donna was a community psychiatrist,' said Fred. 'Apparently, there's a lot of it about in rural areas.'

'Lesbianism?' asked Nel.

'Eccentricity,' said Fred. His partner nodded knowingly. She had lived in rural East Anglia after all.

His aunts might be unconventional, but they were family. And Donna was an excellent baker. Her choux pastry was wonderful (her eclairs and cream buns were astonishingly good) but so were her Danish pastries, her sourdough bread, her Dundee cake, her croissants... As a child, Fred had loved going to see his aunts. He was legendary in the family for the time when, as a small boy, he saw the kitchen table set for the tea they were about to be served, threw up both hands and said, with ecstatic gusto and in a strong Geordie accent, 'Chy-ache!' Now every time he went to tea with his aunts, 'chy-ache' was announced, with appropriate hand movements. He had very few relatives in the world, and one of those was Roderick, who was more like a minor Borgia than a brother.

'Then we were six,' said Nel.

'What?' said Fred, who was still dreaming of patisserie.

'First two, then four, and now we are six,' said Nel.

'Is this a riddle?' asked Fred, bemused. 'Is it something to do with A. A. Milne?'

'No!' said his partner. 'My birthday party has turned into six. Which is almost a crowd.'

'Sorry,' said Fred, who liked people and didn't really understand why Nel wanted a quiet birthday.

Next time they rendezvoused with their friends, Fred explained about Bella and Donna, and also how the ship's loopy quotient had gone up, now that they were liable to be accosted by aunts.

'I think you mean they have psychosocial disability,' said Polly, who wasn't a social worker for nothing.

'It's more a matter of chronic eccentricity than a condition in the *Diagnostic and Statistical Manual of Mental Disorders*. They're lovely, but hanging out with them can be an extreme sport,' explained Fred. 'You'll see,' he added ominously. They'd left him with a few psychological scars. How was it that his nearest and dearest were so markedly unusual? Take Hugh, for example. Maybe it was just his accepting nature. Sometimes Fred felt it would be nice to have friends who were normal. But then they'd be boring.

*

In a luxury suite, elsewhere on the ship, a middle-aged American was unpacking his bags, hanging up his clothes and deciding on his story. He thought he might wear the silk cravat tonight. So far, it had been a successful trip. Very successful. He put his possessions into the safe, although he made sure that the most valuable items were stored discreetly in the secret compartment of his bag.

Nine days on a ship crammed to the gunwales with the comfortably off European middle classes. He felt like an orca who has sighted a seal colony. He slipped in his earpiece, put his special pack of cards into his jacket pocket and cracked his knuckles. Never wanting for a movie cliché, he winked at himself in the mirror and whispered, 'It's showtime!'

Chapter 5

The MV *Queen Ingegerd* felt like a big vessel, although it was smaller than most cruise ships. Everyone had tacitly agreed to banish the word 'boat' from their vocabulary and had begun to deploy terms like 'port' and 'starboard', and 'fore' and 'aft' as if they were old tars. From the shyest, yet strangely forthcoming, member of their party they had learned that Ingegerd had been the daughter of Harald Hardrarda (who the rest were vaguely aware of, although it was news to them that Stamford Bridge was anything other than a football ground), and successively Queen of Denmark and then of Sweden (or was it the other way around? Hugh was a bit vague about that).

In all, there were only 120 cabins on the ship, which valiantly eschewed such frivolous luxuries as cinema or casino. Nor did it have a crèche, because the cruises were not aimed at families and none of these features were needed on what the marketing pitch called 'a voyage'. It was to be all about 'adventure and exploration', which would distinguish it from those top-heavy cruise ships that steamed around the world's tourist hotspots, polluting the planet with noise and rubbish. Nel noted sadly that there were still seven decks, two restaurants and a gym with a sauna, so not all frivolous luxuries had been eschewed. She thought she'd like to do some eschewing. She'd eschew birthdays for a start; they were definitely a frivolous luxury.

The service had gone upmarket in the years since the express boat had been the main way of travelling between towns in Norway. You could now get an eye-wateringly expensive cocktail in the Adventurer's Lounge (where Hugh was not the only one to worry about that possessive apostrophe). Most importantly, on this ship, you could walk around outside at two levels, surveying the seascape and the coastline. A good vantage point for birds, thought Hugh, musing that most of these passengers wouldn't recognise an adventure if it bit them on the bottom. Lounging was what they'd paid good money to do.

The food in the dining room had also gone upmarket, to the delight of the Brits of mature years (by the third night aboard, they had separated into pro-Brexit and anti-Brexit tables). Although certainly a cruise, it barely resembled the type of pensioners' journeys so beloved by one of Fred's paternal uncles, which he had also called 'a cruise'. In reality, he'd spent his time aboard a ferry from Newcastle to the Netherlands and back, benefitting from the duty-free drinks available. Uncle Al wasn't a natural sightseer, but he was quite content to be permanently sozzled. Plus, he'd spent his working life as a policeman, so he enjoyed putting the frighteners on young people on their way back from the cafés of Amsterdam (he would have been on the pro-Brexit table, not least because he was strangely attracted to duty-free booze).

However, this voyage was different. For a start, nobody could afford to get drunk on Norwegian prices, plus you needed a return ticket out of there before you could even buy alcohol on Svalbard. The walls were adorned with original artworks by Sami and Inuit artists, and the line offered cruises to Antarctica and Alaska, as well as to Iceland, Greenland and Svalbard. 'Basically, anywhere cold,' Polly had said, to Nel's approval. Although they were headed to the North, a heatwave was predicted for the Arctic that summer. 'Climate change,' Nel had commented grimly. 'So much for sea ice!'

There were lifts between decks, so most of the ship was wheelchair-accessible. This detail was very important, mostly because Fred wasn't sure how easily he could transfer to one of the Rigid Inflatable Boats (RIBs) for exploring the Spitsbergen shoreline, or the kayaks, let alone the mini-sub, which he suspected involved a ladder into the vessel. These alarming and exciting boats were currently lashed down on the rear deck. Fred felt that he would cross those nautical bridges when the appropriate expeditionary moment occurred. For now, it was relaxing to be on a boat, or rather a ship, and to be away from campaigning about climate change or worrying about the cost of living. That was what Fred looked for in a holiday, and what he thought Nel needed – and Polly, for that matter. Hugh would just go along with what was suggested by the others, although he certainly preferred wild spots. 'The fewer people the better,' was his motto – 120 cabins were about 100 too many, but as Fred pointed out, the numbers were necessary to keep the price almost affordable. Grim reality, as Hugh saw it, was just that: grim.

Fred, Nel and their group had all brought thermal long-johns and waterproof trousers to go with the rugged pair of boots and the branded orange cagoules which were issued to them by the expedition. Even though it was springtime, they were anticipating cold, particularly if they walked over any glaciers on Spitsbergen. Thankfully, none of them would rank style ahead of comfort, because that shade of orange wouldn't suit anyone. Fred had packed his warmest, most waterproof clothes, although he was never sure how to cover up from the weather. His chair and legs got wet if it rained, and ponchos tended to get tangled in his wheels. The wheelchair waterproofs he had seen were distinctly unsexy, and he felt that they were not aimed at his generation, so he was not going to succumb just yet. However, he felt that a waterproof outer layer was definitely needed. At low temperatures, his legs did their icicle impression. Below freezing, the metal push rims of his chair got so cold that he feared touching them. But he had just the thing for this trip: short metal skis that fitted onto each wheel, turning his wheelchair into a toboggan. All he needed now was a gentle slope, or someone to push him over the ice and snow.

Hugh's battered hiking gear was evidence that he was used to roughing it and, together with his tall and thin physique, suggested that someone, somewhere, had mislaid their scarecrow. He had also brought binoculars, both to extend his bird list and to spot polar bears on the ice.

'Best to see them before they see you,' he had joked. The binoculars were a new set, bought by Polly for his last birthday, as advised by another birder at her work. He was impressed by her choice and touched by her thoughtfulness.

Nel had brought a dress as well as her weatherproof outer gear, because you are only forty once, after all, and she thought the others might rope her into having a proper dinner on board to celebrate. Having the charity-shop dress on hand meant that at least she wouldn't be attempting to fashion anything with the shower curtain at the last minute.

Polly had invested in all the right gear, plus she had brought a swimsuit because: a) she had read that there was a sauna, which she was able to pronounce Nordically, and b) given the passengers, she thought that they would shun Finnish-style nudity. In general, she preferred to be too warm than to be too cold.

Nel was a vegetarian, and so was Fred – at least, when she was around. Polly and Hugh were not, so while they were eating boiled cod, pickled herring and bacalao, or salt-cod stew, Nel and Fred would be virtuously vegetarian-only. Fred was rather frustrated by this. On previous Hurtigruten (express boat) journeys to see the Northern Lights or the fjords, the fish had been a highlight. He felt that watching his best friends tucking in was not quite the same, particularly as he would likely be restricted to Quorn and tofu, which even the best chefs could not make appetising. At his age, the attraction of being smug did not overcome a love of food. But the love of a good woman outweighed both.

Although eager to get his share of ozone, Fred also planned to use his downtime to get ahead with that difficult second novel. Writing, not reading. He wanted to write a mystery but show that disability was more comedy than tragedy. Trying to fit in being an author alongside work was a constant struggle, particularly as he tried to write 1,000 words every day. He was reasonably confident that the first book was funny, and the reviews had certainly been kind. His work-in-progress was about as funny as a law tome, in his opinion, and that was a worry. No one wanted a lecture. Not even students. Not all the words were the right words, and he needed to edit out the lectures and edit in the jokes. Plus, have some ideas. Easier said than done, he thought ruefully. Other people made it look so simple.

He and Nel appreciated their accessible cabin, though it was so cramped that one had to inform the other in advance before moving to avoid collisions between titanium and flesh, in which the fleshy party usually came off worse. Meanwhile, they were enjoying their view of endless sea and eternal sunshine through the agreeably circular porthole. It felt rather like a hobbit house. There was no second breakfast on offer, but if they were strategic, they would come away with several bread rolls stuffed with unpronounceable cheeses for their lunch, plus fruit to fend off the scurvy, which of course was endemic to the sailor. Fred was glad that he'd brought an eye mask along, because the darkness and lightness would have played havoc with his circadian rhythms.

Hugh was in his element and was not intending to waste any time. He'd already managed to locate the lifeboats, make an unscheduled visit to the bridge, where Captain Andersson was most welcoming, and spot a storm petrel through his ubiquitous binoculars. It wasn't yet cold enough to make it necessary to wear a coat, but Hugh always wore his battered parka anyway, like a mod who had mislaid his scooter. Although he'd need a better haircut to look like a mod. Polly had done her best with his wardrobe, but certain garments were like comfort blankets, and he would not be parted from them.

His only concern was that he had done a discreet count of his underwear, and he would have to buy some extras in Tromsø. He was not normally bothered by underwear, but it was a nine-day cruise, and he had somehow forgotten to bring sufficient to satisfy his wife's hygiene expectations. Now he was married, that was the sort of thing he worried about: not where to park up the van that night, or how much wood to chop, but whether he was sufficiently sweet-smelling for company. Regularly changing his clothes was a novelty he was still getting used to. Aftershave was still a step too far.

Chapter 6

The advantage of a cruise was that it offered the maximum of nature with the minimum of weather. It was a cross between a luxury hotel and a nature channel on TV. Hugh found Fred upstairs in the lounge, having a break from writing and gazing in the general direction of Norway. The windows offered almost 360 degrees of visibility, although at present the view was restricted to sea (restless) and sky (ditto). In the distance, telltale silhouettes of oil rigs told the North Sea's old story, while bladed ranks of wind turbines spoke volumes about the new. Hugh brought over two mugs of coffee.

'Spot any longboats?' he asked.

'Not so far,' said Fred. 'Plenty of birds, but no Vikings yet.'

Hugh nodded knowingly.

'I was looking for inspiration in the waves,' said Fred. 'Unfortunately, my imagination is as untroubled as they seem to be. How about you?'

'If I had to be another species, I think I'd like to be a bird,' said Hugh, although Fred hadn't actually asked. 'Especially a sea bird. They live much longer than birds on land. Did you know that gulls can live for about thirty years? The oldest known albatross is in her seventies, I think.'

'Don't you think you might get bored? I suspect flying might be rather boring. After the initial excitement at realising that you can actually do it,' said Fred. 'More seascapes than you can shake a fish at, of course.'

'Imagine if you spent all your life soaring,' said Hugh.

'I'd prefer to be in a penguin colony,' said Fred. 'Can penguins even fly?'

'They're brilliant at swimming,' said Hugh. 'But think of the noise! I am not good in crowds.'

'Have you watched *Happy Feet* with Freya? I remember it was brilliant.'

'I think she prefers the sort of penguins that are covered in chocolate and come in a wrapper,' said Hugh, sadly. 'Also, bird flu is ripping through penguin colonies.'

They both contemplated what kind of birdlife would suit them best.

'I've always quite fancied being a puffin,' said Fred.

'Also come in groups,' said Hugh.

'Well, they're a cheerful sort of birds, and I liked the books as a kid.'

'Bet you wore the badge of the Puffin Club,' said Hugh. 'You could look forward to a lifespan of at least thirty years.'

'What would you be?' asked Fred of his old friend.

'I yearn for life as a swift,' said Hugh, glad to be asked. 'There is much to recommend them. For a start, they're loners. Second, they mate for life, which sounds good. And for a finish, they almost never come to land.'

'Life on the wing?' asked Fred.

'Well, twenty years of it,' said Hugh. 'But that would be enough.' Hugh snapped out of his ornithological reverie by coming back to life as a human, here and now.

'I was just thinking that we've done pretty well for ourselves.'

He was about to stroke the ship's cat, then passing on his rounds, but he did not, given that he valued his fingers. The cat flicked his tail in irritation, as if all these passengers on his ship were most tiresome. He was not in a sociable mood.

'You and I certainly have. Look at you!' said Fred. 'Building furniture for most of Hackney and holy matrimony for Mr Appleton. Who would have thought?'

'I am extremely fortunate,' agreed Hugh. 'Although, I do worry that Polly might change her mind.'

'Of course she won't!' protested Fred, loyally. 'You're a great catch!'

'Hardly,' said Hugh. 'I'm not cool. I'm not smart. I'm not even handsome!'

'Rubbish! You're highly intelligent. You dress... well, sensibly. Like Louis Theroux, if he didn't have a stylist,' said Fred. 'And you're a lovely person,' he added. 'Admittedly, an acquired taste, but then, a good man is hard to find.'

'You have to face facts. I am not of desirable appearance.'

'She's not shallow! She goes for more than looks.'

'And don't forget, with Polly, I have to worry about women as well as men,' continued Hugh. 'That's twice the anxiety.'

'But you're married,' Fred reassured him. 'I know Polly, she wouldn't make a commitment lightly.'

'That's true,' said Hugh. 'She did pledge to love and honour, before witnesses. Not obey, of course,' he added. Exchanging rings had been another step too far for Polly, who was as romantic as a sponge scourer. It was down to Hugh to organise their celebrations for Valentine's Day and anniversaries, or else they wouldn't have any. It was just as well that he wasn't holding out for chocolates or cut flowers, because he would have had a long wait.

'Polly isn't the obeying kind,' said Fred, who had been a witness for Hugh, alongside Nel playing the same role for Polly. Nel and Polly saw eye to eye on most things: she also went on Polly's hen do, which, as far as Fred could remember, had been a Reclaim the Streets march. Hugh hadn't had a stag night, though Fred had taken him out for a sly chicken biriani.

'Just be yourself,' Fred said. 'Loved and honoured is all that anyone needs. You can trust Polly. Now, let me get back to writing.'

Hugh wandered off. Being himself was not really a problem. But he wasn't sure that his self was somebody anyone else would want to be with, let alone love and honour. He'd seen the raised eyebrows in his immediate audience often enough to know that most people found him eccentric, at best. It was hard enough even for him to be with himself at times. Goodness knew what it was like for anybody else. For most of the last four decades, he had felt like the lone coloured sock in the white wash of life. He was the cat that walked by himself. But he still yearned for Polly to give him the occasional stroke.

*

Meanwhile, Nel and Polly had found time for coffee together, while the men were busy staring at birds or their laptop.

Given that their partners were best friends, it was perhaps inevitable that they would become close too. It was certainly convenient, although there was far more to their friendship than convenience. Polly had welcomed her new pal to London, and together they had spent time walking Hampstead Heath, looking out from Primrose Hill over London, and exploring the parks around Battersea, Kennington and Brixton. Hills were not Fred's forte, and Hugh was more likely to take the train to some damp fen than enjoy London's green spaces. Polly was determined to show Nel, who had grown up in the Black Country, that London had nature too. Although they'd only met through Fred, Nel and Polly were kindred spirits: they enjoyed the same things and agreed, conveniently, on almost everything.

An afternoon coffee in the Explorer's Bar was therefore a welcome opportunity to catch up, and a cardamom bun seemed the minimum that they could share between them. It felt like weeks since they had last met, and months since it had been just the two of them. A fat cat sat nearby, anticipating affection, and possibly leftovers.

'You must have been busy?' asked Nel, who hadn't been idle herself.

'Busy, stressed and burned out,' admitted Polly. 'Your birthday trip has come at exactly the right time!'

'Burning the proverbial?' said Nel.

'Something like that,' said Polly. 'Thank goodness for Hugh. Not only is he pretty low maintenance, but he's also been taking Freya for cycle rides—'

'In London?' said Nel in alarm. 'Please tell me not on the roads.'

'No, they go somewhere on the train. They take their bikes to Cambridgeshire or Suffolk,' said Polly. 'He's trying to turn her into a bird watcher.'

'Trying?' asked her friend.

'With mixed success,' admitted Polly. 'She'd rather spot something in H&M than in a fen. I don't much care either way, but it's great when they both disappear for most of Saturday, and I can catch up on casework…'

'No lie-in for you?' asked Nel.

'Not for any of us,' said Polly. 'Although Freya has been ominously teenager-ish recently, which means being awake all night and asleep all day. You'd think she was a bat. It's really hard combining parenting, stressful work, having a partner and doing all the usual boring chores.'

'Sounds like a timely warning!' said Nel.

'Meaning?' asked Polly.

'Oh, nothing. It's just that our start-up takes all of our time, and more,' said Nel. 'It's like our baby.'

'You mean it pukes and poos?' said Polly.

'It certainly demands our attention and leaves a mess,' said her friend.

'I wish there were twenty-five hours in the day and eight days in a week,' said Polly. Nel nodded in agreement. Polly thought if she couldn't grumble to Nel, who could she talk to? At that moment, the ship's cat jumped up onto the table between them, glared at them defiantly and continued his walk, before they could even reach out to touch him.

'I'd watch out if I were you,' said a passing member of the crew. 'That cat is more fierce than friendly.' They snatched their hands away and watched the cat stalk off. He was far from impressed that neither of them had left him any crumbs of their cardamom bun.

'I haven't told Hugh yet, but I might be looking for a career change,' said Polly, after the animal had gone. She was not the sort of person who confided in a cat.

'A change to what?' said Nel. She had always thought of Polly as a natural at her job: kind, yet tough – the perfect combination for a social worker. It seemed to Nel that it was more of a vocation than a career.

'Something less pressured! The relentless pace of social problems has broken me. I seem to have every stress symptom going. Fred's aunt always warned me that social work would suck me dry, and she was right. I even grind my teeth in my sleep, according to my dentist.'

'Not good,' said Nel. The pressure of environmental degradation was less intense, she thought. But even if you ignored the climate crisis, it was going to change your life. You couldn't fiddle forever while Rome burned. Which she had pointed out to Hugh, more than once.

'Not good on a regular basis, no,' agreed Polly. 'Of course, I can't help feeling like a failure, but if you spot a good job in the voluntary sector, or even higher education, please tell me!'

'Do the words "frying pan" and "fire" mean anything to you?' said Nel. Some of her friends had gone into higher education, and they always complained of the pressure.

'It's true, nothing in this world is easy, but at least you don't have statutory responsibility,' said Polly, who was now talking so quickly that Nel could almost see her brain whirring. 'Us social workers spend all our time worrying about people. Plus, there's the inevitable complaints, and then the threat of investigations, and there's always the risk of media exposure.'

'But isn't it OK if you're not doing anything wrong?'

'Yes, but our clients are mostly people with problems. We can't solve them all. Not in a world biased against poverty, immigration, mental illness, and so on. Not when we have no budget. And when disasters inevitably occur, it's always convenient to blame a social worker.'

They both fell silent. Polly was remembering near misses. Nel was thinking that while her work could be just as stressful sometimes, it carried far less responsibility. Except that everyone was responsible for the planet, even if most people failed to take their responsibilities seriously. Maybe it was just a matter of timescale.

'Anyway, I don't want to ruin your holiday celebrations – but keep your eye out for a job, any job, that involves people!' said Polly.

'Will do! And don't apologise. Friends are for dumping on,' said Nel, with feeling.

'Your turn next time?'

'Definitely!' said Nel, getting up from the table. It wouldn't be hard to confide in Polly. She'd never had a sister, but Polly, a few years older than her, was as close as she got in terms of friendship.

Chapter 7

The next morning, their first out of sight of land, it was Polly who discovered the Science Centre. This was what the MV *Queen Ingegerd* had in place of the casino boasted by more tropical cruise ships. The centre was staffed with several scientists who researched everything from ocean currents and plankton to polar bears. In the space of twenty minutes, Polly discovered more about meteorology, oceanography and even astronomy than she ever remembered having learned in school. For a start, she'd had no idea there were at least three North Poles. No wonder they couldn't find Santa Claus.

Stuffed with more knowledge than a *Mastermind* finalist, she discovered her friends having a quiet coffee in the Adventurer's Lounge. Their supply of pickled herring was very popular with the cat. Fred, who thought of himself as a dog person, felt disloyal enjoying spending time with a cat, but then he was a rather special cat. He seemed to walk the decks as if he owned them and when he got bored, he would dart up to his friends among the crew for a scratch behind the ears.

'Did you know that penguins lost 90 per cent of their chicks last year? It's so sad,' said Polly.

'Isn't that in the South Pole?' asked Hugh, torn between accuracy and uxoriousness.

'And polar-bear mums struggled to produce milk for their cubs!' said Polly, ignoring, not for the first time, her husband. 'And the Arctic failed to regrow its ice over winter!'

'If we carry on along this trajectory, we're screwed.' Nel sighed. 'No wonder no one wants to have a child, if the future is this grim.'

Fred said nothing. It was a sore subject.

'Sounds like you would be great in a pub quiz, though,' said Hugh to his wife. 'Although, I suspect you're not very good at popular culture,' he added.

'That's because you stop me watching TV!' said Polly (another sore subject). 'We'd need someone for sports, too.' Hugh nodded. He couldn't see it being him.

Polly went on: 'I've just been to the Science Centre. The chief scientist certainly has a strong Norwegian accent. But she was born in Eritrea.'

'How come?' said Hugh, with interest.

'Transnational adoption,' continued Polly. 'It's a big thing here. She likes cross-country skiing, apparently, which is the closest thing Norwegians have to a religion.'

'That sounds a lot like Fleur! One minute,' said Nel, and hared off in the direction of the Science Centre.

'What was that about?' asked Hugh. 'Was it something I said?'

'I suspect we're about to find out,' said Fred.

A few moments passed while they sipped their coffee and Fred tucked into his pastry.

'Fred?' said Polly.

'Yes?' mumbled her friend, with his mouth full. These cinnamon buns really were great.

'I don't mean to be rude, but have you put on a bit of weight recently?'

'Might have done,' said Fred, defensively, wiping icing from his lips. 'It's not easy to weigh yourself when you're paralysed!'

'It's middle-aged spread. It happens to us all when we turn forty, apparently. I think it's something to do with metabolism,' said Hugh, though he was as skinny as ever and could wear the same clothes as when he was at college – and frequently did, to Polly's dismay.

'You could perhaps slow down on the pastries. Have you thought about taking some exercise?' said Polly to her friend.

'It's hard when you're in a chair,' protested Fred. 'But I suppose I really should go swimming more.'

'*At all* would be a start,' said Nel, returning to hear her partner's last words.

'I haven't found the baths near us yet,' protested Fred. 'Except the open-air lido for summer. I didn't think I'd put on that much, but my shirts have got a bit tight,' he admitted. 'I thought they'd just shrunk in the wash...' Everyone else laughed.

'Sorry about running off,' said Nel. 'But I thought the scientist that Polly mentioned sounded just like my friend, and it's Fleur all right. She's as brilliant as she is gorgeous. I did my Masters with her.'

'Who?' said Hugh, who had forgotten the previous conversation. Fred was just pleased to change the subject.

'The head of the Science Centre!' said Nel, in exasperation.

'Did you meet in London?' asked Fred, who was still wondering when Nel had fitted in a Masters.

'Yes, during my Science Communication class. It was years ago. Fleur Kidist Kristiansen. She chose her own first name. The second name is Amharic, and it means "darling", apparently. And her surname comes from her adoptive parents.'

'You studied in London?' asked Hugh, still trying to catch up.

'Yes. I went to UEA after that for the biology doctorate. Although I never finished mine. Fleur did, at Southampton. She's a star, especially if you're interested in marine biology. What she doesn't know about lugworms isn't worth knowing!'

Fred wondered whether there was anything worth knowing about lugworms.

'Did you know that Norway has two languages?' said Hugh, for whom no tangent was a cul-de-sac. 'First, Bokmål, which dates from when Norway was part of Denmark, and second Nynorsk, which is the more right-on nationalist version that was constructed from dialect in the nineteenth century.'

'A bit like Old English and Norman French?' suggested Fred.

'Yes, but the divide goes right up until today,' said Hugh. 'That's why the stamps say *Noreg* as well as *Norge*. It's now the language of about 10 per cent of the population, and part of everyone's schooling. That guy, Jon Fosse, who won the Nobel Prize for literature, he writes in Nynorsk.'

Neither Polly nor Nel showed any interest in these fascinating philological matters, so Hugh stopped his lecture. He was becoming more sensitive to listeners. Fred, his old and loyal friend, smiled at him. At least Hugh wasn't going to accuse him of being fat, or tell him to eat or drink less.

Fred blamed cheese for the extra pounds he'd gained. Thanks to Nel's influence, he had reduced the amount of meat he ate. These days, he never cooked it at home. The problem was, he just ended up eating his body weight in cheese instead. Which he had to admit was causing a problem with his body weight. The trouble was, cheese was so addictive, especially the chunks of Cheddar and Lancashire, which he inhaled as if they were manna in the wilderness. It was like dark chocolate: a chunk became a slice became a bar – or a block. But when it came to cheese, there was toast involved, or worse, crumpets. Some people eschewed butter with cheese. He was not one of those people. So much the worse for his waistline.

Queen Mary once said, 'When I am dead and opened, you shall find Calais engraved on my heart.' In his case, he suspected it would be 'Mrs Kirkham', the provider of the best Lancashire available – only, her traces would be engraved in cholesterol-congested arteries. Thankfully, he took his daily 'cheese pills', as he called his statins, but he feared blood tests more than he had once feared the driving-test examiner.

After lunch, the four friends joined many of their fellow passengers at a lecture in the Science Centre entitled: 'The ice caps: where are they now?'. Nel introduced Fleur to her friends, who liked her immediately. Fleur was a tall woman with cornrowed hair, wearing a shimmering suit of blue-green silk; one could sense she would excel at whatever she turned her hand to. But her chosen field was science, or rather science communication. She knew her stuff, having given lots of talks over the years, and just as importantly, she knew her audience. She made people laugh, connected with them and took them on a journey. It was as if you were watching a powerful TV nature documentary, but in the flesh.

Fred and Hugh watched as Fleur took them through a series of slides and factoids on climate change. She was impressive, but also horrifying. Or rather, she was great, but her talk was horrifying. There and then, sixty middle-aged people clad in brightly coloured puffer jackets resolved to do better with recycling and composting, and possibly even to go on a demo, as long as they weren't too busy. Who knew where the time went?

'Playing havoc with the birdlife, global warming,' whispered Hugh. 'Although we do get to see more accidentals these days.'

'Accidentals?' asked Fred. He preferred eating his birds to watching them, if truth be told. He glossed over that point at work, although on nights when Nel did taekwondo, he was a regular at Nando's. It was his only guilty secret.

'Non-natives who are blown onto our shores in search of more congenial weather,' explained Hugh. 'There are some benefits, at least.'

Better bird-watching did not count as a tangible benefit of global warming to Fred, but he let it pass. He saw Ingrid sitting beside the lectern, watching everybody through narrowed eyes. Didn't cats kill an astonishing quantity of birds? He might not remind Hugh, who probably knew the exact number.

Having waved happily at her friend at the beginning of the lecture, Nel was listening carefully. Fleur was staring at her significantly and indicating to stage right.

'Polly, do I have something stuck in my teeth?' hissed Nel.

'No. Why?' said her friend, having a look.

'Fleur is trying to signal something, and I thought it must be something about me.'

Polly looked at Fleur, and then at where she was trying, rather indiscreetly, to point while explaining the impact of global warming on the Arctic's flora and fauna. Meanwhile, Nel was handing onwards a cardboard box of dried-up polar bear dung, which she'd been given by a guy behind her. She had heard him take a snapshot of the poo. She looked carefully, but it didn't seem photogenic to her, so she was happy to pass it on.

'She's pointing at that guy in the second row. The one with the horn-rimmed specs and the Assyrian beard. Wearing a face mask.'

Nel glanced over and froze.

'Oh. My. God.'

'What? What?' said Polly, trying to spot what her friend had seen.

'I think that's Cyril Earther,' said Nel.

'Really?'

'Definitely.'

'I've read his pieces in the *Guardian*,' said Polly.

'I get his emails,' said Nel.

'He emails you?' said Polly, not sure whether to be impressed or outraged. She thought there were laws about that.

'No, not personally. I've signed up to his mailing list about climate change. He has thousands of subscribers.'

'Didn't he use to be called Cyril Towner, until he changed his name by deed poll?' asked Fred.

The allure of people like Cyril is one of the great unexplained mysteries of the world, along with the Loch Ness monster, extraterrestrial intelligence and the hairstyle of Donald J. Trump. Cyril was neither physically nor intellectually commanding. In a former life, he had been an environmental science lecturer, and it showed. Cyril was a humourless man of great stubbornness, who could turn out a scary op-ed at a moment's notice. Yet, he was astonishingly popular as a campaigner, and his celebrity could induce swoons in otherwise robust listeners. In that, he resembled Jeremy Corbyn.

Perhaps it was something to do with beards – Cyril Earther's was his most memorable feature. It had become his trademark. Other people had glasses or bow ties: he had his luxuriant beard, which he had vowed not to shave until net zero was achieved.

'Yes, that's the one. Cyril Earther. He's big in Oil Emergency.'

'They're the ones who do those outrageous protests? Slow walking, and silly costumes?' said Hugh. 'Not big fans of global warming?'

'You could say that! He's their brains. Their Gandhi. Only, with a beard,' said Nel.

'What on earth is he doing here? Is it an ice-cap thing? He must want to see for himself. No wonder Fleur is off her stride,' said Polly.

With a flourish, Fleur brought the lecture to an end, and there was a ripple of applause. As people queued to leave,

Nel saw Cyril Earther approach the lectern. A few moments later, at the bar, Fleur rushed up to them all. Waving aside their congratulations, she beamed at Nel. She was in full fangirl mode.

'It *was* him! Apparently, he really enjoyed my lecture. I got him to sign my notes! He promised we can have a one-to-one later in the cruise. He's here to see the Arctic for himself.'

'Wow!' Nel looked at Cyril Earther's name, signed roughly on Fleur's papers.

'I reckon he must be single,' said Fleur, who had clearly taken an interest. 'If he had a companion, they'd have put a stop to that beard…'

'What's the big deal?' asked Fred, a bit put out that his partner was also swooning over such an odd-looking guy. 'If it's to do with his work, it's probably a tax-deductible trip to go to the Arctic.'

'Avoiding tax is the last thing on his mind,' said Nel. 'He wants us all to pay more of it.'

'I am so excited to find that he's on this cruise,' explained Fleur, reverently. 'I've read all his books!'

'Really lives what he preaches,' said Nel.

'That beard does make him look like an Old Testament prophet,' said Hugh, siding with Fred. 'More Jeremiah than Jonah. He's already wearing the sandals. I can imagine him being fed by ravens. Or setting the bears on people who laugh at him. Was that Elijah or Elisha? I always get them mixed up.'

His companions thought that Hugh was being rather too flippant regarding Cyril Earther, whose prophecies were based on science and in imminent danger of coming true. Forget the beard and the socks, let alone the sandals – Nel and Fleur were united in admiration. Clearly, Cyril had guru status. Polly was impressed, despite herself.

Fred just caught Hugh's eye and shrugged. He had read Cyril's pieces, and generally agreed with them, but was not a groupie. Fred sent money to Oil Emergency, but did not go on marches or demonstrations. Hugh, who probably knew more about nature than all of them but had scant interest in politics, had no idea what all the fuss was about. But when lunch came, Fleur was sitting with her hero, nodding at his every word, with barely any time for her friends, old or new. Polly was engrossed in a chat with his sidekick, a young Asian person of indeterminate gender and with many piercings. Hugh looked as if he would prefer her to be less engrossed.

Chapter 8

That afternoon, Fred lunched with Aunt Donna, who liked her food too. She was paying, and Nel was nowhere to be seen, so for once, he thought he'd be safe with fish. Donna had followed his career with interest. She was certainly someone in whom to confide, and he did. But that done, he was curious to know what she and Bella were doing on the Spitsbergen cruise.

'I wouldn't have thought it was your thing,' he said.

'I'm giving a few talks,' said Donna. 'Hence the cheap holiday. It's a retirement hobby.'

'Oh, I see,' said Fred. 'We all saw Fleur do her bit this morning. It was eye-opening! But what are you talking about? I thought you were a psychiatrist. Surely, you're not also an expert on Arctic flora and fauna?'

'No, I'm not,' replied his aunt. 'But I am getting to be an expert on isolation. From the mental-health perspective.'

'Loneliness?'

'Exactly. You probably don't know, but in my talk – which I expect you and your buddies to attend, by the way – I will discuss the Russian hunters who overwintered on Spitsbergen from the seventeenth century onwards. Plus, many of the polar explorers would have experienced extreme isolation…'

'Frozen into their ships?'

'Exactly. Or in freezing-cold huts.'

'Sounds awful,' said Fred, shivering in sympathy with Shackleton's men. 'I am glad this ship can break through ice. I doubt your lecture has many jokes.'

'Which reminds me: how is the writing coming along?' said Donna. 'I loved the first novel.'

'Slowly,' admitted Fred. 'I'm still trying to work out the plot of the second.'

'The first one made me laugh so much that my tea came out of my nose.'

'Great to hear,' said Fred. 'That's a good benchmark.'

'Though I don't think that there's much to make jokes about these days. We seem to be going to hell in the proverbial handcart. No wonder depression is on the rise…'

'No, the news *is* mostly awful, but think of the last century: that was dreadful too, but P. G. Wodehouse still made people laugh.'

'What's awful?' said Bella, appearing as lunch was ending, with an eager glint in her eye and a Scrabble board under her arm. She was wearing a thick sweater in orange and blue stripes, not unlike a furry caterpillar, albeit one who was wearing glasses and prone to gambling.

'The news?' offered Fred.

'We were talking about isolation in the Arctic,' said her partner. 'You know, my lecture?'

'Got us a free holiday,' said Bella. 'I'm not complaining. I'm happy to be a plus one, just as long as I don't have to stay in a hut.'

'You'd last twenty minutes in a freezing-cold hut,' said Donna, lovingly.

'None of them even took a Scrabble board!' said Bella.

'I am hoping to write a book on polar exploration,' said Donna, 'using my lectures as the basis.'

'That's a fantastic idea,' said Fred. 'No wonder you're interested in my book. Well, writing is a dog's life but the only life worth living, as Flaubert said.'

At that point, Bella and Donna greeted their new friend Paul, who was passing, and introduced him to Fred, who shook his hand. He had grown up in the Scottish Borders, not far from the Tyne Valley.

'Always happy to meet someone from nearby,' said Fred. 'Us North Britons should stick together!'

'Lockerbie is a fair distance from Newcastle,' said Paul. 'Not to mention being in a separate country. But I'm always happy to talk to someone with Northern vowels.'

He might enjoy talking to them, but Paul seemed wise enough to avoid the inevitable invitation to Scrabble. He smiled, shook his head and went on his way.

'At least you're ready to be trounced,' said Bella, turning to Fred. 'I've done my steps, and I'm taking on all comers.' She guided the three of them to a table in the lounge.

'Oh no,' said Fred. 'Am I doomed to play with you both?'

'You certainly are,' said Donna. 'Consider it a cure for loneliness.'

'But I'm not lonely,' protested Fred. 'And I wouldn't mind it if I was,' he added.

'Scrabble is protective,' said Donna. 'Well, probably. Maybe the manufacturer would sponsor a randomised controlled trial,' she mused to herself.

'Shall we play for a penny a point?' asked Bella. She hoped one day to get to the National Scrabble Championships, where this sort of behaviour would be frowned upon, but in the meantime, she liked a flutter. Fred looked around for his companions, in search of moral support, but they had all mysteriously disappeared. Now he really was isolated. He sighed.

'Yes, I'm ready. But let's not play for money. Not even with you,' he added, although he could be forgiven for thinking 'especially not with you'.

The Grassington Ladies' Club was notorious for gambling. It wasn't just Bella; it was all of them. Pool, cards, bingo or Scrabble – they were all the same to the GLC. Not that there was much else to do in rural North Yorkshire, unless you were a farmer, and most of them were on set-aside, or whatever the equivalent was now. No one could keep up with agricultural policy post-Brexit. Grassington was where the recent *All Creatures Great and Small* was filmed, which was rather entertaining for the locals, although being chosen did rather suggest nothing had changed there since the war. Wensleydale was not far away, so Fred was always friendly to the local cows, whose milk was a constituent of the famous cheese, always best eaten with cake, which was killing two birds with the same stone, as far as Fred was concerned.

The GLC had been known to operate a sweepstake on the belated arrival of the weekly bus and, in the dying months of the last UK administration, their Hon. Secretary had opened a book on which cabinet minister would have to resign next. But gambling was not for everyone. Fred's father had regarded it as sinful – profiting from another's loss, he had said. The liberalisation of the gambling regulations had been a subject that could be guaranteed to get him hot under the collar in his old age. Another was the use of the National Lottery to provide arts and community funding. 'A tax on the poor!' he'd thundered. While not sharing his nonconformist faith, Fred shared his disgust with the lottery, and governments in general.

'I know your late dad disapproved of games of chance. But it's not a game of chance, not the way that we play it!' was Bella's rationalisation. 'It's all about literacy and ingenuity! Who among us can put down the most seven-letter words?!'

All Fred knew was that it wasn't going to be him. Right now, the only words which came to mind had four letters. His Scrabble prowess had limits, and his aunts were two of them.

'You're just frit!' said Bella, which, he admitted to himself, was probably right. 'I need all the practice I can get,' she said. 'I need to win a qualifying tournament for the National Scrabble Finals when I get back home.'

'Look, I've learned all my two-letter words since we last played,' said Fred, defiantly. 'I don't think this is going to be quite the walkover you expect.'

'No one in Scotland uses "ch" for loch, by the way,' said Paul, passing them again with another cup of coffee.

Well, it certainly wasn't the walkover that Fred had expected. They seemed to have compendious knowledge of the English language. The two aunts were like goats on a climbing wall. As he fell further and further behind, Bella took pity on Fred and fished a well-thumbed book out of her bag.

'Here. Take the OWL. There's no way you're going to put up a fight without it.'

'Owl?' asked Fred, mystified.

'Official Word List,' explained Bella. 'It's not allowed in a proper tournament. But you need to learn a few words. I read it on the loo sometimes.'

Fred looked at them from behind a rack of letters that might as well have spelled MR LOSER.

'I always have a dictionary to hand when I play,' he said, plaintively. 'And I read my phone on the loo.'

'That's because you aren't a competitive Scrabble player,' said Bella. 'As if there was any doubt in the matter.'

'Thanks a bunch,' said Fred, weakly. 'I thought I was holding my own.'

'Just look at the scores,' said Donna, putting down another seven-letter word.

'I don't even know what that word means,' protested Fred, who was trying not to think about the scores.

'Nor do I. All I need to know is whether I can put an S on the end,' said Donna.

'At least you don't play like an American,' said Bella, as she consulted her letters.

'Of course not,' said Fred. 'I'm from Northumberland.'

'She means you don't try and stop other people making good words,' said Donna.

'Is that a rule I don't know?'

'Which makes it all the better for us,' said Bella, putting down a vastly ingenious word that also created three shorter words running across and came to an impressive total. 'Us Brits leave opportunities for other players. Those Americans just stop you making good words.'

Fred looked at the scores. After eight turns, he had only just gone past 100 points. His aunts were each several hundred points ahead of him. He was glad that he'd said no to gambling. It was like playing croquet with his father, only indoors. He wondered if he could accidentally-on-purpose jog the board. Or would that be childish?

A shadow fell across the table, just as Fred put down a four-letter word that he wouldn't say in public but was fairly sure was proper English, albeit Anglo-Saxon.

'Oh, hot diggity dog! You dirty hound! You've made The Word!' said the stranger, in mock horror. 'Where I come from, no cuss words allowed.'

Fred had seen the perma-tanned figure before somewhere. It was not a big ship. Certainly, this stranger pumped his hand as if he were an old friend. He was middle-aged, smooth verging on oily, and wearing a bolo tie.

'Are you a Scrabble player yourself, mister…?' asked Aunty Bella.

'Am I a Scrabble player?' drawled the stranger. 'Marvin G. Ridley III, admired for my vocabulary across the Southern Yewnited States.'

'And where in America might you be from, Mr Ridley?' said Aunt Donna.

'The Lone Star State: Texas. We call it the friendly state. Who do I have the pleasure of meeting this evening?'

Bella seemed flattered, but also irritated, as if she couldn't make up her mind what to think. Donna just beamed. Marvin was broad-shouldered and twinkly, wearing an expensive-looking polo neck. He was muscular but not paunchy; attractive, but not threatening, and a considerable improvement on his compatriots on the ship.

Charmin' Marvin G. Ridley soon had them laughing and eating out of his hand. To Fred, he was disarmingly friendly. He was soon playing the next game of Scrabble, and then buying them all a round of drinks. Relieved to have someone to take his place, Fred made his apologies and went off to find Nel.

As he wheeled away, he wondered if Marvin would turn out to be as American in his Scrabble style as he was in his approach to making friends. Fancy having a number as part of your name, as if you were a monarch or a Pope. Marvin was obviously from a proud Texan family, probably very rich from the look of him. Americans were just as status-bound as the Brits, even if they wouldn't admit it. As he left them, Fred heard a conversation starting about Texas oil and nodding donkeys. He hoped that neither Cyril Earther nor Fleur Kristiansen heard them.

Chapter 9

The friends who had deserted Fred at lunch had gone their separate ways. Nel had headed off to see Fleur at the Science Centre to talk about old times and new possibilities. Hugh had gone to play his fiddle in his cabin. It's what he did instead of talking about his feelings; a few jigs would clear his head and calm his fears. It saved him a fortune in therapy bills, although didn't solve any of his problems.

Polly had already fetched her swimming costume and bottle of water and disappeared to the sauna. After months of work, she badly needed to relax and de-stress. Her strategy was to start perspiring gently on the bottom bench, and slowly work her way up to high-level sweat. A bit of peace and quiet was demanded if this was to be her holiday. She was just settling down, eyes closed, when the door opened. She sighed internally. It would probably be a chatty North American couple, or a naked Northern European who would insist on his right to dangle his bits in her general direction. Perhaps if she kept her eyes closed, the other person would get the message.

'Do you mind if I splash on some water?' said a youngish-sounding British woman, whose voice seemed familiar. She was clearly on her own, thank god.

'Not at all. Not now I've had time to get used to this temperature,' replied Polly, hoping she'd get the message. Polly heard the splash of water over the coals, and felt the heat level slowly increase. Thankfully, chatter didn't follow. After ten minutes, Polly thought she could risk opening her eyes. In the dark, she could see a naked figure lying on her towel on the top bench. Well, well, well, she thought to herself. The other woman was obviously used to sauna etiquette.

Polly lay down on the middle bench, feeling conspicuous in her swimsuit. Well, she was almost middle-aged, dammit. She was entitled to be a bit saggy. That perky young woman was at least a decade her junior. Or possibly two. And who knows what lowlifes are on this cruise, she thought. You might prefer to be wrapped-up in a mixed-sex sauna. It didn't mean you were a prude. When she next opened her eyes, after what felt like another ten minutes, but could have been twice that, the younger woman was smiling at her.

'Please tell me I wasn't snoring,' said Polly. She felt relaxed, and less chat-phobic.

'Nope,' said the young woman. 'No snoring – no dribbling either, so far as I noticed. But I wasn't looking closely.'

'Thank god for that!' Polly thought she'd encountered her before. 'Weren't you there at the end of Fleur's lecture?' she asked. 'I'm Polly—'

'How could I forget? I was with Cyril and I was looking for kindred spirits,' said the other. 'And in case you don't remember, I'm Lu. Short for Lubna. My pronouns are she/her.' She had obviously taken out her piercings for the sauna.

Polly sighed. Please don't let her be a social-work student. She couldn't bear it.

'Polly. Also she/her. From Hackney, before you ask.'

'Oh, I live up your way, in a Crouch End collective,' said Lu. 'I'm actually here because of Cyril Earther,' she said proudly. She didn't mind bathing in his reflected glory.

'Oh yeah, I saw you sitting with him at Fleur's lecture...'

'Isn't she brilliant!' said Lu. 'I have such a girl-crush on her already. She's funny and clever and gorgeous!'

Polly chuckled.

'I'm surprised you have time for girls, if you're with Cyril.'

'He's a nightmare,' said Lu, firmly. 'And I'm not *with* him, not in that sense.'

'That's bad news – and, of course, good news,' said Polly, diplomatically. 'His articles and books are spot-on, so I was a bit star-struck to meet him.'

'Yeah, they're all right,' admitted Lu. 'They're most of the reason I'm here.'

'To hang out with the man himself?' said Polly.

'Something like that. Except that he really is a nightmare. As I have discovered through extensive personal research.'

'Not too extensive, I hope,' said Polly.

'No.' Lu looked revolted at the thought. 'Though we are going back to England by train,' she said morosely. 'I am not looking forward to it.'

'Feet of clay?' asked Polly.

'Very much so. Think ankles of clay, calves of clay and knees of clay.'

'Oh dear,' said Polly. Metaphors had rarely been overextended to such great effect.

'Men are mostly bleugh,' said Lu. 'Which is why I have more time for girls,' she added.

'They are, in general,' agreed Polly, who had some experience with males. 'Although I'm here with a couple of nice ones,' she added, feeling disloyal.

'Gosh, it's getting hot up here. Mind if I come down to your level?' said Lu.

'Not at all,' said Polly, sitting up just in time to see the naked twenty-something woman scramble down to sit next to her on a folded towel. This was not an everyday occurrence. She couldn't say she minded. It reminded Polly of being that age herself, and her Interrail trips around Europe. Lu was slim, and her dark hair was cut short. On her shoulder seemed to be a double labrys tattoo. I bet she kept that hidden from her parents, thought Polly. But you could be anyone you wanted to be in London.

'You in a tour group, then?' said Lu, after a few more moments of synchronised sweating.

'Sort of,' said Polly. 'It's my friend's fortieth birthday trip. We want to see the Arctic before it's all gone.'

'Are you forty too?' asked Lu in wonderment.

'I was two years ago,' said Polly.

'I hope I look as good as you when I'm forty-two,' said Lu, admiringly.

'Flattery will get you everywhere,' said Polly.

Lu giggled. 'Everywhere?'

Polly left the suggestion hanging. Admittedly, Lu was lovely, but she wasn't about to flirt back. She was a married woman, although she was glad she had never opted to wear a wedding ring.

She smiled at her new friend. 'I had better go back to my room and shower.'

'Bye, then,' said Lu, who sounded disappointed.

'I am sure we will meet again,' said Polly. She was quite enjoying being found attractive again. It was good practice. She knew Hugh desired her, but it was mostly a matter of assumption, not demonstrativeness.

'Anytime you want to work up a sweat,' said Lu, smiling.

'Definitely. I'm always up for a sauna,' said Polly. 'And now I know you don't have to wear swimsuits, it will be even nicer.'

Oh god. There she went.

'Oh, I always go naked,' said Lu. 'I think it comes of having dance training. You're much less bothered about bodies.'

Polly nodded and waved a cheerful goodbye as she opened the door. She happened to know this was mostly rubbish. The rate of eating disorders among dancers, especially ballet dancers, was notorious. Though she got it that arty people were less bothered about being naked. Especially arty people who were young and gorgeous. But, Polly thought, I bet she's bothered about other people's bodies. Better not mention her to Hugh: it was likely to make him draw all the wrong conclusions. She loved him dearly, but he did need a lot of reassurance.

Chapter 10

Hugh paced around the deck, steering well clear of Ingrid, who was sprawled out and getting some rays. Hugh approved of the cat, with whom he had come to an understanding: he, Hugh, would ignore Ingrid, and in return Ingrid would ignore him. It was better that way. But now he was looking for his friend, because he had come to a decision.

'Oh, there you are!' said Hugh as he found Fred nursing a quiet coffee in the lounge.

'Were you looking for me? I am just recovering from a Scrabble game.'

'I wanted to run something past you.'

'Don't tell me, you want to become a vegan?' said Fred.

'What? No. It was about my business,' said Hugh. Humour was not his strong point.

'Hit me with it,' said Fred. Hugh stared at him in alarm. 'Tell me about it,' clarified Fred. He had forgotten how literal Hugh was about metaphors.

'Well…' said Hugh. 'I reckon that the market for shelves cannot continue forever.'

'Not unless you do more advertising,' said his friend.

'You know what I think of marketing,' said Hugh.

'I know you're no good at marketing,' said Fred. 'Which is a different thing.'

'Anyway,' said Hugh, ignoring him. 'What about playground furniture?'

'What?'

'You know, wooden playground furniture. Slides, climbing frames, all sorts.'

'Oh, I see. For children. Yes, I can see you'd be good at that.'

'A vast turkey, with a slide coming out of its bum. An eagle that you could clamber over…'

'Or a huge polar bear come to that.'

'Exactly. Lots of colourful wooden animals that could be very popular in children's playgrounds. My ideas have mostly been for birds so far.'

'I think that's brilliant!'

'I could do it pretty easily. Of course, there must be all sorts of rules about safety.'

'And Freya would have plenty of suggestions,' said Fred.

'I've got plenty of thoughts myself, thank you.'

'But do they include a name for the business? I've got just the idea for one,' said his friend.

'Have you?' Hugh answered warily.

'Fowl Play. With a W! Get it?'

'Better than Play Zoo, which is all I had thought of.'

'Carved Capers?'

'Maybe. I will sleep on it. Do you think I should tell Polly?'

'Not yet. Work it all out. Then tell her.'

'Sensible.' Hugh nodded.

After Hugh had wandered off, Fred thought more about his rehab novel. So far, it was a series of situations in need of some comedy. And a plot would help. Perhaps his literary career was doomed after one book?

The mystery to be solved after an injury, he thought, was getting better. Nobody knew how that would end. But what would be stolen or who would be murdered? And why? Rehab was full of black comedy, thought Fred. Usually, people falling out of bed or having toilet emergencies. You had to be there. Or rather, you'd prefer not to be.

The problem, as usual, was a plot. His family and friends were falling over themselves to provide him things to write about. Usually without meaning to. They just couldn't help themselves. All that had worked perfectly for his first book. People had been so impressed that he'd got into print that they didn't mind recognising themselves in the Threepwood capers.

But was it fair to use them again to comic effect? Was there some sort of ethical code about that? Did you have to wait until people died to use their life stories? He might be waiting an awfully long time if so. And what if people who weren't included complained?

For that matter, would it be possible to write a novel about someone who bumped off his friendship group so he could use them as characters? That plot was more like Patricia Highsmith than P. G. Wodehouse. He wasn't certain he could be so vicious. It was hard enough coming up with a villain who wasn't out of Central Casting.

The physios he had encountered in hospital may have been tough on their clients, but they weren't nasty. The only unbearable feature had been the cooking. Maybe his villain could be a catering assistant with a grudge against people with an appetite. Never knowingly having had a grudge, Fred found this difficult to write. Maybe a character was in rehab because someone had tried to kill him... and maybe they were now bringing him poisoned chocolates? Promising, thought Fred, promising.

*

At dinner that evening, the four friends sat together again, and the cooking was great, even for vegetarians. The cruise included half-board, while the midday meal cost extra, which explained why they all ate a substantial breakfast and were planning on making surreptitious sandwiches for lunch. None of them was paid what they were worth in their jobs, living in London was expensive, and all this science did not come cheap. The gravadlax, boiled cod, potatoes and spinach (with egg salad for vegetarians) were very welcome at supper time. As was the almond cake, and the sweet soup, once they had got used to the idea. Walking the decks and all that fresh sea air were good for the appetite.

Polly said she had spent much of the afternoon in the sauna. She didn't mention who else had been there. Nel had been reading Barry Lopez's wonderful book about the Arctic, which she'd recommend, and Hugh had used his binoculars to examine the rocky Norwegian coastline for sea birds. In turn, Fred had written several thousand words of his new book. He had swallowed his conscience and blatantly stolen life events from his nearest and dearest. He'd changed their names so, surely, they'd understand? Nobody would ever know. Except them, sadly.

'Do you know…' said Hugh. 'People in Greenland eat fermented little auk at Christmas.'

'If this is research for pub quizzes, I think you're going a bit far,' said Polly.

'It's called *kiviak*,' said Hugh.

'First, thank goodness we're not going as far as Greenland, and second, I am glad we draw the line at roast turkey and mince pies,' said Fred. 'You certainly win the trivia prize for unlikely things to do with rare birds.'

'The great auk, of course, is extinct,' said Hugh. 'It was like a penguin, completely flightless, and was last seen in 1852.'

'Probably by someone hungry,' said Fred.

While they were eating and talking, Fleur walked past – with Cyril and Lu in tow, each of them carrying a tray.

'Mind if we join you?' she said.

'Not at all,' they all replied. Fred and Hugh answered automatically, Nel with genuine warmth and Polly with some anxiety, in case Lu mentioned the sauna. There was silence for a moment. What did gurus eat?

'Most of us are British,' said Fred, suddenly. 'We should discuss the weather.' The others groaned. Lu winked at Polly. Luckily, Hugh was staring at some bird out of the window.

'I think we can do better than that,' said Cyril, absent-mindedly munching a stick of celery. 'It's the climate we should be discussing.'

Fred felt outdone. Cyril was eating boiled potatoes and salad, as well as pudding. Fred guessed that he boycotted fish. At least there was feta with the tomatoes and lentil salad, otherwise he'd be worried about Cyril's protein levels. Hugh didn't like the noisiness with which Cyril was eating celery, but did not want to sound like a fascist.

'Fancy a glass of wine?' Fred said to Fleur and Cyril. 'It's biodynamic,' he added, to show he was really quite right-on too. He'd had a compost bin before it was trendy.

'Yes, please,' said Fleur, holding out her glass. Cyril examined the label on the bottle before agreeing. 'Sometimes they use fish-derived products to strain wine. But this brand only produces vegan wine.'

Fred filled up Lu's glass. She smiled at him.

'I brew my own beer sometimes,' volunteered Hugh. He didn't say that the only meat he ate was roadkill, first, because he thought it very likely that Cyril disapproved of both omnivores and the internal combustion engine, and second, because it wasn't totally true, now that he lived with Polly. Fred wasn't about to disclose his Nando's addiction either. It was neither cool, nor right-on.

Cyril nodded approvingly. His vision of the future was small communities living artisanal lifestyles, so brewing and baking were very much part of that. He could talk for hours about composting. He would have approved of Hugh's carpentry too, if he'd known it was all reclaimed timber. Hugh was slightly jealous of Cyril's evident appeal to his wife. Fred didn't much like his beard, because it felt a bit like showing off. But maybe it disguised a weak chin.

'We were just arguing about rewilding,' said Fleur.

Cyril nodded.

'Britain should reintroduce wolves,' he said, which seemed a bit impractical to Fred, but maybe good for writers of children's books.

'In Norway, we have brought back lynx already,' said Fleur, proudly. Mystified, Fred thought for a minute that they were referring to the aftershave, before remembering the wild feline.

'Isn't the lynx a member of the cat family?' asked Cyril suspiciously. Fleur nodded.

'I myself am very keen on beaver,' said Cyril, so seriously that Fred only avoided giggling by chewing his own cheek. He just hoped that Cyril avoided saying things like that in public. The man seemed devoid of a sense of humour.

'Don't beavers just build dams and end up flooding everywhere?' he ventured. He'd been to Canada, between school and university, to visit his father's cousin. She still sent him a magazine about British Columbia, and he knew that some found beavers a curse.

'Yes, they do, of course, but it's natural, and it helps wildlife rather than working against it,' retorted Cyril.

'In Canada, apparently they have baffles, so beavers can't hear the running water and respond to their instinct to build dams,' said Hugh.

'I love the idea that the beavers can see the water, but not hear it. Must be very confusing for them,' said Fred, who was sure he'd told Hugh about the baffles in the first place. Hugh hadn't been on a plane since childhood, and not for the right reasons either.

'We need something like that for men,' said Lu, changing the subject. She smiled at Polly.

'Beavers are not great for global warming actually,' said Fleur. Fred was relieved to see that the conversation was back in safer waters. 'Because of warmer temperatures, they're moving into Alaska and Northern Canada. And of course, they cause ponds, which are dark and therefore absorb heat from the sun. It's a vicious cycle.'

'I hadn't read that,' admitted Cyril. 'But it makes sense.' He brooded.

Fred was secretly delighted that their new friend had shown up the eco-guru. This competitive environmentalism was fun.

'One of the biggest Norwegian rewilding projects is on Svalbard, in fact,' said Fleur, diplomatically. 'They have removed a whole town, and all traces of the mining they used to do there. They have made way for the polar bears and reindeer and Arctic foxes. We are going to visit it on Spitsbergen.'

Cyril nodded his approval. Fred thought that Norway was evidence that if you had enough oil wealth, and a small population, you could do these sorts of things. He couldn't see it working in Swindon. Not that there were many polar bears in Swindon.

'I saw a film about a bunch of wolves being reintroduced into Yellowstone Park in the 1990s,' said Polly, not wanting to be left out. She wasn't going to admit it was a film she'd watched on a flight. 'For a start, I hadn't realised how much bigger than dogs they were. They're huge! But it was also fascinating what impacts the reintroduction had had on the other flora and fauna. It even indirectly changed the landscape. It was very positive for the other animals.'

'Except for the ones they ate,' pointed out Hugh. He believed in nature red in tooth and claw. He was scornful of 'all things wise and wonderful' versions of flora and fauna. Nature could be vicious and cruel. It was not always about gorillas and other charismatic megafauna.

'Of course, wolves do eat a lot of elks. But that's good for other animals, like bears and coyotes,' said Cyril. 'The bears frighten off the wolves and eat the carcasses.'

'And they even eat their nephews and nieces, as far as I remember,' said Polly. The others looked at her in horror. 'I mean the other wolf cubs,' she clarified.

'Not something I'd recommend myself,' said Fred, thinking of Andy and Gerry – his brother's sons – who were both extremely lacking in taste.

'Anyway, good to meet you all. I have got to go and file a piece,' said Cyril, getting up and stroking his beard. Fred shuddered and tried to avoid catching Hugh's eye. Not only was Cyril rather self-important, but he also obviously had no clue about the effect of his facial outgrowth on other members of the party.

'Would you mind coming along, Lu?'

Slightly sulkily, because she was enjoying making friends, Lu joined Cyril as he left. She followed him like a grumpy teenager trailing behind her father to a parents' evening.

'I could listen to Cyril all day!' said Fleur, breathlessly. 'I am so glad he is on this trip!'

'Me too,' said Nel, almost as enthusiastically.

'He'd be much better with a less bushy beard, though,' said Fleur. 'Or, in fact, no beard at all.'

'Perhaps it's to hide a weak chin?' said Fred hopefully.

'I'm glad I actually met him,' said Polly.

Fred couldn't help glancing over at Hugh at this moment. Polly was clearly much too reverent for his liking. Hugh raised his eyebrows and gestured with two fingers at his open mouth, as if feeling nauseous. Thankfully, Cyril's fans did not see Hugh's uncalled-for gesture.

'I'm going to reread his stuff on rewilding,' said Fleur. 'It's all evidence-based, you know. Which makes a change, given that he's a journalist as well as an activist. Although he clearly doesn't know the latest beaver science.'

Fred thought of the journalists he knew: his old friend Heather, and his brother's ex-wife, Charlie. They were certainly good on anecdote and found plenty of interesting people to talk to. Not much data, though. Perhaps Cyril was different.

'You need both, don't you?' said Hugh. 'Strong stories backed up by good data. If you have just data, it gets pretty dry. If you have just stories, it can get unrepresentative. Or so I'm told. I suspect those rules don't apply on the channels where you just fuel your viewers' prejudices.'

Sometimes, thought Fred to himself, Hugh was surprisingly insightful. Nel and Fleur nodded seriously. Polly beamed at her husband. She liked it when others realised how much he knew, because otherwise he just risked coming across as an oddball. Which he was, of course, but he was more than that. Polly liked his directness, and didn't mind his shyness or oddities. The more he mumbled, the more she loved him. Which was why she had married him in the first place. And no scantily clad women in saunas could tempt her away from that.

Chapter 11

That evening, on his way to their bedroom, Fred wandered past the bar. He was surprised to see a familiar face with a glass of what looked like whisky in his hand, sitting opposite Paul, who was similarly equipped and smiling. Fred had never seen Captain Andersson looking relaxed before.

'If you're here, I hope someone reliable is steering the ship!' said Fred.

'It's my evening off. The first officer is in charge,' said Captain Andersson, shaking his hand. He wasn't wearing his uniform, but his blue eyes, and blond hair and beard made him unmistakeable.

'We were talking about seafaring,' said Paul. 'I've done a bit myself.'

'I'll have what these two gentlemen are having,' said Fred to the barman. He could smell the whisky on the captain's breath.

'It's good malt this,' said Captain Andersson, indicating his glass. Paul raised his glass in salute.

'How did you develop the taste for whisky?' said Fred, sipping his drink. 'I'd have thought you'd prefer aquavit?'

'I used to have a fishing trawler,' said Captain Andersson. 'Sometimes we'd offload our catch in a Scottish port, so we had two chances – out and in – to make some money.'

'Which is why he knows Campbeltown, Oban and Skye, but not the Highland malts,' said Paul. 'This is an educational session.'

'Where did you sail out of?' asked Fred, thinking about the Swedish captain's exile.

'Different places,' said Captain Andersson. 'We were after the skrei, the codfish wandering from the Arctic to Lofoten to mate or spawn. We used to sail up to the islands, for Lofotfiske, which is what Norwegians call fishing in Lofoten, at the beginning of the year.' He had a wistful look in his eyes. 'In the fjords, we'd fish for salmon. Lots of them, too.'

'Norway is good for fish?'

'The best!'

'It's got a lot of coastline.'

'It must be that,' said Captain Andersson, pointedly finishing his glass and putting it down. Paul just smiled at Fred. His glass was empty too.

'Oh, that'll be three more of the same,' said Fred to the bartender, thinking of the hole these whiskies would blow in his budget.

'Sweden is good for lake fishing. Something like 100,000 lakes, you know. But I prefer sea to lakes,' said the captain.

'England only has about a dozen lakes,' said Fred.

'Though Scotland has lots of lochs, and Northern Ireland has loughs,' interjected Paul.

'Most of the lakes in Wales are reservoirs, I think. It rains a lot in Wales,' said Fred. 'Where we English get our water.'

Captain Andersson nodded.

'You can go offshore in Sweden, of course. But Norway is the best fishing in the world.'

'Which is how a Swede got to be captain of a Norwegian ship?' asked Fred.

'Something like that,' admitted Captain Andersson. 'But fishing got so many regulations, I switched to the passenger ships. Fishing is still great if you've got a rod and line...'

'Good for the fish, bad for the trawlers?' asked Fred.

'Probably,' growled the captain into his whisky. He had such a long, sad face that he looked a bit like a codfish.

'I should be eating that fish,' thought Fred, although he said it aloud.

'You should,' agreed Captain Andersson.

'My friends are enjoying it, and I am eating the vegetarian options,' said Fred.

'You're really missing out,' said Paul.

'No more!' resolved Fred.

'Plenty more fish in the sea,' agreed the captain. Fred wasn't sure whether that was strictly true but wasn't going to point it out. There was an agreeable silence while they finished their whisky. Swedes were good at agreeable silence. Possibly not as good as the Finns, thought Fred.

'Well, I'm going to leave you to it,' he said. 'If I don't get an early night, I won't get my 1,000 words written tomorrow.'

'And if I don't get to bed, I will be grumpy as hell on the bridge tomorrow,' agreed Captain Andersson. He shook Fred and Paul by the hand.

'Goodnight, Fred,' he said. 'Goodnight, Paul.'

'Goodnight, captain,' said Fred, and nearly saluted.

'Thanks for the drink,' called the captain, as he wandered unsteadily off.

'Don't mention it,' replied Fred, equally politely. He thought that he shouldn't get used to Norwegian bar prices. That was the whole point of having a bottle of malt in his cabin. But it was good to be sociable, and how else would he get material for books? He wandered to the elevator, wondering what a Swedish sea captain could get up to in his novel.

Chapter 12

At breakfast the next morning, Fred was the first one to arrive. Thankfully, the whisky he had drunk had not left him with a sore head. He sat on his own, because he didn't see any of his friends in the dining room. Hugh would probably be out, spotting birdlife, Polly would be having a lie-in, and he knew Nel was out jogging around the ship. He had no idea where his aunts were, and he felt breakfast was far too early to find out. Really, he was just surprised that the Norwegians seemed to sprinkle hundreds and thousands on their breakfast. Freya might like it, were she here, but his idea of a morning meal was rather less frivolous. Toast and some sort of egg. Possibly a crumpet. If Nel wasn't looking, then bacon, though not on the crumpet, of course. You couldn't put just anything on crumpets. Some people (he shuddered at the memory) put baked beans on crumpets. Naturally, here they had no crumpets, but they did have hot pancakes with syrup, which were not bad at all. And he spoke as a breakfast aficionado, indeed almost a breakfast connoisseur.

When Marvin G. Ridley asked if he would mind if he brought his coffee and oats to eat opposite him, he couldn't object. Another culture with the wrong idea about breakfast, felt Fred. No feeling for tea, for a start. After all, their revolution had started by throwing the stuff in the harbour. And their coffee was dreadfully weak stuff, poor benighted souls.

'So, what brings you on this cruise?' Fred asked, to break the silence. He thought he would keep his observations about American hot beverages to himself.

'I wanted to see the Arctic, Fred,' said the American. 'I figure, you need to know what you're letting yourself in for. Before you make a move, as it were…'

'Make a move?' asked Fred, lost. 'Are you planning to date someone in these latitudes? Do you have a penchant for snow?'

'Let me be straight with you, Fred. You don't mind if I call you Fred? Good. You can call me Marvin, or Marv if we're drinking. Well, Fred, I'm from Texas, as you know, and I'm an oilman. Ever since we finished with bison, we took up with oil. I'm the sort of man who counts nodding donkeys to fall asleep.'

Fred nodded. It didn't surprise him. He'd overheard Marvin enthusing to his aunts.

'I just love West Texas Crude,' said Marvin, sounding more and more like a street-corner evangelist. 'I live for it. I've got it all here, on my Apple watch, and I have these earbuds to feed me prices, that's what I'm listening to, constantly. Trading, trading, trading… Every minute of every day I know what I'm worth. And let me tell you, that's a big number, believe you me. Think of a big number, and multiply it by ten, you might come close.'

Fred raised his eyebrows. Was that the way to show you were impressed? Really, he couldn't approve of anyone showing off about their wealth.

'This Arctic here, all around us, it may be very cold now, but you'll see the ice is melting, year on year. Temperatures are going up. Less and less of it is ice again each winter.' Marvin spoke as if the climate emergency was just one of those things. 'A big thaw is happening. Sad for the bears, of course. We're all going to miss those bears, Fred. But an opportunity for the likes of me...'

'You want to get your hands on Arctic oil?' asked Fred, grasping Marvin's meaning. He didn't like the sound of this. He knew Nel definitely wouldn't like the sound of this. He was breakfasting, quite literally, with the enemy.

'I do want,' said Marvin G. Ridley III. 'I didn't get into fracking, didn't like the sound of it, and frankly the sums didn't add up. But the Arctic is different. Fred, the Arctic is the new Paradise. A whole new world. The Geology Survey back in the US of A reckon that one quarter of the world's remaining oil and gas is about to become accessible, any minute now.'

'Which is where you come in?'

'Fred, you've got it in one. It's why I'm here. Let me be frank with you, this is no tourist caper. The Arctic seems to me to be just like a big sponge oozing oil, and I am the man to squeeze it, ice or no ice. Cometh the hour, cometh the sponge squeezer!'

Fred didn't think much of this play on words, nor did he think Marvin would appreciate criticism of his plans. In his limited experience, millionaires just expected you to say 'yes, sir' in the right places, and nod occasionally. Two-way dialogue wasn't their thing. But now he worked in sustainability, he wasn't going to give the oilman a free pass.

'I thought we didn't need oil anymore.'

'Don't need it? You think we don't need it?' exploded Marvin. 'Who the hell doesn't need oil?' Fred seemed to have touched a nerve. Marvin was continuing: 'Sure, there may be a few more Teslas about, one plane may have crossed the Atlantic on fat from a deep fryer or something, and a few folk in Norway might have hydro and heat pumps, but most of the rest of the world still needs oil for its cars and gas for its homes. We all need plastic, and where do we get that? Yes, good ol' oil, mostly. We need to keep drilling all right, at least for our lifetimes and probably beyond too. What line of business are you in yourself?'

'I'm a lawyer.' Fred did not think it was the time to tell his new friend that he was specialising in environmental law.

'Well, you'll know all about deals, contracts, obligations, options…'

'A little,' admitted Fred.

'Well, that's what I'm all about!'

'Good,' said Fred, uncertainly.

'I have more millions than I could possibly need. I have more stock options, profit-related pay and performance bonuses than my army of lawyers and accountants can keep up with!'

Marvin G. Ridley sat back with a broad smile on his face, as if he was lord of all he surveyed, which he probably soon would be, if he got his way. Marvin G. Ridley had two favourite topics of conversation, the first being himself. The second was energy (the non-renewable type). From the tar sands of Alberta to the gas rigs of the Gulf, he knew a hydrocarbon when he saw one and had an oil-slicked finger in almost every pie.

'I'm about winning, Fred. Because I'm an American. We like winning.'

'Except Vietnam,' muttered Fred under his breath. 'And Afghanistan.'

Luckily, Marvin didn't hear, because he had now moved on to sports.

'Even American games don't end in a draw. If the teams are drawing, you carry right on playing until there's a winner. We love a winner!'

'In my country we have score draws and no-score draws,' said Fred politely.

'That's why you're losers. Who put a man on the moon?'

'Lots of women doing maths, as far as I know,' muttered Fred.

'The Yewnited States of America, that's who!' said Marvin, ignoring him. 'And that's why we are going to come first in the Arctic. You'll see. It will be the American majors. We're going to boss it.'

Fred didn't like the sound of this.

'Now, if you'll excuse me for just a few hours,' said Marvin, 'I have to issue some instructions for my people. I'll see you at lunchtime!'

He marched off, shaking a few hands as he went, genial as anyone could be. A Texan to the core, with cowboy boots to match. Fred shook his head. He knew Nel would have had a go at Mr Ridley. Even Polly, and certainly Cyril. But Fred preferred a quieter life. Let sleeping hound-dogs lie. Even if Marvin G. Ridley was as oily as a serving of triple-cooked fries in Pam's Bar, Austin.

Chapter 13

Soon after Marvin left, Nel arrived, hungry for her breakfast. Purely out of courtesy, Fred was having a second breakfast with her, when they were both waylaid by Bella and Donna. The older women were wearing matching leisurewear, in lilac brushed cotton.

'Something really strange has happened!' said Donna.

'Stranger than meeting you here?' said Fred.

'Much stranger than that!' said Bella. 'How good are you at anagrams?'

'I'm hopeless,' said Nel. 'It's probably why I hate Scrabble.'

The two older women recoiled in shock, but let the comment pass.

'We left the board and letters out last night, in the corner of the saloon. Not far from the bar—' said Bella.

'And this morning, when we went to finish our game and tidy it away, we think we found a message left for us,' said Donna.

'What did it say?' asked Fred.

'It's hard to tell. That's why we need to solve the anagram,' said Donna.

'The rolling of the ship in the night has messed up the letters,' said Bella.

'I told you we should have brought Travel Scrabble,' said Donna to her partner.

'I'm getting too old to read the letters,' said Bella, 'let alone fiddle around with them.'

'What's the anagram?' said Fred. 'It was probably just Marvin or someone fooling with you.'

'I brought the letters to show you,' said Donna. 'Here they are.' She placed them carefully on the table.

STAY NOW DEW I BEAT IS CUS

'But that makes no sense,' said Nel.

'Is it Multicultural London English?' asked Fred. 'It might mean something in some sort of rap? I could try to message my nephews. Slang is their thing.'

'Have you tried singing it?' suggested Nel. 'Could it be some sort of chorus?'

'No, I think it really is an anagram,' said Donna, firmly. 'Leave it to me.' Having prior form with anagrams, she began to scribble on a scrap of paper, while Bella watched her adoringly. Fred looked at Nel and shrugged his shoulders. His aunts were always up to something, but as he tried to express, it wasn't usually his fault.

At that point, Polly turned up to breakfast, looking very worried. Her lie-in had been ruined, which was the least of her problems.

'What's the matter?' asked Nel, seeing her friend's distress.

'Georgie has lost Freya!' she said. 'At least, that's what her text said. I tried to phone her, but there's no signal at the moment.' Georgie was her ex-partner.

'Lost?' said Fred. 'How can you just lose a nine-year-old child?'

'Our dog Fenner was with Georgie, and Freya was meant to be staying with her friend Wildeve,' explained Polly. 'Except she wasn't. When Georgie and Fenner went to pick her up, it seems that she had never gone there. She's pulled the wool over all our eyes. Lisa is distraught to think she might have done wrong. She had no idea Freya was meant to be going home with them.'

What a nightmare, thought Fred. No wonder Polly was frightened. Freya was quite possibly his favourite child in the world. Although she'd clearly been extremely naughty on this occasion. She was nine going on nineteen. But in this latest emergency he wondered what he could do to help. All he could offer was support, and sometimes that's all people need.

'Oh my god!' said Nel. 'Do you have to go back?'

'Shouldn't you alert the authorities?' asked Fred.

'Georgie's already done that,' said Polly. 'I feel completely powerless! What can I do?'

'We're stopping at Tromsø in a few hours,' said Fred.

'That's true,' said Polly determinedly. 'If need be, I can get a flight back to London from there.'

'That makes sense,' agreed Nel. 'But what a disaster! I can only imagine how desperate you feel.'

Bella gazed at Polly in sympathy. But Donna, having decided that there was nothing she could do to help, was still puzzling away at the anagram they had been left on the Scrabble board.

'Wait everyone!' she said, as the group was dispersing after a gloomy breakfast. 'I think I've got it.'

'What?' said Fred.

'The anagram,' said Donna. 'I think it reads STOWAWAY NEEDS BISCUIT.'

'Stowaway?' said Nel. 'This isn't *Treasure Island*. It must be a joke.'

'Or a message,' said Polly, slowly. 'Might it actually be Freya?'

'It would be just like Freya,' said Hugh, who'd joined them, clutching his bird list, to have a rushed cup of coffee. 'She would love playing at stowaways.' He didn't seem half as alarmed as his wife.

'She does have a very vivid imagination,' admitted Polly. 'It must be all the books she's read.'

'Although Hugh's read loads of books,' said Fred. 'And his imagination is rubbish.' His friend glared at him.

'Couldn't it be Marvin, or someone else, pulling our leg?' said Bella.

'Where would she hide?' asked Polly.

'There must be a hundred places,' said Donna. They thought for a moment.

'The sub?' suggested Fred. It was lashed down on deck.

'The lifeboats?' said Hugh. They were hung along the sides, neatly covered.

'An empty cabin? The sauna? The kitchens?' said Polly, turning about to peer in every corner.

'But who was the message for?' asked Donna, looking around their group.

At that moment, Paul passed with a cup of coffee, giving them a wave. Thinking he might be good at anagrams, and possibly stowaways, Fred wheeled after him before he could leave the Adventurer's Lounge and brought him back to where they were sitting. Paul looked at the paper where Donna had been puzzling out the anagram. They could see him trying out alternative combinations under his breath. Finally, he turned back to the others round the table.

He said, 'First off, it wasn't me. I can see it might be fun to put the wind up your aunts, but it's not my style. This seems like it is for real. Unless you have got other new friends on board, with a poor sense of humour?'

Donna and Bella shook their heads, and the others shrugged. Fred wondered about Marvin. Nel was thinking she now knew far too many people, on what was meant to be a quiet cruise.

'Then in that case, I reckon we really have got ourselves a stowaway somewhere on the vessel,' said Paul.

'Trying to save on the high prices!' quipped Hugh, whose sense of humour did not always suit the situation. 'Let's see if we can find her.'

'In this situation, you have to tell the captain,' said Paul, ignoring Hugh.

'Really?' said Polly.

'Is that absolutely necessary?' asked Hugh.

'Can't we just find the person who's left this message?' asked Fred. 'Or work out who it was intended for?' He gave Hugh a long, hard stare.

'I'd certainly recommend that you do,' said Paul. 'And I'd be glad to help. But you still have to tell Captain Andersson. It's his ship. He needs to know.'

'I'll go and do that,' said Donna. 'The message was sent in our Scrabble tiles. And I'm a guest of the cruise line, so maybe that counts for something. Plus, I'm a doctor. I once swore an oath to uphold the highest ethics.' She marched off to the bridge, with her professional face on.

'I suggest we take a deck at a time, inside and out where possible,' said Paul, who seemed to be taking charge. 'Let's start here and work our way down.'

Hugh disappeared for a minute in the direction of the buffet. He came back with a selection of biscuits and cereal bars. He distributed them to the search party.

'The message did mention biscuits,' he said. 'I think the stowaway might be hungry...'

'If it really is Freya, she's in such trouble,' said Polly. 'Biscuits are the last thing she deserves!'

'Though she's probably starving,' said Bella. 'I think Hugh's right. There are very few questions for which cake is not the answer.'

The group armed themselves with prophylactic snacks and fanned out to search all the places where a stowaway could hide. It was not an untidy ship, so it was hard to find any nooks and crannies. Anyway, reasoned Hugh, the stowaway, if hungry, could surely not be near the kitchens, where there was plenty to eat. After they'd surveyed the canteen and the viewing area, they went out on the deck. As well as the rigid inflatables and the mini-sub behind the observation room, there were lifeboats hanging from davits along the sides of the ship. It would not be hard to pull up the cover and hide inside one of them, thought Hugh.

The party were joined by Donna and one of the crew, in her navy sweater and woolly hat. Her uniform announced that she was H. Halvorsen. She went down the row of boats, each hanging neatly, and after Hugh had roughly pulled off each of the covers and rummaged, she made the contents shipshape and safely re-covered the lifeboat.

It was becoming tedious, until Hugh suddenly revealed, curled up asleep under rugs and blankets in the bottom of the eighth lifeboat, a nine-year-old girl with two plaits. Either she had put on weight recently, or she was wearing all her clothes. Hugh gently shook her by the shoulder. She woke up, slowly, and smiled as she recognised him.

'Have you brought the biscuits?' she asked. Hugh handed over his stash and it didn't take her long to devour it.

When she looked up again, Polly was glaring at her.

'What are you doing here?' said Polly, asking a rhetorical question in the tradition of irate mothers everywhere. As she explained to Fred later, at that moment she felt a mixture of bone-melting relief and incandescent fury.

'Everybody's got to be somewhere,' said Freya.

'Said like a true philosopher,' said Hugh, doing his best to defuse the situation.

'But. You're. Meant. To. Be. Back. In. England. With Georgie,' said Polly, enunciating every word precisely. This was not the moment for philosophising.

'I wanted to come with you!' protested Freya, defensively. 'I brought my passport! I wrapped up warm! I have been sleeping all day, and creeping inside all night. Look, I have blankets!'

'Your other mum is beside herself!' said Polly. 'How could you lie to her?'

'If only I didn't read so many books,' moaned Freya, ignoring that point. 'My books are full of stowaways. I think it's really your fault for feeding my imagination. If you had only got me an Xbox, I would never have done this.'

'This isn't a book or a game. It's real life. Actions have consequences!' snapped Polly, still very cross, but at the same time relieved beyond measure to have found her.

Freya burst into tears. She wasn't up to defying her mother. After all, it had been an awfully big adventure.

'We need to go and see Captain Andersson,' said Paul, trying not to smile. Sailor Halvorsen nodded seriously.

Chapter 14

Captain W. Andersson was on the bridge. When Sailor Halvorsen approached him, she saluted. He came over to meet Polly, who was gripping Freya by her shoulder, and Paul. Freya had stopped crying, but was still rather emotionally fragile. And the captain was a huge man, who could be very scary for a nine-year-old girl to confront.

'This is our stowaway?' he said sternly. 'Miss Freya.'

'Yes, captain,' said Polly, pushing her forward. 'We've told her off.'

'I am glad to hear it.'

'I'm very sorry,' said Freya in a small voice. The captain appeared stiff, stern and unforgiving.

'I normally put stowaways in irons,' said Captain Andersson in his deep bass voice. 'You have a good name, Freya, so on this occasion I had better let you go free,' he said, showing a different side to his personality and winking at Polly. 'But only if you promise never to do it again?'

'I promise!' Freya said eagerly.

'And not to go out of your mother's sight,' added the captain.

'I won't,' said Freya, who was so intimidated that she even forgot to cross her fingers.

There was a pause for thought.

'We've never had a stowaway before,' said the captain, ruminatively. 'At least, not in my time.'

'I always wanted to be a stowaway,' admitted Sailor Halvorsen.

'Me too,' said Captain Andersson. 'I blame Pippi Longstocking. I was a very impressionable boy.'

'It's very easy really—' said Freya, brightening up. She was more than willing to share her technique.

'*But it will never happen again*,' said the captain sternly, cutting off the nine-year-old. Freya shook her head and stared at her feet. Paul stood in the background, trying not to laugh. Polly was quite happy for someone else to be cross with her daughter.

'Now, would you like to see the bridge?' said Captain Andersson.

'Yes, please!' said Freya.

And, aside from a text to a relieved, but angry, Georgina – and an apologetic phone call once they finally reached Tromsø – that was the last of it.

*

The birthday party were having lunch with the stowaway. Or rather, she was having her first proper hot meal, and they were eating their filled rolls, their relief tinged with a bit of envy. She was clearly quite the celebrity on board already, despite being in big trouble with her mother.

Passing crew members who knew all about it were stopping to take photographs on their mobile phones. Several Americans had even asked for her autograph. Her story and her photograph were in the photocopied news of the day. As the only child on board, and an actual stowaway, she was enjoying being the centre of attention. Polly felt that Freya should not be further rewarded for her bad behaviour. She was also worried about whether she would be allowed on excursions.

'What did you live on?' asked Nel.

'Haribo, mainly,' admitted Freya.

'Well, that accounts for the twitching,' said Fred.

'It's very clever of you,' said Hugh. 'Giving Lisa the slip and remembering to wrap up warm!'

Freya beamed.

'No, it's not!' said Polly, sternly. 'It's extremely naughty. Plus, it's a nutritional disaster.'

'I'm impressed,' said Hugh, who had always wanted to be a castaway, like Ben Gunn, although stowaway came a close second. 'However did you do it?'

Fred gave his old friend another long, hard stare. Something told him that Hugh knew much more than he was letting on. For a start, he was terrible at acting.

'The child protection issues alone are scary as hell,' said Polly, who had not noticed anything.

'Oh, I can defend myself,' said Freya. 'I have a knife.'

'That's a paper knife, darling,' said Nel. 'Not sure it would be sharp enough.'

'Maybe you're right,' said Freya. 'Perhaps I should have a Taser...'

'Nine-year-old girls do not have Tasers,' said Polly, firmly.

'Maybe they should?' said Hugh.

'Would certainly make a difference to gender-based violence,' said Fred.

'Maybe I should just change career,' said Polly, mournfully. 'It's not too late. What future is there in social work for someone whose own child runs away?'

'Do I see a workshop coming on?' said Fred, looking over to the crowd that was gathering. 'Or a conference even?'

'What are you going to do aboard?' asked Nel, turning to Freya.

'Stay in the cabin?' said Polly hopefully.

'I could teach you all I know about sea birds?' said Hugh, also hopefully.

'That's awfully kind, Steppy…' said Freya, seriously.

'Steppy?' asked Nel, in a whisper.

'Stepfather,' said Fred. 'It's what they agreed.'

'…but mainly Captain Andersson is going to teach me about steering the ship,' Freya continued.

'He is?' said Polly, rather stunned.

'Oh yes,' said Freya. 'He reckons I could go to sea properly when I leave school.'

'We'll see about that,' said her mother sternly.

'And Sailor Halvorsen is going to teach me some useful knots,' continued her daughter.

'They might come in useful if we need to tie you up,' said Polly.

'I can't decide between the merchant marine or the navy…' said Freya, ignoring her mother. 'What do you think, Uncle Fred?'

'Depends which has the best uniforms,' suggested Fred. Polly was kicking him under the table, but luckily not in a place he could feel.

'I think you only have to be sixteen to join. I have the hat already!' Freya pulled on a blue woolly hat, like the ship's crew members.

Polly groaned.

'Oh, and you don't need to worry about child protection,' said Freya airily. 'There are always at least two adults on the bridge. And Sailor Halvorsen has said I can call her Helga.'

'Child protection is the least of my worries,' said a reluctant Polly. 'It's crew protection I'd be concerned about.'

Chapter 15

That afternoon, the ship puffed along slowly until it finally came to a stop and anchored fast in Geirangerfjord, a long and very picturesque inlet, just North of Bergen. Most of the passengers were on deck or at the windows, open-mouthed, as idle as their cameras were busy. The deep sides of the narrow fjord had been cut by a glacier tens of thousands of years ago. This was one of the highlights of the cruise, a UNESCO World Heritage site no less: in its unspoiled, primal glory it was indeed a memorable place, and not only because it starred in Disney's *Frozen*. Waterfalls of melting ice cascaded photogenically down the dark rocks, and the crew member at the helm obligingly steered in close enough that the scenery could be captured on phones and digital cameras to be proudly shown to less adventurous friends and relatives.

Here some of the passengers were to kayak for a couple of hours, while others remained on the ship to photograph the steep sides of the fjord and those charming waterfalls tumbling into it as the inlet snaked its way through steep cliffs. The kayakers were easily spotted, wearing the matching branded orange cagoule under their life jackets. Fred felt that this was a chance for him to come into his own, given that he was an experienced kayaker with strong arms and good technique.

Nel had given her apologies for the trip. She had kayaked many times with Fred before, in Norfolk and also on the Thames above Teddington Lock (although icebergs were less of a hazard in the Home Counties). She would see the fjord from the ship and have a relaxing sauna. Polly had also said she wouldn't go, because her hands were full with Freya, who now had a custodial sentence with no time off for good behaviour. They had been warned that there was a known risk of landslides and even a tsunami if the whole mountain of Åkernes fell into the fjord. Although Fred felt they were all quite safe for one afternoon, it was a not totally improbable disaster, because it would happen one day, and Polly didn't want Freya at any further risk. Fred didn't point out that if the mountain fell into the fjord at that moment, they would be in nearly as much danger on the ship as on the kayak.

Because the others had cried off, Fred was now taking Hugh on the trip. They had not been out kayaking together since they were both sixteen, and Fred was looking forward to it. He hoped that the two of them would have some good conversations as they wended their way through the fjord. They had a double kayak, and they were both wrapped up in storm gear to avoid any possible splashes, although their life jackets would not be much good if they were hit by falling rocks, let alone if there was a tidal wave. Anyway, it was Norway, and they had signed the usual disclaimers.

Hugh had his field glasses around his neck, because he was eager to see the sea eagles which Polly had been describing, or any other fjord-based birdlife for that matter. As a consequence, Fred felt he might end up as the engine of their boat, given that he was less keen on bird-spotting, but really, he didn't mind. It was a good opportunity to get active and off their ship for a while. Nel and Polly each photographed their partners in the double kayak; Fred was smiling at the camera phone, whereas Hugh remained entirely oblivious. Freya waved, impressed and slightly jealous. Whatever her mum said, she saw no reason why stowaways could not also be champion kayakers.

Fleur, trained in marine biology, was there to explain anything they found, and give anyone listening a short lecture on the geology of fjords. She was in a single kayak, so that she could nimbly paddle over to any of her party. Fred noticed that his aunts were in a double kayak too, having left their beloved Scrabble set behind. In their matching yellow sou'wester hats, they were hard to miss. Paul was out there too, weaving around as if he was in a kayak slalom – showing off a bit, thought Fred, who was proud of his own prowess. Marvin was conspicuous by his absence.

As they glided along through the still waters of the fjord, Hugh was more interested in what he could see through his glasses than in contributing to their collective momentum. Nor was he holding up his end of the conversation. The sides of the gorge towered high above them, dangerously photogenically. Far above, there were goats, rocks and presumably people, possibly with cameras. As he paddled, Fred watched the other kayakers. His aunts were on a quest for spring flowers on the slopes of the mountainside, but seemed to have had a difference of opinion. As he got closer to them, he heard Bella trying to get Donna to agree to move out into the centre of the fjord. If anything fell from above, she was saying, they were sitting ducks. But Donna was busy photographing wildflowers and paid no attention at all.

Fred looked up. He couldn't see anything coming their way. But, presumably, if there was a real avalanche or tsunami, it would be over in a second. Perhaps Donna would be better in a boat with Hugh next time. Then they could both dawdle all they liked. Just extremely slowly. He rather envied Paul his dashing around.

While Fred paddled gently along, he saw waterfalls flowing down the rocks and into the fjord, and far above them the green of farms, which had once been tended, despite their altitude and the steepness of the mountainside. Put a foot wrong, he thought, or be a bit absent-minded, and you would fall to your death. Certainly, no good for wheelchairs. As he looked up, he spotted a large rock in the act of tumbling down from on high. Fascinated, he watched it rolling faster and faster, bouncing from slope to slope as it came. Their own boat was quite safe, well out of the way of the impact, which was why he could look on calmly. A moment later it fell, with a loud splash, into the fjord. A wave of water went up and their kayak rocked.

Hugh looked around at the sudden sound, more bemused than anxious.

'What was that?'

'A rock,' replied Fred. 'Pretty big. About the size of a door, I think. Sent up a sheet of water, rather spectacular. But we were quite safe!'

'My list is looking better by the minute,' said Hugh. 'I'm going to bring it up to date when we get back on board.'

'Good to know!' said Fred, who was not in the least interested in Hugh's bird list. But he was happy to be his friend's navigator through the chilly waters of the fjord.

Then he suddenly thought of his aunts and glanced around for their boat. They were nowhere to be seen. Surely, they hadn't been caught in the wash of the rockfall? Had they capsized? Nobody might have noticed them sinking. He looked around again, more anxiously this time. There was Fleur, giving her lecture to some of the other kayakers. She would surely have been keeping an eye on everyone. There was their ship, a few hundred metres away, standing at anchor in the deep water of the fjord. In the distance there were other cruise ships, and other tour boats, and even other kayak parties. But no aunts to be seen. He began to panic about them. Where could they have gone?

He was about to alert Fleur, when his aunts' double kayak came into view again from the direction of the mountainside from which the rock had tumbled. The lead kayaker, who he thought was Bella, waved at him. He paddled in their direction. As he reached them, his two aunts were keen to explain.

'We found a sort of cave,' said Bella, excitedly.

'It was an overhang of rock,' explained Donna.

'Really very precarious!' added Bella.

'Certainly not the sort of thing that is covered by travel insurance,' said Donna.

'Probably some nesting bats?' enquired Hugh, but everyone was too taken up with the drama to respond.

'Guess who we saw in the cave,' said Bella.

'Saw?'

'Yes. Marvin! He was handing over cash to someone else!'

'Cash?'

'Yes,' said Donna. 'Not card. We wondered if he had been betting on *Eurovision*.'

'We've been known to,' said Bella, in explanation.

'There was no sign of a Scrabble board,' said Donna. 'And the other guy was a local, we reckon. He certainly wasn't from the ship.'

'Not that you were spying or anything,' said Fred.

'Anyway, as we were passing under there,' said Bella, 'we heard the splash of that falling rock!'

'It would have killed us instantly!' said Donna, not without relish.

'Only if it had hit you on the head,' said Fred. 'You'd have been in big trouble, then.'

'Well, we had been in that very spot where it fell,' said Bella. 'We saw the ripples as we came out from under the overhang. Neither of us is a strong swimmer.'

'Well, thank goodness you are safe,' said Fred, entering into the spirit of the drama. 'For a moment, I thought you were goners.'

'They are never going to believe this, back in Grassington,' said Donna, who wrote amateur dramatic plays and had a vivid imagination. What with the rock and Marvin's surreptitious rendezvous, it had been quite a theatrical moment.

Fred could see how the story would gain in the telling. No doubt his aunts would try out their experience around the dinner table. By the time they got home, the rock would have become a boulder and eventually it would end up being a big chunk of mountain. Marvin would turn out to have been handing over thousands of kroner. He was probably being blackmailed by a local. At this rate, the episode might end up on stage.

Fred obligingly took a photograph of his aunts sitting in the kayak with their paddles, to attention, the fjord rising steeply behind them. Maybe they could Photoshop in the boulder afterwards. But in real life, could they really have seen Marvin handing over money? Was it something to do with oil?

Chapter 16

That afternoon, it was sunny and quite warm, considering they were steadily steaming North towards the Arctic, and it was only April. Perhaps it was due to the Gulf Stream? Fred thought he'd been colder on an English summer's day. Global warming was changing everything. He'd read about, and shivered at, the likelihood of the Atlantic currents changing, and how all the weather they were used to would change as a result.

The coast of Norway was looking rockily interesting as they chugged past, as if someone had done a really bad job of making pastry, as Bella suggested. Many of the ship's passengers were taking the chance to get some air, neglecting the Science Centre's afternoon talk on: 'Everything you want to know about auks'. Fred thought that Hugh might be the only taker for that one. While the tiny gym was quiet, Polly and Nel were using the running machines, and chatting as they panted.

Fred was sunning himself on the rear deck, after his kayak exertions, when Cyril approached; he was wearing shorts and a singlet, and carrying a mat. He took off his shoes and unrolled the mat in the centre of the deck. He began by squatting on his heels and bringing his hands together in prayer, and then he slowly started making moves, in what was plainly his own version of yoga.

Although Fred felt it was rude to stare, it was difficult to ignore his contortions, given that Cyril had placed himself in the centre of the deck, and he was making quite extraordinary movements. While he may have been stubborn in public dialogue, Cyril was clearly very flexible when it came to his body. As the ship's passengers were middle-class and polite, they pretended none of it was happening – particularly the ones who were English – or refused to look, if they were from Nordic countries. For Cyril's admirers, his exercises were further evidence, if any were needed, of his saintly status.

Freya came and sat with Fred. She seemed unabashed about staring at Cyril, and indeed imitated some of his more outré movements. When he had finished, she asked him if he was a dancer.

'No,' he said. 'That was my daily Iyengar yoga practice.'

'Wow!' she replied. 'You do all that every day?'

'Most days,' he said.

'What would happen if you got stuck?'

Many people on deck were listening in, keen to hear the answer to that question.

'I don't.'

'But if you did? Or maybe someone burgled your house when you were doing your exercises? Or if you realised that you had left something on the stove? Or you did a fart?' She giggled. Cyril tried to ignore her.

These seemed quite reasonable questions, and Freya's fellow passengers were agog to know more, although Fred guessed that

Cyril felt somewhat ambushed by this impertinent nine-year-old. He lay peacefully, as if he were a corpse, on his mat.

'I'd rather not continue this conversation,' he replied. Fred guessed that Cyril was infuriated at having to break off his practice. Cyril Earther's fabled stubbornness left his fellow passengers disappointed and Freya feeling short-changed. Even his admirers felt he could have been less abrupt with the child. As he rolled up his mat and stalked away, Freya could be heard telling Fred: 'I bet he does tie himself in knots some days! I wonder who unties him? Can you do Iron-girder yogurt, Uncle Fred?'

This was not the general approbation that Cyril had hoped to receive as a result of his public display of Iyengar yoga. It was as if Thoreau had been asked who did his washing. Cyril had aimed to impress his public. It would probably be sunny another time, so he could try again. Perhaps he'd wait until the child was busy in the Science Centre or otherwise engaged. Cyril liked an audience, but preferably one which was more admiring than inquisitive and didn't ask him questions during his corpse position. Laughing at himself was not something that Cyril was in the habit of, and he saw no reason to start now.

For his part, Fred suggested that Freya might be a bit gentler in her interrogation of other people.

'I think he looked silly,' said Freya. Fred conceded that she might have a point, but added that even silly people deserved consideration. Freya screwed up her face and ran off to see what was happening on the bridge. Fred sighed. Having a nosey nine-year-old was a mixed blessing on a cruise.

*

After supper that evening, they joined a roomful of their fellow voyagers to hear Fleur talk about polar bears, which was a favourite subject of hers – and theirs. The voyagers learned about the largest land animal and biggest carnivore, and about the jet-black skin which underlay all that fur. They learned about the polar bears' dependence on sea ice to catch seals. They learned how polar bears were going into Canadian towns, eager for food, and how they had been airlifted away from humans. They learned about the nineteen subpopulations of polar bears, and how the withdrawal of the ice was leaving them isolated, despite the fact that polar bears could swim 150 kilometres, over days at a time, using their front paws to paddle and their hind paws like a rudder. Although they spent half their life looking for food, only 2 per cent of their hunts were successful (which Fred thought was very unfortunate).

As well as climate change, oil exploration was hazardous to polar bears: not only was oil toxic to ingest, but it also made their fur less waterproof. Hugh was interested in the grizzly-polar bear hybrids, known variously as 'grolar bears' or 'pizzly bears', which were names that Freya enjoyed. He set her to coming up with a name for wolf-coyote hybrids, which kept her quiet for the rest of the lecture.

There were 2,600 polar bears left; of the nineteen subpopulations, only one was increasing and four were in decline, although, as Fleur pointed out, more data was needed.

'All scientists say that,' suggested Nel afterwards. 'More data is needed.'

'Not sure I want to be the one collecting data about polar bears,' admitted Fred.

'What you want is Interferometric Synthetic Aperture Radar,' said Fleur, coming up to them. 'Sensors on aircraft wings which can map the maternal den habitats of polar bears.'

'In other words, you need more funding,' said Nel. 'Because more data is needed.'

'Exactly,' said Fleur. 'And in the meantime, we can use these voyages to collect data and do conservation projects. We do usually see a bear on Spitsbergen.'

'As long as it's from a distance,' said Polly, thinking of her daughter.

'I don't have the balls to get up close and personal,' said Fred. Freya giggled.

'Balls are exactly what we need for conservation,' said Fleur. 'As you may well see!'

*

As they filed into the bar, as had become traditional after a lecture, Fred saw Marvin in a corner of the room. He seemed to be doing magic tricks for a small party of Germans, who were clustered around him. At least, whatever he was doing certainly involved cards. Fred thought he heard the phrase 'Persian monarchs' as he came back to his group with the drinks, one at a time. The Texan was smiling broadly but the Germans did not seem so enthusiastic. Out of curiosity, he kept an eye on Marvin's huddle. Money seemed to be changing hands, but it was only going in one direction, so he was not surprised that the huddle broke up, leaving Marvin standing there, smiling, riffing his cards between his hands. He looked like a shark who has scented blood in the water.

Chapter 17

For the next few hours, the birthday party did what had become habitual: Hugh was on deck, looking for birds; Fred sat in the corner of the Adventurer's Lounge, tapping away at his novel and trying to resist the temptation of pressing the 'Word Count' command every ten minutes. Polly and Nel were always off, probably taking exercise in the gym or relaxing in the sauna, or wrapping themselves around a coffee or a glass of wine, endlessly talking. Meanwhile, Marvin was roaming the ship with a pack of cards, willing to bet on anything. At one point, he had sidled up to Hugh, looking to open a sweepstake on how many birds he could tick off, but Hugh had not understood what he was suggesting, so Marvin had marched off in disgust and in pursuit of less other-worldly prey.

They had been concerned that Freya's presence on board the adults-only cruise would have caused upset, but everyone seemed to be minding the nine-year-old, from her mother to the ship's cat, Ingrid, who had taken a liking to her. As Polly said, any danger was to Freya's companions, not to her. For example, at that moment, she was busily teaching Helga Halvorsen how to make friendship bracelets. Their interaction had started out with Helga spending her morning off showing Freya how to make knots: but having made bowlines, reef knots and a round turn and two half hitches on their pieces of string, they had got on to the much more important topic of friendship bracelets. It was typical: nobody could tell Freya anything these days. Certainly, Helga was not escaping until lunchtime, but she seemed to be enjoying herself.

Freya was the interesting new arrival among 100 pairs of people, many of whom were in an advanced state of relaxation. Thankfully, nobody worked out whether she had had an accomplice helping her to stow away. Freya was making the most of her status as the only child on board to be friends with everyone. Other people's children are so much easier than your own, and other adults are very much more acceptable company than one's own parents. Only one person shunned her company: Cyril, who thought her directness did not accord him the respect which he expected.

*

It was after lunch on day three (or it may have been four) when the ship slowly steamed alongside the quay in Tromsø. They had been heading North up the coast of Norway, and unless they were keeping a diary, it was hard to be sure exactly how many. This time it was reassuringly Arctic weather out there: −10°C and a howling gale. Yesterday's sun could have been a different world. Although they were stopping for a few hours, most of the passengers preferred discretion over valour, and viewed the quayside curiously from the safety of the saloon, well wrapped-up in their fleeces.

Marvin had been telling anybody willing to listen that Norway was safe and secure and rich, thanks to their new-found oil. Fred mused that Marvin was certainly somewhat richer, now that the spare cash of several Germans was locked away in his safe. Cyril ostentatiously jotted down notes from a report on sea temperatures, presumably for an article. At the other end of the saloon, Bella and Donna were playing Scrabble, without a word list in sight. Out on the main deck, Lu was doing her tai chi practice, and teaching Fleur the moves.

Polly and Nel, with Freya in tow, and their oilskins on, went out sightseeing. A few minutes after they left, Hugh jogged down the gangplank, looking slightly furtive, thought Fred. Was he trying to catch up with the others? Because the others had gone towards the Troll Museum ('The first and only troll museum in Norway to use augmented reality technology.'), and Hugh went in the opposite direction, towards the shops. He probably didn't think much of trolls, let alone augmented reality technology. Fred definitely wanted to hear more about both these excursions.

Fred had a coffee and typed away on his laptop, sitting and enjoying the quietness in the saloon. There was a background hum of conversation, but no sound was distinguishable, which he preferred to the quiet of a library. Even Bella's and Donna's voices did not stand out, for which he was grateful. After half an hour, a small gaggle of new passengers made their way up the gangplank towards the ship, wheeling bags behind them like penguins on parade. So much for quietness.

There was a woman on the quay with a very smart and highly fashionable grey wool coat, black leather boots and waterproof-yet-chic cloche hat, joining the queue of new voyagers embarking. She had a certain elegance and demeanour about her, which Fred instinctively admired, and then half-recognised. Could that be his college friend Heather? Surely not? For a moment, he thought he must be seeing things, but then realised it was definitely her. He'd recognise that hair anywhere. Part of him was thrilled, and all of him was mystified: what on earth was she doing here?

Until he had met Nel, he had nursed a crush on Heather, which started when they were both university students at St Warburg's. Nearly half his life! He thanked his lucky stars that Heather had proved impervious to his charms. Although he was much better off with Nel – for a start, she was a kind person – Heather still retained the ability to stop him in his tracks. As she queued up the gangplank, Fred had time to admire her. What was it that made her so distinctive? Perhaps it was the auburn hair streaming in the wind, despite the woolly hat. Perhaps it was the black leather boots, and the confidence with which she owned her surroundings. She seemed to travel light, no doubt because her producer was struggling behind her with boxes of equipment and their cases. At least, Fred hoped it was her producer, given that Heather was married to his own brother.

As she boarded, Fred wheeled to the entrance door of the saloon.

'What on earth are you doing here?' he asked, not unreasonably.

'Well, hello there, Fred!' said Heather, kissing him warmly on both cheeks and seeming unsurprised by the coincidence. 'Can't a busy girl have a break from time to time? I've just learned more about the Norwegian hydroelectric industry than is good for anyone, so I need a holiday.'

'Are you on assignment?' asked Fred suspiciously. 'Or is Roderick with you?'

'News never sleeps,' replied Heather, who was as fluently clichéd as the finest estate agent. 'But occasionally it takes a day off. I wanted a cruise, and this is the easiest. Roddy is on a state visit to somewhere dull. I've taken a suite with a hot tub, and apparently there's a sauna on board. So I am making the very best of a bad job. I've always wanted to see the Northern Lights.'

'Wrong time of year for that,' said Fred, still puzzled by the coincidence. 'You'd want to go in the winter, not spring.' Fred thought that, since some people had now seen the aurora as far South as London, a major motivation for a winter Norwegian cruise had been removed.

'Silly me,' she said, flashing the flawless smile that had made her orthodontist considerably richer. 'Whatever. Here I am in the Arctic. It makes a change. Get me a coffee, would you? Black?'

Heather was used to people obeying her requests. Men generally did. Even men with partners. Fred felt uneasy, but did it anyway. Carrying hot liquids while wheeling was not his strong point, but he got the coffee, and she came to his rescue, at least once she noticed him spilling some of it.

'How is Roddy anyway?' asked Fred of his brother, as he relinquished the Americano. He did not see much of him these days, despite them both living in London.

'As you know, he's just been appointed Shadow Secretary for Energy, or something,' said Heather. 'He's certainly got plenty of that. We're like ships in the night. He's either haring back to Stoke for a surgery on a Saturday morning, or he's off to inspect a new power station or wind farm. He mumbles ministerial questions in his sleep. It's really quite fascinating. I'm sure he was saying, "Order, order!" the other night.'

She took a grateful slurp of her black coffee, made a face, and then reached for her bag and clicked two artificial sweeteners in.

'Anyway,' she said. 'I'm not here to talk about Roddy.'

'Has he worked out what his Party think about non-renewables?' asked Fred.

'I am absolutely 100 per cent in favour of the environment,' said Heather in a self-important voice. She could certainly do a good impression of Roddy. 'But you can be sure that Labour will not wage war on the motorist, let alone the homeowner.'

'Talking of having your cake and eating it too.' Fred sighed. 'Charlie Howells has just moved to the drive-time slot on Universal Radio, you know.'

'I know,' said Heather shortly. 'I also heard the good Lord has lightened up.'

'A younger gentleman friend, I hear,' said Fred, who found Charlotte's mid-life transformation astonishing and rather admirable. She'd been his friend since college, had once been married to his brother and had two sons, and now had resumed where she'd left off, aged twenty-one. It was as if all that wife-and-motherhood had been left behind her. Not to mention the Bible-bashing. Anyway, she seemed happier this way, that was the main thing. And wasn't she training to be a celebrant now or something?

'Good for her,' said Heather, distracted.

'Good for who?' said Polly, joining them and doing a double take. 'Oh hello, Heather, what on earth are you doing here? Is there a war happening we don't know about?'

'Almost certainly, but if so, I don't know about it either – and I would rather not,' said Heather. 'Just having a wee vacation between assignments. And here I am.'

There was a moment's silence. Clearly, Polly was still unconvinced that it was just a coincidence that Heather had joined them.

'Are you here because of Cyril?' asked Polly, persisting.

'Cyril?'

'Cyril Earther.'

'Oh, him,' said Heather. 'Is he here?'

'He is,' said Polly, less and less convinced.

'I would certainly like to have his take on things,' said Heather. 'But no, he's not why I am here.' In this, she was being completely honest, for once, but sounded as insincere as she always did, which was not the impression she wanted to convey.

'Nel's taking Freya round the shops. Not much more in the city centre than you can see from the ship,' Polly told Fred. 'We thought we'd give the Troll Museum a miss, not having infants. I think it's a tourist trap, it's certainly very expensive.'

'Oh, is it real trolls, not internet trolls?' said Heather.

The others just stared at her. Sometimes she seemed very dim.

'More folkloric than real,' said Polly. 'But yes, the old kind, not the recent version.'

'That's rather sweet,' said Heather. 'At least for kids.'

'I see what you did there,' said Fred, smiling appreciatively.

'What?' said Heather.

'Goats? Billy Goat Gruff...' started out Fred. Heather looked at him nonplussed and he gave up.

'Fred here has become a novelist since you last saw him,' said Polly, changing the subject.

'How could I miss that? I do go to lots of airports, you know,' said Heather. 'Well done! Not read it yet myself,' she admitted.

'We were all sent presentation copies,' said Polly.

'So thoughtful!' said Heather. 'It really was. But who would I present it to?'

Polly turned and grimaced at Fred. How had they ever been friends with such a shallow dimwit? She was clearly better doing pieces to camera than analysing world events. Fred just raised his eyebrows. Although it was a little insulting, it was a relief that Heather hadn't yet read it. It saved the embarrassment of discussing exactly who 'Mary' the foreign affairs journalist was based on. Even though he'd changed her look, there were several telltale features of Heather parodied in the character. He thought it was impossible to tell that he'd had a crush on her for a couple of decades. Now it was as if the scales had lifted from his eyes. She was as shallow as a paddling pool with a slow puncture. And she was up to something, for sure.

He was glad his brother seemed happy. Heather might be the ideal partner for Roderick. A generous assessment was that they were both movers and shakers, one in politics, one in the media. A more critical voice might point out that they were both operators who could not be trusted. In the old days of student life, they would have been called a hack, someone in the world of politics or media who was only in it for themselves.

Fred felt much better off without Heather dominating his thoughts. Polly, who did not much like her, had always said that she was unworthy of him and that he could do much better than that. And indeed, Nel was perfect for him: interesting, but unselfish. Never predictable, but always loyal.

'Let's have a drink together tonight?' said Heather, smiling at her old friend. 'Got to unpack my stuff and take a rest.'

Fred didn't need much persuasion. It would be a good way to wriggle out of another Scrabble game with his aunts.

'Goodbye, darling,' said Heather, and touched cheeks.

After Heather left, Fred found himself alone with Polly and the faint aroma of expensive perfume. The two old friends looked at each other in shared amusement.

'Don't you think it's a bit of an unlikely coincidence, Heather suddenly turning up in the Arctic?' said Polly.

'Is it?' asked Fred, distractedly. He had started reading Barry Lopez's book about the Arctic. 'She has a plausible reason.'

'It was an excuse, and not a very convincing one,' said Polly. 'I'm keeping my eye on Ms Crisp, you can guarantee that. And I wonder whether she has designs on you.'

'Me? I very much doubt that,' protested Fred, in surprise. 'Do you think Freya and Nel will be back soon?' he asked, thinking it best to change the subject. Heather had never been Polly's favourite person, and he rather knew what she'd say about her. In his heart, he knew she was right.

'Nel said she'd take her to get some more clothes,' said Polly. 'I just hope they're waterproof. Freya always wants skimpy numbers these days. Nel's got her orders!'

'What's Cyril up to? Why aren't you shadowing him?' said Fred.

'I do not shadow Cyril!' retorted Polly.

'You very do!' said Fred.

'She's great, Fleur,' said Polly, changing the subject.

'Yes, she is,' said Fred. 'She should be on telly.'

'Lu seems lovely too,' said Polly.

'Do you think Lu might have a crush on Cyril?' said Fred.

'Definitely not.'

'How can you be so sure?'

'Because I happen to know she doesn't much like him. She told me. But it's meant to be a secret, so please don't repeat that,' said Polly.

'Well, I wouldn't much like him, if I were her,' said Fred. 'He seems a bit of a self-important know-all. Plus, he's got an awful beard.'

'That's what she said. I got the impression that he is a bit of a chauvinist.'

'Why does she suddenly confide in you?' said Fred, curiously. Then he remembered Polly's past predilections. 'Oh, wait a minute. Please don't tell me you've got the hots for her.'

'Certainly not!' said Polly, not entirely convincingly.

'You're a married woman! To my oldest friend!'

'I am aware of that. Lu is a bit of a flirt,' she admitted. 'We met in the sauna. But I am not going anywhere near her. You're going to have to trust me on this. And you're no saint either, when it comes to that. I seem to remember you went to bed with your brother's wife.'

'Woah, this isn't about me!' retorted Fred quickly. He preferred to draw a veil over that part of his fortieth birthday weekend. Although he wouldn't be the man he was today without Charlotte.

'Which Nel does not know,' said Polly.

'And really it would be much better if she never knew,' said Fred, suddenly alarmed. Nel was very easy-going, but even she might get the wrong idea. 'It happened before we got together. I'm trusting you! Anyway, please don't give Hugh the wrong idea. He's very insecure, you know, and it's not as if you don't have form.'

'You know me, I hope: I keep my promises. So, if Hugh ever worries about Lu, please put him right. Nothing is going on.'

'And don't you mention Charlotte to Nel. That's ancient history.'

'I believe I am right in saying, "The past is a foreign country: they do things differently there",' concluded Polly.

Chapter 18

Nel returned with Freya, and was followed soon after by Hugh, their various shopping trips complete, carrying bags. Ten minutes later, they all felt the engines shuddering as the ship moved out into the channel, and then into what Hugh told them was the Barents Sea. It was early afternoon, and already dark. The lights from the city and across the cantilevered bridge were reflected against the inky water and glowing against the sky of the polar night (like pearls on an embroidery, thought some of the travellers; like *Revenge of the Zombies III*, thought others). Soon, spray from the open sea smashed against the windows of the saloon, and they felt the ship rolling with the swell. They were finally off, leaving Norway behind. Next stop, Spitsbergen!

First, though, it was time to have a picnic lunch. Nel had bought baguettes, and sliced cheese and fruit in a supermarket.

'The bread may be trying to be French, and the fruit is imported from Southern climes, but I also bought some typical Norwegian sausage, Morrpølse,' she said. 'In case any carnivores want to try it.'

Hugh cut the end off with his penknife and chewed. The sausage was definitely smoked.

'Not unpleasant,' he reported. 'Tastes of nutmeg and aniseed.'

'That'll be the juniper,' said Nel. 'The meat is mostly offal, and tripe.' Freya turned up her nose and decided to pass on the sausage.

'Charming,' said Fred, also declining to try it. 'Makes me glad you made me a vegetarian.'

'I'm having second thoughts myself,' said Hugh.

'I guess that's what foreign travel is all about. Strangely delicious food made from offal,' said Polly.

'You've obviously been to some unusual places,' said Fred, slightly envious.

'Talking of strangely delicious, guess who I saw?' said Hugh.

'Heather?' ventured Fred.

'How on earth did you guess?' said Hugh. 'She's the last person I'd expect to see here.'

He seemed peeved that his mystery turned out not to be one.

'Well, she came aboard, of course,' said Fred.

'Oh, she's on the ship?' said Hugh.

'Isn't that where you saw her?' asked his wife.

'No, I saw her in a coffee shop – the one in the street to the main shopping area,' said Hugh. 'She was talking to that bearded guy, the one who puts the mental into environmentalist. The one you like.' He pretended not to know his name.

'Sounds like Cyril,' said Nel. 'Anyway, why were you going to the shops, Hugh? You hate retail.'

'I had to buy underwear,' admitted Hugh, sheepishly.

'Is the underwear something I want to hear about?' said Polly. 'Are you into lingerie all of a sudden? Your Y-fronts are certainly full of holes, but it isn't exactly sexy. Please don't say you were getting it for me. You know I hate all that stuff.'

'To be quite frank, I ran out of pants. So I had to buy some more,' admitted Hugh. 'For me, not for you.'

He'd bought Polly lingerie early in their relationship, a mistake he wasn't going to make again. It was embarrassing and complicated to buy, and turned out to be wrong anyway. She just laughed. He planned to stick to flowers in future. Although Cyril probably disapproved of them, given the air miles and water, and the fact that they weren't very nourishing. Maybe chocolate would be better.

'The Tromsø Underwear Crisis,' said Fred. 'That might make a good title.'

'Arctic Pants?' suggested Hugh.

'No, that sounds like a porno,' said Nel.

'To be honest, it's quite a relief you've invested in some more,' said Polly. 'I don't really like you washing your underwear in our handbasin. Although they can't have been cheap, I'm guessing.'

'Yes, a packet of three boxers was incredibly expensive,' said Hugh. 'Maybe I should make someone some furniture.'

'Or even a whole kitchen!' said Polly. 'Lingerie might have been cheaper.'

'Why's Heather talking to Cyril?' asked Hugh, changing the subject.

'Well, he's an environmentalist,' said Nel.

'Even I had noticed that,' said Hugh.

'I think she might be here to film him protesting,' said Fred. 'She's certainly up to something. Although she denies it, of course. But her denials are about as believable as yours.'

Hugh ignored the jibe. He thought he deserved it.

'What would he protest about? Isn't Norway an ecological utopia?'

'Drilling, of course,' said Nel. 'We think that Oil Emergency are going to protest on Spitsbergen. We reckon it's about Arctic drilling or something. We'll have front-row seats.'

'Just don't tell Marvin,' said Fred. 'He likes the idea of Arctic drilling.'

'Oh, now it all makes sense. Most of Norway's wealth comes from oil,' said Hugh. 'At least they aren't interfering with traffic again. Oil Emergency,' he added. 'Not Norway.'

'Sometimes you're extremely dim,' said Polly. 'For a clever person.'

*

That afternoon, Fred was having a coffee in the Adventurer's Lounge, watching the sea, in a vacant sort of way. While for the first day or two, the sea had seemed boringly unchanging, Fred was beginning to realise that it was different, minute by minute, and the sight was endlessly enthralling. Depending on the time of day, the sun's or moon's action, or the wind, the sea contained a multitude of moods. It could be as daunting as the new job for which one is utterly unqualified, as tempting as the blank sheet of paper, or as calm as a concert hall before the pianist has played the first note of the sonata and a mobile phone has gone off. Above all, it was so relaxing that sea-watching should surely be prescribed on the NHS. Perhaps that was the point of Bournemouth.

Having left mainland Norway behind, they were heading North to the Svalbard archipelago. As the poet Coleridge opined, there was indeed water, water everywhere, but as they moved North, more and more of it was frozen. The ship had an especially toughened hull at the front to break through the ice. Thankfully, Fred was better hydrated than the Ancient Mariner. He needed a break from writing, and he had no idea where everyone else had gone. Jogging around the deck? Doing an experiment in the Science Centre? He was watching out for Marvin, largely because he didn't want to be caught in another conversation.

'Hello!' He swung around just in time to see the smiling face of Lu, Cyril Earther's partner in crime. He felt it might be rude to ask what crime they planned to commit. As a lawyer, he wondered if they were currently on the high seas and so, technically, out of anyone's jurisdiction. Though presumably Spitsbergen itself had Norwegian law, and Danish law applied to Greenland. Where were they exactly now?

'Would you mind if I joined you?' she said, breaking into his musings. 'Lu. She/her,' she explained.

'Fred,' he responded. He added afterwards, 'He/him.'

He was still not sure what was a pronoun and what was a preposition. And it was no use saying they didn't have pronouns in his day, because it made him seem like a dinosaur. It wasn't his fault that he was on the other side of the great gender politics rift valley. Everyone younger seemed to take gender identity for granted, whereas everyone older was either a confused liberal like himself, or a conservative culture warrior, or the third possibility, which they couldn't even agree on a neutral name for. He had resolved not to get involved. Which wasn't easy. Even Nel and Polly, who were great friends, had agreed never to discuss gender for fear of falling out (one, a biologist; the other, a social worker). Being male was certainly easier in that respect. He certainly wasn't an *it*, although disabled people were often thought of as asexual.

'I'm not going to be patronising or try and score brownie points,' Lu said, indicating Fred's wheelchair. 'I am mainly here because I don't think you're going to hit on me.'

'Because I'm in a chair?' asked Fred, interested and a bit annoyed.

'No, of course not,' said Lu. 'Because you are with that other one...'

'Nel,' supplied Fred.

'And I think you already know I'm a lesbian.'

'Ah, yes,' said Fred carefully. 'Polly did mention it.'

'You can't tell by looking these days,' said Lu. 'We don't wear badges. Let alone dungarees.'

'So...' said Fred, as he tore apart one of the excellent cinnamon buns that had been put out. He searched for conversational gambits like a dog-walker who can't see where his dog has just pooed. 'How's Cyril?'

'Don't ask,' said Lu, sipping her black coffee.

'You've had a row?' said Fred with interest. It seemed much safer to discuss the famous environmentalist than to talk about the sauna, which he knew more than enough about already. And he was keen to get the inside story on the great man.

'Put it this way. We were together a whole lot in London… preparing climate actions, that sort of thing. After all this, I have to go home with him by train. And of course, Cyril doesn't fly. It takes ages to get overland from Norway to London. And I'm meant to sit opposite Cyril all the way. I'm going to end up feeling like a poorly attended public meeting.'

'Is he inclined to lecture?' asked Fred, sympathetically.

'Is he? In London, I had to hide in the loo just to get a break.'

'I could imagine that would get wearying,' Fred said.

'I already know how to suck eggs. Down with the kids? Not,' said Lu, with feeling.

'Oh dear,' said Fred, fearing he was guilty of this in the way he spoke to his nephews.

'He expects me to be at his beck and call 24/7,' said Lu. 'I hate it. I am planning on going on strike. I've been to college, you know. I'm not stupid.'

'What did you study?'

'Dance.' She stared at him defiantly. He thought he wouldn't ask. Everything was theoretical, these days.

'Aren't you here as his assistant?'

'Sort of. The protest group pay the costs,' she said.

'Group?' said Fred. She didn't provide further details.

'I'm here as a volunteer,' she explained. 'I do it for expenses. And I don't like being ordered around. So I might quit.'

'Friendly requests are more appropriate with volunteers,' said Fred.

'Exactly. Respect.' She looked at Fred demolishing his second cinnamon bun. 'Do you think those buns are vegan?'

'Yes, I imagine so,' said Fred, wiping his sticky fingers. Were they buttery? He wasn't sure, and felt he'd better not mention it, as Lu was already getting stuck in.

'Anyway, better get back,' she said, licking sugar off her fingers.

'Bye for now,' said Fred, as she pirouetted and skipped away.

*

Fred was lucky that Nel, let alone Polly, was not there to see him succumbing to a cinnamon bun. Polly had taken advantage of the ship's Wi-Fi to download information about nutrition, exercise and qualifying as a personal trainer. Hugh might not approve of the current fad for gyms, but she could see it was good that so many people wanted to be fit and healthy. She was a healthy woman, and she already ate well – as for exercise, she had always liked walking and cycling all over London. Couldn't she turn her hobby into a career? Maybe this was an escape out of the stress of social work? It was never too late, and all that. She was trying to think of some suggestions she could give to Hugh, but he was already wiry and fit. So she thought that it would be good practice to try out dietary advice on Fred and walk around the ship with Nel.

That way, all of them could steer clear of middle-age spread! She thought it would be good if she could consider disabled people and older people, not just younger folk, in her plans. After all, they were more likely to be rich enough to pay for advice. Well, older people were, anyway. For now, she was not going to talk to her husband about her new idea.

He would probably scoff, thinking personal trainers just a middle-class fad, not a new type of health worker.

In turn, Hugh was not going to tell his wife about his career plans, just yet. He had borrowed a notebook from Fred and was quizzing Freya about children's play preferences. He imagined he could combine his knowledge of birdlife with his carpentry skills to build a series of ornithologically accurate slides. He was sketching them out and asking Freya what she thought children might like. A pirouette around a pigeon? A slide down a skua? A climb up a condor? (He wasn't sure if he was going to restrict himself to British birds.)

For now, he had sworn her to secrecy, which of course Freya loved. He had promised his stepdaughter that he would of course be telling Polly in due course, once he had the details ironed out. But for now, it was their secret. Well, theirs and Fred's. But after coming up with the name Fowl Play – which Freya agreed was brilliant – Uncle Fred had been a sad disappointment when it came to children's playground suggestions. Hugh was worried that his new idea might be laughed at. He wanted Nel and, particularly, Polly to admire the plans, not poke holes in them. He wanted to think it all through before telling them. That's why it was useful to be reminded by Fred that a play area had to have something for kids in wheelchairs. He wanted his idea to have legs. Was that metaphor disablist? He certainly didn't want it to be shot down in flames.

Chapter 19

It was back in the Science Centre, that evening, when Fred realised that Marvin had all the popularity of a C. difficile bacterium on their Arctic voyage. Aunt Donna had just given her lecture on the psychological effects of isolation in the polar regions, taking in Russian hunters on Spitsbergen, Ernest Shackleton and his men on Elephant Island, and the search for the Northwest Passage.

She was introduced and thanked by Fleur, and Fred noticed Marvin's eyes on Fleur throughout. She must have been aware of his interest, because she acknowledged his gaze with an embarrassed wave. After the lecture, Fred made his way forward to congratulate his aunt. Cyril was there before him, ever serious, thanking her for the lecture.

'Do you know of Barbara Hillary?' asked Cyril, stroking his beard.

'Yes, I certainly do,' said Aunt Donna, enthusiastically. 'I've just written a chapter about her. The first African American woman to reach both the North and South Poles. You know she was in her seventies when she did it? Amazing story, I don't know why I didn't mention her.'

'She was very concerned about climate change.'

'She was indeed. May I send you my chapter? I would be most interested in your view of it.' After they exchanged emails, Cyril saluted her with a clenched fist. Fred watched the interaction, amused. It was a typical gesture but, coming from Cyril, it looked wrong, like he was trying too hard. Fred struggled to understand why Cyril had so many fans, when he could make more people cringe than a fingernail on a blackboard. He even had an irritating way of stroking his beard. He was naff, that's what he was. Impossible perhaps to define, but he was certainly it.

When Fred finally spoke to his aunt, he was aware of a slightly awkward encounter between Fleur and Marvin occurring to the left of the stage. He couldn't hear what was said, though the body language suggested Marvin was introducing himself. But his expansive Texan drawl was not having the desired effect on the Norwegian. It looked as if she came as close to cold-shouldering a guest as a crew-member of the *Queen Ingegerd* was contractually permitted to do. She was saved by Cyril, who engaged her in a detailed conversation. She seemed very grateful to be immersed in marine biology.

Looking rather embarrassed, Marvin waited for a few minutes, pointedly ignored by Fleur and Cyril, before beating a retreat. He looked around to see if anyone had noticed, before leaving the Science Centre. Fred wondered if it was his manner or his profession that had so alienated Fleur.

'Fleur doesn't seem to like our new friend Marvin,' said Donna, following his gaze.

'Is it his personality or is it his being an oil millionaire that she objects to?' said Fred. 'Marvin can certainly be a bit much, but maybe this is our chance to re-educate him.'

'Not sure. I'll find out over dinner,' said his aunt. 'I'll report back.'

'Please be discreet,' said Fred. 'I don't think she'd appreciate us staring at her.'

'She certainly seems to appreciate Cyril... Quite the saviour...' Donna left knowing pauses.

'Surely, she isn't keen on him?' said Fred, in shock. 'That beard...'

'Well, put it this way, she admires him more than she likes Marvin,' said Donna. 'Leave it to me to find out.'

Leave it to you to tell everyone you know, thought Fred. He knew his aunt of old. But his friends were beckoning and the evening meal awaited. Just as well, as he was feeling rather peckish.

At eight p.m., the party had finished dinner and were sitting around with their coffee. The carnivores could now say they had had reindeer meat. The vegetarians were feeling superior, but hungry. There were a limited number of different things to do with potatoes, and a cuisine based mostly on foraging wasn't much good out at sea, unless you were prepared to serve seaweed. The berries were good – whether red, yellow or blue – and nobody could object to ice-cream, particularly if dairy-free frozen yogurt was also available. Freya in particular was mainly dining on pudding, as far as Fred could see.

Hugh, Polly and Nel were now discussing nutrition, and whether a hunter-gatherer lifestyle was healthier than an ultra-processed diet. Polly thought it might be, while Hugh had read that famine was not good for anybody, and life expectancy of prehistoric people was low. Fred didn't want to point out that Polly's daughter was hunter-gathering ultra-processed food as fast as she could. Drawing attention to himself might just end up in another unwelcome lecture on nutrition. Fred considered this inappropriate on holiday; diets and exercise could surely begin back in London. Polly seemed to have developed all the zeal of a convert, and he was worried she might take him as her first subject for improvement.

Aunty Bella and Aunt Donna had already shouted, 'Yoo-hoo!' from across the dining room, and shaken their letter bag at him impatiently. Hugh and Polly and Nel didn't look as if they'd be very good opponents, so it was him they had in their sights. He didn't like what they seemed to be suggesting. There was no sign of Marvin, which was one blessing, but that meant that Fred might get stuck playing Scrabble with his aunts.

At this point, Heather materialised in a cloud of expensive scent, wearing a thick white woollen sweater. She was clad in olive-green trousers and her customary black leather boots. She even had a pair of binoculars to complete the picture. That Nordic sailor look was a dangerous one to try and carry off, and Fred thought it wasn't the time to point out that she looked like a very *femme* U-boat captain. She tossed her head, and her auburn hair cascaded around her shoulders to complete the look of crack reporter. More like cracked reporter, thought Fred, disloyally.

'Heather Crisp, war correspondent, how do you do?' said Fred, grateful to be rescued from Scrabble. It sounded like a contagious disease, which in a way it was.

'Heather Crisp, *Europe editor*, thank you very much. Hello Polly, hello Nelly,' she said. She caught sight of Freya.

'Hello,' she said cautiously. 'Isn't it past your bedtime?'

'I am allowed to stay up late on holiday!' said Freya.

'I was just going to put her to bed,' answered Polly, who did not like aspersions being cast on her parenting. She headed off with her protesting daughter.

'What's Freya doing here?' asked Heather.

'Long story,' said Hugh.

'Did she bring her recorder?' asked Heather warily.

'She's moved on to the trombone,' answered Hugh.

'Oh god,' said Heather, with feeling.

'You're quite safe,' said Fred. 'She didn't bring it with her.'

'It does make it somewhat perilous being in the same house as her,' admitted Hugh. 'Same street, really,' he added.

Heather turned to Fred. 'Are you still eating? I just had room service in my cabin.'

Fred thought her cabin was probably rather more de luxe than theirs.

'All finished,' he said.

'Ready for that drink?' said Heather. 'It's on expenses!'

Although her friendliness made him slightly suspicious, it was nice all the same. Polly and Nel were wearing identical scornful expressions as he wheeled off. Heather was not their favourite person. Polly knew Heather from college, whereas Nel just knew that Fred had once been keen on her. Heather getting her name wrong wasn't calculated to endear. Luckily, Heather had already turned away, so she did not see their faces. Fred shrugged in their general direction, as if to disown responsibility. He followed Heather towards the bar, feeling guilty for hanging out with her, although at least she was not armed with a Scrabble set.

'There are several bars,' he said, as they reached the lifts. 'There's one on this deck. Then there's one upstairs, with a better view.'

'And that's exactly where we're going,' said Heather. 'You can count on me for the best views!' She laughed at her own joke and put her arm around his neck in a style which she thought of as affectionate, but he thought of as annoying. Fred no longer had romantic thoughts about Heather, but still found her fascinating. She was so driven, seemed to know exactly what she wanted, and then had no qualms in going out and getting it. Most people he knew reacted to whatever happened, sometimes rather passively. Heather seized control of events and made them serve her purposes. His poor brother. Fred felt rather guilty for thinking he had fallen victim to a praying-mantis. Feeling sorry for Roderick was not an emotion he was used to. He hoped it would all work out. His brother clearly had ambitions of his own, mostly to do with being a cabinet minister, it seemed. Or maybe even prime minister? Fred shuddered. Politicians seemed to have no idea about their own limitations.

'So, tell all,' said Heather, once they were settled over a rather good but very pricey dry white wine, with the most impressive of scenes in front of them. The ship was ploughing through the night, spray churning to right and left. Snow was falling, and the lights of the ship caught it turning and falling like confetti. Outside, nature was looking very cold: inside, civilisation was the usual toasty warm. It worried Fred that they all seemed to have become blasé about some of the best landscapes and seascapes on the planet, after a mere few days on the ship.

'All is great,' said Fred. 'The flat in Kennington seems to be working out, I get buses all over London and only drive if we're going down to an SSSI or community meeting.' He thought Heather was sitting rather too close to him for comfort, and he didn't want anyone to see them.

'SSSI?'

'Site of special scientific interest.'

'Oh, I see. Natterjack toads, wild orchids, that sort of thing?'

'Exactly. The wars we fight are rather more humble than yours!'

'And things with Nelly? Has she fully adapted to South London domesticity?'

'*Nel*. Yes, so far so good. We see eye to eye on most things. She likes the parks,' said Fred, tearing up a beer mat. 'We have a cat. It has a bell,' he quickly added. 'So the birds hear her coming.'

'Not eye to eye, clearly, on everything, if the state of that beer mat is anything to go by,' said Heather. 'Is she meeting all of your needs?'

Fred had never seen Heather as an agony aunt, but she had been a good friend the last twenty or so years. He sighed.

'Well, I would like us to have a baby.'

'Whatever for?' asked Heather in astonishment. 'Nasty, sicky, pooey things. Surely you don't want one of those?'

'I like babies!' said Fred defensively. 'The mess doesn't bother me.'

'Well, you've had plenty of practice with that pug you used to own. He seemed to spend most of his time busily sniffing bottoms.'

Fred ignored the slurs she was casting on Humphrey.

'Babies don't sniff bottoms.'

'That's only because their own bottoms are quite sniffy enough.'

'But they grow up into endearing toddlers, gorgeous children and interesting nine-year-olds. Think of Freya.'

Heather shuddered.

'I'd rather not. And please let's not talk about the teenage years.'

Fred remembered that Roderick and Heather had regular custody of two teenage boys, possibly not a fate you'd wish on your worst enemy. Even he had to admit that his nephews were better in small doses.

'Anyway, we're here celebrating Nel's fortieth, which is lovely, but the clock is ticking.'

Heather groaned.

'I can't tell you how much I hate that expression.'

'I don't use it in front of Nel, of course…'

'Thank goodness for that! Makes her sound like an unexploded bomb!'

'But I would like us to have one, if we can.'

'And she's not keen? Most women tend to be…'

'Not if they think too much about climate change,' said Fred. 'Having a baby is the single worst thing you can do for the planet, apparently.'

'To be honest, the single worst thing you can do is blow it up, which various autocrats seem hell-bent on at the moment,' said Heather. 'I speak as a former war correspondent. And I've been to Pyongyang, remember.'

'But given that we're not autocratic dictators, reproduction is right up there,' said Fred. 'Consuming resources, and so on.'

'So, you don't have a baby because there's a danger of us going extinct, but then there's a danger of us going extinct if everybody gets that idea... Seems contradictory to me,' said Heather.

'You have a point,' said Fred sadly. 'But it's not me you have to persuade, it's Nel.'

'Back in the day, I was keen on having a kid. Until I actually spent time with one,' said Heather. 'I still can't hear the tune "Frère Jacques" without an involuntary shudder.'

Fred thought he knew the young person in question. Giving her a recorder was like committing a public order offence. At least the trombone was less portable.

He couldn't see Heather being a very great mother of any kid, nor her ever wanting to have one. Nel, on the other hand, would make a wonderful mum. When they did talks at schools, the kids all loved her, and she was able to speak to them without seeming patronising, which was far from easy.

'Another drink?' offered Heather.

'I don't think I should,' said Fred.

'I was rather looking forward to getting drunk and talking about the old days. Isn't alcohol good for the old sperm count?' Heather joked.

'Ha, bloody ha!' retorted Fred. 'No, I had better be getting back to see if Nel is doing OK. Having spent half my adult life trying to become part of a couple, I don't want to blow it now.'

'Suit yourself,' said Heather. 'But she sounds rather high-maintenance. Talking of which, any messages for your bro? I should really give him a call, when I get a signal.'

'Just send him my best,' said Fred. 'I haven't asked you how things are... Not that you have to tell me, of course.'

'Oh, it's all fine – when we actually see each other. If our careers are going well, we don't tend to,' said Heather, a bit sadly, Fred thought. Maybe she was looking for something too.

'At least there's no time for it to get boring,' he said.

'That's true,' said Heather. 'And I haven't had to open any fêtes or anything. But he's far too principled to tell me any Party gossip, sadly. Call me old-fashioned, but I want to know who's shagging whom. Or who's about to be arrested with suspicious substances and/or a rent boy!'

'I think that's the other lot,' said Fred, hoping that was the case.

'I'd still rather they were using contraceptives,' said Heather. 'Or if not, that I was the one to find out about it.' She thought better of trying to make an elaborate but off-colour joke about scoops.

'At least with this lot, you aren't physically sick at the thought of them shagging,' said Fred, thinking of the various members of the Cabinet.

'Let's move on,' said Heather.

'I am just glad Roderick has good boundaries,' said Fred. 'And being the partner of a journalist, I'd imagine they're rather important.'

'He doesn't want to get caught and have to resign is all,' said Heather, who knew exactly how her husband thought, which was very close to her own thinking. Scandals were what other people suffered. What you had was good news management.

Chapter 20

The next morning, Fred was with Nel at breakfast, drinking strong coffee and eating savoury things with unpronounceable names, when an excited Polly found them, with Freya trailing behind. As usual, Hugh was trailing along in turn. They sat across from them at the table, and Polly launched in: 'You'll never guess what I saw!'

'On the ship?' said Fred, who usually enjoyed Twenty Questions.

'I think she meant it rhetorically,' said Hugh, who generally didn't. 'Because you'll never guess.'

'It looked like there was a polar bear in the corridor in the early hours!' said Polly, going straight for the reveal. She was so excited that she didn't even lecture Fred on sprinkling hundreds and thousands on his bread and butter.

'I think that's very unlikely,' said Nel, who knew her zoology. She was eating some Russian salad. These Nordic types had strange ideas about what constituted breakfast.

'Were mind-expanding chemicals involved?' said Fred, who had some experience of these on his own fortieth birthday weekend.

'I realise it wasn't a real polar bear!' said Polly in exasperation. 'I'm not that daft. Plus, I was sober, and us social workers can be struck off for taking illegal drugs.'

'Was it you, Freya?' asked Fred. The girl screwed up her face in a scowl. She was on best behaviour!

'Not this time! She was asleep in our room,' Polly replied.

'If it wasn't real,' said Nel, ticking the choices off on her fingers, 'and you weren't drunk, and it wasn't Freya, then either you've had a psychotic hallucination, which I would say is very unlikely, or this was someone dressed as a polar bear.'

'Exactly what I thought!' said Polly. 'The latter option!'

'A polar-bear impersonator,' said Hugh, thoughtfully. 'Which I've heard of before. I just can't think where…'

'Is there a fancy-dress evening on the cruise?' asked Nel, shuddering at the thought of the last fancy-dress party she had attended.

'I don't think it's that sort of cruise,' said Fred, who had read about furries, people who identified as animals rather than, well, people.

'I am simply being methodical,' said Nel. 'When you have eliminated the impossible, whatever remains, however improbable, must be the truth.'

'Oh, very good!' said Hugh, impressed. 'Did you learn that on your science degree?'

'I was quoting Sherlock Holmes,' said Nel.

'Or rather Sir Arthur Conan Doyle,' said Hugh.

'You don't always have to have the last word,' said Polly to her husband. 'The point is that I saw someone dressed as a polar bear, and I think they must be planning some sort of stunt.'

'Bet it's rather sweaty inside a polar bear outfit,' said Hugh. 'All that fur fabric.'

'Perhaps it was Father Christmas?' suggested Freya. The others pondered.

'I don't think so, darling,' said Polly gently. 'It's the wrong time of year.'

Freya nodded wisely, and the others breathed a sigh of relief. It seemed unlikely that Freya still believed in Santa Claus, but now was not the time to break it to her. One of the attractions of coming to the North, Freya had said, was seeing where he lived. She seemed to be trying to have her Christmas cake and eat it too.

'Do you think it was Cyril Earther?' said Fred. 'Is that the sort of thing he'd do?'

'Quite possibly,' said Nel slowly. 'It's just the sort of thing which Oil Rebellion might do.'

Hugh didn't like the idea of Cyril Earther in only his knickers. And that beard would be hot in an animal costume. Plus, he was sure that dressing up as a bear had bad associations, if only he could remember what they were. It wasn't because of Bungle from the TV programme *Rainbow* – that was part of people's childhoods, and therefore untouchable.

'It would explain why he was on this cruise. Unless he's just here for the rewilding on Spitsbergen,' said Polly, excitedly. 'Lu must be part of the plot. In fact, perhaps that was Lu under there when I saw the bear?' She didn't like to say she was more familiar with Lu with her clothes off.

'And that might just explain why Heather and her camera operator are here too. I thought what she said about needing a holiday sounded a bit far-fetched,' said Nel.

'Did you? I thought it seemed fair enough,' said Fred.

'That's because you generally believe people,' said Nel.

'And we generally don't,' said Polly. 'You don't last long in social work if you believe what everyone says,' she added.

'Thinking the best of people is an endearing trait, Fred,' said Nel, lovingly. 'But we'll knock it out of you eventually.'

Nel and Polly smiled at Fred, who shrugged.

'But more to the point, are we going to do anything about it?' said Hugh, carefully peeling a boiled egg.

'Well, we're certainly not going to report him,' said Nel. 'I think we're all on the same side.'

'Perhaps we should offer to help?' asked Polly. 'Or join in?'

'We might not get much choice,' said Nel. 'If we're all in the same RIB.'

'She means boat,' whispered Fred to Hugh. 'It stands for Rigid Inflatable Boat. For going ashore. Like a Zodiac.'

'Should we talk to Fleur?' said Polly. 'Or do you think she already knows?'

'Please, let's not tell my aunts,' said Fred, now making his lunchtime sandwich. From previous coastal voyages, he had remembered a fondness for brunost: a caramel-tasting substance which was more cheese-adjacent than actual cheese, but ate well with some lettuce in a bun. Oh god, now he sounded like Nigel Slater. What a Guardianista he was.

'Don't tell my aunts, because first, they'd love it,' said Fred, 'and second, because they're incapable of keeping a secret. I once told them about seeing Daniel Craig in Hexham Waitrose, and thanks to them, the news was all over the Tyne Valley in twenty-four hours. It must have ruined his chances of a peaceful weekend break.'

Freya nodded wisely. She would keep the secret from the old ladies.

Fred had steered clear of gamalost, literally 'old cheese', on the buffet counter. He'd learned from his mistake, on a previous trip to Norway. The stuff smelled of old socks and you couldn't forget the mouth-feel all day. It was like eating cobwebs. Not that he'd ever voluntarily eaten cobwebs. Fred put a satsuma and a banana in his zippable back pouch to prove that his diet was not nearly as bad as Polly said. He intended to eat the fruit ostentatiously. He also added a cupcake, when she wasn't looking. One good thing about being in a wheelchair was that you could stow quite a lot of provisions. You just had to remember what you were carrying: Fred had had disasters with forgotten pears before. Not to mention bananas. Before you knew it, you were sitting on a compost heap.

'Let's watch and wait,' said Nel. 'Keep your eyes skinned for more Arctic animal impersonators!'

'If I talk to Heather again, I'll play innocent, and she might not be able to resist giving the game away,' said Fred. 'She's pretty hopeless at keeping secrets, and she is my sister-in-law. She can't resist gossip.'

'I don't think impersonating an Arctic fox would work,' said Hugh, thoughtfully. 'Unless you were a small child. And there'd have to be two of you to impersonate a reindeer, even these small ones... Maybe a seal would work, but they're no good on land.'

'Then they might all have to be polar bears,' said Nel, firmly.

'Except me!' said Freya.

'Yes, you could possibly impersonate an Arctic fox,' said Hugh. 'But I don't think you should. Fur trappers are probably around.'

Freya shuddered. She already knew about fur trappers from books. She was going to be as careful about traps as her mum was about Lyme disease.

'If I meet Lu again, I'll see what I can discover,' said Polly. Fred, guessing she was referring to the sauna, made faces at her. Luckily, Hugh seemed to ignore both of them. He was often away in his own world, and he was probably still thinking of how to impersonate Arctic wildlife.

'See if you can find out if she's made up with Cyril,' whispered Fred, to Polly's surprise. 'Because if they're still having a row, that might make it difficult to do an action together.'

'OK,' said Polly, also sotto voce.

Chapter 21

It was lunchtime, and Fred was sitting at a table, having coffee with Heather. Nel had dragged Polly along to hear a lecture in the Science Centre about Arctic marine biology and Hugh had joined them. As Hugh observed loudly, he was more interested in Arctic ornithology, but as Nel pointed out, most of the ornithology grazed off the marine biology, which was basically a wet bird-buffet. Hugh grudgingly saw the relevance of that and tagged along with the others. Freya had complained that it was too much like school. But everyone pointed out that it had been her choice to be a stowaway, so now she couldn't complain if she ended up having to go to a talk.

Fred wondered if Heather had driven them off. The others certainly took every opportunity to avoid her. Although, she seemed very eager to spend time with him. She could be rather loud and was happier talking about her exploits than listening to others. Her conversation revolved around wars she had witnessed, scoops she had had, and media gossip too tedious to relate. Perhaps that was why she was keen to find a good listener.

He remembered, in amazement, how for many years he had hoped for her to share his life, and now it was as much as he could do to share a table with her. It would be a relief later to sink into bed with Nel, who was much quieter and more well-rounded than Heather. Not for the first time, Fred wondered about Heather's home life with Roddy. Did they even have a home life? He had opened their fridge on a recent visit to their flat to find it empty, except for the remains of a chocolate gateau and a bottle of champagne. At best, they had an extremely unbalanced diet.

As Heather talked of great natural disasters she had witnessed – surely the conversational equivalent of doomscrolling, and no cheerier – Marvin went past with a full tray. He had obviously passed on the healthy items, and gone straight for the burger and chips, Fred noticed, enviously.

'Marvin!' said Fred. He was clutching at straws, and even Texan oil magnates would make a change. 'Why not join us?'

Fred introduced Marvin to Heather. She was immediately interested, especially when Fred hinted that his new American friend was a millionaire businessman. She turned on the charm, and Marvin was the focus. Fred was impressed with her.

'Your company is in the energy sector?'

'Companies,' corrected Marvin. 'Yes, that's right. I'm in hydrocarbons, for my sins!' He laughed heartily.

'I don't suppose you know the property field?'

'No, can't say as I do,' said Marvin.

'Oh,' said Heather, disappointed. 'I was looking for someone who knew the American president. Who had been to Florida, to his resort.'

'The president?' said Marvin. 'Oh, we all know the president!'

'You do?'

'Sure. Been to his hotel too,' said Marvin proudly. 'Florida ain't so far from Texas, and we have various concerns in the Gulf. It's a short hop from Houston to Palm Beach.'

'I guess it would be,' said Heather. 'It's very lucky I met you.'

Fred thought it was less 'very lucky' than his doing. But he seemed to have been written out of the situation. Certainly, it wasn't him that Heather was currently flashing her smile at, but then nor was he having to keep the conversation going. At least he couldn't be blamed for the American president getting more media exposure.

'Billionaires aren't so very different, whether they're in oil or real estate,' said Marvin.

'I was hoping for an introduction,' said Heather. 'I'm a journalist, you see. I'd just love to get an interview. One-to-one.'

'Well, you've come to the right person,' said Marvin. 'If you mention you've met me, it should get you past the executive assistant, secretary, chief of staff, and what have you. Get you straight to the man himself.'

'I can't tell you how exciting that would be,' said Heather, her eyes shining.

'Don't mention it!' said Marvin, smiling broadly. 'Just glad to be of service.'

Then he grinned at Fred and added, 'We're all friends here.'

Fred hoped that he wasn't assuming they were all Republicans. Heather might be happy sucking up to big money, but it wasn't part of his plan. He loathed the American president. Plus, he disapproved of the whole oil industry. Perhaps he should scowl more. His aunts had evidently gone soft. He didn't want his friends to catch him out making compromises as well. Marvin was quite literally The Man, and Nel would hate him.

But it wasn't easy to be unfriendly. Marvin's bonhomie, however generously lubricated by dollars and non-renewable energy, was hard to resist. Arrogance with a faux humility, nastiness with a smile. He was a mess of contradictions – evil behaviour, but with a friendly face. This made him hard to make out. And anyway, Fred found it hard to be hostile to anyone. He knew this wasn't necessarily a good thing. He needed to develop the killer instinct. He wondered if he should go on a course. Perhaps he could practise on Marvin.

Chapter 22

That afternoon, Fred and his friends were having a cup of what passed for tea outside the British Isles while staring at the sea – an occupation which they had become very good at – when Aunt Donna found her nephew and demanded his immediate attention. Shrugging his shoulders, Fred made his apologies to everyone else and went with her back to the cabin she shared with Bella. He was shocked to see his aunt crying.

'Whatever is the matter?' he asked with concern.

'We've lost everything!' she wailed.

'Now, stop being silly, Bella!' said Donna. 'We've hardly lost everything.'

'Well, we've lost all our travelling cash,' said Bella, tearfully. 'We won't be able to eat or drink or go on excursions.'

'What happened? Were you robbed?' asked Fred.

'We might as well have been,' said Donna. 'It was playing Scrabble with that terrible Texan!'

'Marvin?' asked Fred. 'Why is he terrible all of a sudden? I thought you liked him!'

'He turns out to be nothing but a gambler and a cheat!' said Bella.

Fred didn't say that the mistake might be gambling in the first place.

'If Marvin won your money honestly, then it's hard to argue with. He might just be better at Scrabble than you.'

'But he didn't and isn't!' wailed Bella. 'He was looking up words all the time!'

'Calls himself a Southern gentleman,' said Donna. 'Well, he isn't.'

'Are you sure?' said Fred. 'Wouldn't you notice someone cheating like that?'

'We think that his Apple watch gizmo has a word-list program on it. He was consulting it all the time,' said Donna grimly. 'He said he was keeping in touch with his office in Houston, but we think he was coming up with good words. It's quite subtle, so you might not notice at first.'

'He got bingo after bingo!' said Bella.

'I've never seen someone get so many seven-letter words,' explained Donna. 'When you get an extra fifty points for every single one, it soon mounts up! Who on earth gets a bingo almost every turn?!'

'So he won all your money?' said Fred. 'Which means no more snacks or drinks for you! Unless you do what we do, and make lunch at breakfast!'

'It was our lunch money,' said Donna miserably. 'And for us to do the excursions!'

'I can easily make you a financial advance,' said Fred. 'But what else can I do about it? Fair play or foul, he has it now…'

'Couldn't you get it back for us?' said Donna, eagerly.

'How?' said Fred. Aunts, he thought bitterly. More like stinging nettles than family members.

'We want you to burgle his cabin,' said Bella, as if this was a completely reasonable suggestion. 'We are owed our £500. It's a big amount – he won't carry it around with him, so it must be somewhere in his cabin.'

Fred sighed. He knew his aunts meant trouble. But what they expected this time was really too much.

'Oh, no,' he said. They had got him into hot water before, but this was the worst scheme they'd tried to strong-arm him into.

'It's not theft, if he cheated,' said Donna, forestalling his objection.

'Well, technically it is,' said Fred, who wondered whether they were still in Norwegian territorial waters. 'It's highly risky. I could be caught red-handed. If I get caught taking his money, I'm finished. It's all very dodgy. I really don't like the idea.'

'We'll distract him, so you'll be quite safe,' said Donna, in a wheedling tone. 'We've already "borrowed" a master key off the maid.'

'You did *what*?' Fred certainly didn't want to hear of anything that sounded criminal.

'Well, I could see she needed some medical advice, so I had her sit down in our cabin, and while her trolley was unattended, her master key fell into Bella's pocket. We'll slip it back afterwards,' said Donna, shamelessly.

'Isn't that covered by the Hippocratic Oath?' said Fred. 'Not tricking your patients?'

'Now I'm retired, I am no longer on the register,' said Donna.

'You're incorrigible!' said Fred, exasperated.

'Remember Katharine Hepburn: "If you follow all the rules, you miss all the fun,"' said Donna.

'If you follow all the rules, you don't end up serving three years for aggravated burglary,' said Fred.

'Pshaw,' said Bella. 'A mere bagatelle. Anyway, there is no chance of you being caught. He'll be busy playing Scrabble with us.'

'You remember, I'm a lawyer – you get disbarred for this sort of thing,' protested Fred.

'Hush, hush,' said Bella. 'A child of ten could do this. Really, it's as safe as houses. I'm quite surprised you're making such a fuss about it.'

Fred remembered one of them saying this last time they had him do something for them. They had wanted to borrow his Blue Badge to nip into Newcastle city centre. It wasn't OK then, and it certainly wasn't OK now.

'My safe isn't the same as your safe,' he said firmly.

'Your safe, our safe – it's his safe that we're interested in,' said Bella.

'You leave me no choice. No more cakes!' said Donna, wagging her finger. This was the nuclear option.

Fred swallowed hard. Staying at his aunts' was such a treat because of the extravagantly elaborate breakfasts. And every time they came to London, there was always a box tied up with string for him. He was already looking forward to the Nordic treats that she would bake after this trip. His mouth watered thinking of the cardamom buns she would undoubtedly offer on his next visit. The threat was like a blow to the very soul.

'No more patisserie?' he said, weakly, thinking of Donna's walnut Danish.

'Not one crumb shall pass your lips again!' said Bella firmly. 'Unless you do this teensy tiny thing for us!'

Fred sighed. These two aunts had always been very kind to him, particularly since both his parents had died. Plus, cakes were his Achilles heel. Now he was a healthy vegetarian, he had few treats left. He still dreamed of bacon sometimes, and sausage rolls were a thing of the past. He could surely ignore the rules just once. Nobody would know back home. And morally, it was *their* money. Very different from actually stealing. It was just a matter of taking back what belonged to them.

Chapter 23

Later that afternoon, Fred found himself using the purloined card to open the door to Marvin's suite, while the occupant was out playing Scrabble. The Texan certainly had much more room in his quarters, thought Fred enviously, as he wheeled through and quietly closed the door behind him. For the first time, it suddenly occurred to him that one trouble with being in a chair was that there was no way he could hide under the bed if someone came.

Fred opened the closet and saw several jackets on the rack, next to their respective neatly folded trousers. The drawer of identical socks and white branded underwear was similarly arranged. Fred felt rather uncomfortable looking at another man's pants. It felt rather intimate. Was Marvin married? he mused. Fred rifled through each drawer, as he had patted down each jacket, looking for a bulging fold of money. Nothing there. Perhaps he had taken his winnings with him?

He looked about the suite. There was a guidebook. There was a novel, by Javier Marías, which was far more highbrow than he'd expected: not exactly the latest Jack Reacher. And it was actually in Spanish! Marvin clearly had hidden depths. Next to the novel on the bedside table was the Apple watch. Not the money, but a chance to check whether it really had the Scrabble word list on it. He picked it up. Of course, it was password protected. He put it back.

Fred quickly searched through the rest of the drawers and cupboards. If the money was here, it must be in the safe, he thought. The safe was the usual small metal box in the wardrobe. Fred shook it and heard a reassuring rustle and clunk. The box was firmly closed and did not respond to Fred's primitive efforts to unlock it. He'd have to take it with him and hope one of his aunts could help. Luckily, it was small enough to stow in the bag behind him.

Looking around to ensure things were left as he'd found them, including on the bedside, Fred took the safe, turned off the light and wheeled backwards out of the door, shutting it quietly behind him. He stowed the safe in his own cabin and went to find his aunts. They were safely in the throes of a game of Scrabble with their mysterious nemesis, and neither of them could get away. Bella nodded encouragingly to her nephew.

'Everything well?'

'Quite well. But *the cleaner has put the towels out of reach and I would like a shower.*'

'Shall I come and get the towels down from the rack?'

'Nel is out somewhere, so it would be very helpful. If you can be spared for a few minutes?'

'Neither of you would mind, would you, if I absented myself for as long as it takes to get the towels down for Fred? I've just taken my turn.'

'Not at all,' said Marvin. He smiled easily at Fred, who smiled back, although he was getting a bit narked with all the faux gentility. He preferred people to smile when they really meant it. Fred was beginning to think that Marvin was a fake, playing a game with them all. How much of what he said was a front?

The two of them bustled along to Fred's cabin, although he didn't really like showing his aunt where he was staying. Bella whistled when she saw the strongbox.

'Do you reckon our money is in there?'

'Can't be anywhere else,' said Fred. 'I searched everywhere.'

'You sure it wasn't just a boy look?' asked Bella.

'No!' retorted Fred indignantly. 'Anyway, what should we do with this box? I should take it back before it's missed. I tried the obvious number combinations, and it won't open.'

'Oh, I think it will open,' said Bella calmly. 'Can you pass me a hairpin?'

'No, of course not,' said her nephew. 'You can see I have a short back and sides, and Nel has her hair cut short too. Why would either of us need one?'

'For this,' said Bella. She pulled a pin from her own bun, and her hair started collapsing. With one hand she held it in place, and with the other she probed the lock of the strongbox. Fred watched in fascination as he heard each tumbler fall in place with a click. When she finally turned the dial, opened the catch and pulled, the door opened. There was a sound at the door to the cabin, and it opened. Nel walked in to find Fred feeling inside a strongbox, as his aunt rescued her bun. The cabin was now rather crowded, with three occupants.

'Thank god it's you!' said Aunty Bella, both hands doing her hair.

'Quick, close the door!' said Fred. Nel paused at the entrance, shocked. She sat on the bed and stared in amazement.

'We'd rather no one saw this,' said Aunty Bella as Fred withdrew a wad of cash. She nodded her head in satisfaction, took the money from Fred, withdrew £500 in Norwegian kroner and put the rest back. Aunty Bella put the box down on the bed, went to the bathroom and came back with a hand towel. She carefully wiped everything she had touched. Then she left them to return to the Scrabble table, after one final shot.

'Go on and put it back! I reckon you've got twenty minutes until the end of the game!'

Nel looked at Fred and raised her eyebrows.

'Should I ask who you're robbing and why? It looked just as if you were stealing something. Which I would not have expected from you.'

'Probably best you don't ask,' said Fred. 'My aunts would say it's not really stealing. It's regaining. Blame my sweet tooth. Long story.'

The box was still open. To look inside one more time was so tempting. Fred fumbled in confusion with the other contents of the box and withdrew them one by one. There were two US passports, one in the name of Marvin G. Ridley III and one in the name of Curt Wrigley. The photographs both looked like the man they knew as Marvin.

Nel whistled.

'I can see why you don't know who they're robbing!'

But Fred was staring at the final item in the strongbox, the thing that had rattled as he had brought the box into his cabin, the thing that looked exactly like, but couldn't possibly be, a gun.

'Bloody hell!' said Nel. 'Isn't that a Glock pistol? I've seen those in films.'

'Let me put it all back now!' said Fred, now in even more of a hurry. 'I thought that guy was dodgy!'

'But who is he?' asked Nel.

'I've absolutely no idea. He just seems to be very keen on drilling in the Arctic,' said Fred.

'Which suggests he's an oil magnate, like he says,' said Nel.

'Anyway,' said Fred. 'I'm a lawyer, but I am not sure I will be one for much longer, if I carry on committing burglary.'

'But is he Marvin or is he Curt?' said Nel. 'And why the hell does he have a gun?'

'Questions later,' said Fred, and quickly wheeled back to the suite.

In a rush, Fred returned the strongbox to the wardrobe, though he did take the precaution of wiping it with his own handkerchief. Satisfied, he reversed out of the suite. It all looked just as he had found it. He even saw a cleaner's trolley in the corridor and dropped the master-key card into the top compartment. As he wheeled away, everything was left just as it had been before. But now it felt quite different. And all sorts of new questions suddenly demanded answers.

Chapter 24

That evening, Fred was having his supper when he saw his friend Polly. On his own, he felt like Billy No-Mates, but at least he hadn't been spotted by Bella, Donna or, worst of all, Marvin/Curt. Nel was having a drink with Fleur, and while she hadn't exactly told Fred not to come, he was tactful enough to know when he wasn't wanted. Polly's hair was damp.

'I saw Lu.'

'I am not sure I want to know this,' said Fred, forking bean salad into his mouth.

'No, it wasn't like that! And anyway, as I said to her, I'm a married woman.'

'And don't you forget it!'

'Oh, do shut up.' Polly rolled her eyes. 'Or I'll start talking about nutrition.'

'Where is your daughter?'

'With Hugh, looking for birds. I'm not sure he's a good influence.'

'Each to their own.'

'I talked to Lu about Cyril.'

'Now, that is interesting,' said Fred, putting his fork down. 'I'm all ears.'

'You are right, there was a row. She's really upset.'

'Oh no...'

'Yes, he's been very autocratic and laid down the law.'

'No animal fats?' said Fred, toying with an unappealing piece of smoked tofu. He was getting a bit fed up now. He didn't want to start eating pudding in front of Polly.

'Don't be silly. About where, when and how they should do their action. She was a bit vague about that.'

'Probably didn't want to give the game away,' said Fred. 'I don't know exactly what they're going to do.'

'I'm not sure they're going to *do* anything.'

'Really?'

'Well, Cyril might jump up and down on the tundra, brandishing a placard. But it won't get on the global news.'

'He may be famous, but he's not exactly prepossessing. Not with that beard.' Fred shuddered at the thought.

'I think he's a fine-looking man,' said Polly, inexplicably. 'But it's hardly riveting footage, is it? Bearded white man gets cross about drilling. Seen that, done that. No, it has to be very surprising and preferably funny to go viral. For which he needs Lu.'

'He doesn't have her imagination. Or her looks. And she moves like a trained dancer,' said Fred. 'Whereas he moves like a narcissistic gibbon.'

'Exactly,' said Polly, ignoring Fred's jibe about Cyril. 'Because she is a trained dancer.'

'She did say her degree was in dance,' said Fred.

'Do you want their plans to succeed?'

'Definitely. As you know, Nel and I spend most of our lives working against climate change. Plus, I give money to Oil Rebellion. I want to amplify their message.'

'Which is why I need you to persuade her to take part. I've tried and failed. For a flexible woman, she's rather inflexible.'

'Me?' said Fred, surprised. 'Why me? I don't really know her.'

'Well, would you rather it was Nel, dressed only in a towel, in the sauna?'

'I see your point,' said Fred. 'I don't trust what I've heard of Lu when it comes to semi-naked women!'

'Which is exactly why you're going to have to do it. Hugh will just get all insecure on me, if he knows I have been meeting her. You know what he's like.'

'Ridiculous! You've simply been meeting a flirtatious young woman dressed only in a towel,' said Fred sarcastically. 'He's got nothing whatsoever to feel jealous about.'

Polly ignored him again.

'I have made an assignation with her for 7:30 tomorrow morning. It will probably take less than take thirty minutes, so you'll still have time for breakfast before we see Spitsbergen.'

'Joy in the morning,' groaned Fred.

'Well, I know how much you like your breakfast,' said Polly. Fred thought it safest not to answer that.

'It will take most of the day to steam around the island, especially if we have to break through some ice,' said Polly. 'Fleur said the next day we might get some kayaking done, or go out in the mini-sub, and then we'll land in the afternoon for our first stop,' said Polly firmly. 'By which time we need Lu to have made up with Cyril and to be ready to do whatever they are planning to do. One more thing: I think that's the real reason why Heather and her camera operator are here. They're not on holiday. They're here to get the scoop of the demo. And I am thinking it's something to do with that polar bear I saw the other night. At least, that's what Lu has hinted at.'

'I think you're right on all counts. It all makes more sense now,' said Fred. 'I had better go and talk to Lu tomorrow,' he said, sighing. It didn't sound like he had much choice. But did he ever have a choice in these matters? It was a bit like breaking into Marvin/Curt's cabin. He generally went along with whatever was suggested. Which might be where he went wrong.

'What are you going to do tomorrow?' said Nel, joining them.

'Show off my kayaking?' said Fred. Well, it was not untrue, although it was not the whole story.

'I'm going to rescue Hugh from Freya,' said Polly. 'We're taking it in turns to make sure she doesn't get up to mischief.' With that, she zipped up her coat, pulled on her cap and disappeared in the direction of the upper deck.

'Are you finished?' said Nel to Fred. 'Do you want that croquette? Only, I missed supper.'

'Help yourself,' said Fred. 'And then let's go outside. We might find Hugh and Freya.'

Chapter 25

'So who do you think he is? Marvin or Curt?' asked Nel, on the rear deck. It was getting cold, but not chilly enough that they had to cuddle together for warmth. No wonder loneliness could be a problem for polar explorers, thought Fred sadly, thinking of his aunt's presentation. He blamed the bunks.

Fred hadn't told Nel about his assignation the next morning. Nor had either of them mentioned what they had seen in Marvin's strongbox to Hugh and Polly, let alone Freya, although, as Nel remarked, both their friends had prior form as burglars, and no doubt they were bringing up Freya to be the next Raffles.

'More to the point, what's his game?' asked Fred.

'Maybe this is all standard stuff for an international businessman?' said Nel.

'You think? Two passports and a pistol?' said Fred. 'I bet they don't mention that in Rotary International.'

'But they all have guns in America. Certainly in the Midwest.'

'True. But the passports would be harder to explain,' said Fred. 'I don't think that's normal.'

'No, you're right. He must be either a criminal or a spy,' said Nel, with confidence. 'A Texan accent is surely about the easiest to fake. Remember *Pillow Talk*?'

'He's no Rock Hudson. And I'm not sure he's a criminal, despite the Scrabble,' said Fred.

'Then he must be an agent,' said Nel 'But what's he doing here?'

'Even agents have holidays?'

'No, I reckon he's keeping watch on someone,' said Nel.

'On the ship?'

'Must be,' said Nel. 'Unless he's on his way to do his spying on Spitsbergen.'

'Who is that someone?' asked Fred.

She stared at him as if he was of weak wits, which he didn't like.

'The obvious person is Cyril,' she said, continuing her withering stare.

'What makes you think that?' said Fred, although he was inclined to agree. He thought Nel should save the withering stare for people she opposed, not for her nearest and dearest. Even the Medusa kept herself veiled in company.

'Well, we strongly suspect that Cyril is planning something. Although, of course, we have no idea who else is among the passengers,' said Nel. 'Any from hostile nations?'

'Not obviously,' said Fred. 'But there are at least 150 passengers, I reckon. Maybe as many as 200. They said all the cabins were full. I am sure we haven't seen everyone. And there's no shortage of nations which might like to make mischief.'

'Well, keep your ears… whatever you are meant to keep your ears. The equivalent of keeping your eyes peeled,' said his partner.

'To the ground,' said Fred, glad that Hugh wasn't part of the conversation.

'Don't forget to ask Hugh if he has seen anything suspicious. He is always looking out through those binoculars,' said Nel. Although she liked Hugh, she found him frustrating to interact with. It just went to show that while science was just pedantry with qualifications, all pedants were not necessarily scientists.

'We're not far from Russia here,' said Fred.

'Or America,' said Nel. 'Do you think it's about the Northwest Passage?'

'The plot thickens. Mysteries are afoot,' Fred added.

'This isn't Miss Marple.'

'I was being Hercule Poirot, actually.'

'More like Inspector Clouseau. This might be an espionage thriller, not a whodunnit. Anyway, he'll know someone has been into his room,' said Nel. 'As soon as he counts his money, he'll know. You-dunnit.'

'Not my problem. Nobody saw me, so he won't know who did it. I say we lie low and play the innocent.'

'Certainly a better idea than playing Scrabble,' said Nel.

Chapter 26

Lying low was not an option when they went back into the Adventurer's Lounge. Marvin was at the bar, with his eyes on the door. Fred worried he had been waiting for them.

'Come with me,' said Marvin, more like a command than a request. Trapped, Fred wheeled along beside him. Nel took one look at Marvin, decided that his instruction was not directed at her and made her escape. He led him, not to his suite as Fred has expected, but to the upper-level bar where Fred had talked with Heather.

'Double bourbon,' he instructed the bartender. 'Hold the ice. You?' he asked Fred.

'Can I have a whisky and ginger?' asked Fred.

'Give him that. Make it a double.'

Fred winced as he saw the credit card come from that wallet, but he sipped his drink as calmly as he could, while wondering what he'd let himself in for. He wished he had edged out of it with Nel, but it was too late now. Judging by his garrulity, Marvin – or Curt, or whoever he really was – was well on his way to being drunk, presumably having had pre-dinner drinks and wine with his meal.

'Have you been to the Science Centre?' Marvin demanded.

'Of course, we went on the second day,' said Fred.

'And there was a lecture?' he demanded.

'From Fleur? Yes, she's good. She spoke about climate change. The differences she could see in the Arctic,' said Fred.

'She's brilliant,' said Marvin, in a reverential tone. 'Although she's wrong about climate change…'

'She is definitely brilliant,' said Fred, preferring not to quibble about global warming with a man who had a gun on board. 'She's an old friend of Nel's.'

'And beautiful,' said Marvin, admiringly. 'Fleur, I mean. Great hair.'

'Brains and beauty,' agreed Fred. 'The whole package.'

There was a pause before Fred saw the complete picture, as Marvin stared brooding into his glass, like a man contemplating a future which didn't have a happy ending.

'Wait a minute!' said Fred, who could put two and two together as well as the next man, even after a double whisky. 'You like her! You like Fleur!'

'Who wouldn't?' said Marvin, shrugging his shoulders.

Fred thought for a minute and realised why this might be a problem.

'And she hates you because you're an oilman, and she's an environmentalist.'

'She's lovely,' slurred Marvin, his head resting on his hands.

'She may well be, but you'll never know,' said Fred, triumphantly.

'Do you think the age difference is a problem?' asked the American, suddenly.

'Well, she's late thirties, I'd guess. Maybe forty. At least, Nel's just turning forty.'

'And I'm forty-seven.'

'Really?' said Fred, looking him over. 'I had you down as older.'

'It's all about… how you come across,' said Marvin, suddenly seeming proud. He was good at what he did. Which was mainly impersonating people.

'It must be.'

'The dress and the walk and the talk… Can you keep a secret?'

'I think so,' said Fred. Looking around first, Marvin spoke to him quietly: 'I am not as old, nor as oily, as I look.'

'Really?' Even Marvin's voice sounded different now. Fred had no idea what he was.

'Oh, very good, play the innocent if you want,' said Marvin, now looking Fred right in the eye. 'But I know you've been in my cabin.'

'What?' said Fred, giving his best impression of a rabbit in a trap.

'You have,' said Marvin confidently.

'I don't know what you mean,' said Fred, blushing despite himself.

'I know a set of wheelchair tracks when I see them.'

'Damn!' muttered Fred, knowing he'd blown his cover. 'I tried so hard to leave no trace.'

'You don't have to be a tracker to know it was you. Nobody else on this ship leaves those marks. But if you got your aunts' money, you would have found out the rest…'

'I have literally no idea what to think,' said Fred, wondering where the gun was. This man was clearly drunk. Fred was beginning to get frightened.

'I'm one of the good guys.' Marvin looked at him. 'Believe me.'

'You're not really an oilman?' Fred wondered if he was talking to a Curt, not a Marvin. Was he still conning him?

'No.' The American spoke patiently. He was obviously Curt. It sounded as if he was telling the truth.

'Who are you, then?'

'One of the good guys, as I said. From the Agency,' he clarified.

'Oh, you're trailing Cyril?'

'I couldn't possibly comment,' said the American, but Fred thought his smile said it all.

'And you like Fleur?'

'Yes.'

'But she doesn't like you. She hates oilmen.' Fred felt that a recap was called for.

'So you keep on reminding me,' said his companion.

'Why are you pretending to be an oilman?'

'It seemed like a good cover. For why I was going to the Arctic.'

'Hmmm.' Fred was glad he wasn't in Curt's shoes. Or Marvin's. Presumably, they wore the same shoes. This was the sort of thing that Freya would love. She was very into spies.

'I want you to help me win over Fleur,' said Curt. 'OK, she may still not like me,' he acknowledged. 'But at least she would dislike the *real* me. That feels important.'

'You have to be the real you. If you pretend to be someone else, you've got a scandal on your hands.' Fred had read stories about undercover police who led a life of lies.

'Exactly.'

'You can't be Marvin G. Ridley with Fleur. What does the G stand for, by the way?'

'Garrett. Do you like it?'

'I do, actually. Didn't you shoot Billy the Kid?'

'No, it's a city in Indiana. Where I come from.'

'Where who comes from? Marvin or Curt?'

'Curt. I don't even have a middle name. Let alone a number. Anyway, you know all my secrets now.'

'I do.'

'I'd be grateful if you kept them to yourself,' said Curt, looking at him seriously.

'I will,' promised Fred. Although he thought that telling Nel was surely OK.

'And you're going to sort things out with Fleur.'

'I'll try.'

'And in return, we'll forget about the little bit of breaking and entering you did.'

'Thank you,' said Fred, fervently.

'That's a felony in any jurisdiction. I could get you struck off.'

'Please don't!' said Fred in alarm.

'I won't. Because you are going to make everything right with Fleur,' said Curt. Was that a threat? thought Fred. Sort of. Blackmail? And Curt had a gun, he couldn't forget that.

'I will do my best. And now, don't you think I'd better walk you back to your suite?'

'Take me to my bed, Fred.'
'Just stay alert, Curt.'

*

Later in bed that night, Fred lay awake. Nel had fallen asleep almost immediately, probably because of all those circuits she'd done of the deck with Polly, in the fresh Arctic air. Fred had things on his mind. He wasn't sure that Marvin was to be trusted. First, who was he really and what was he up to? Was he really a CIA man? If not, what? He certainly wasn't an oilman. Maybe he was just a Scrabble hustler. Did they even exist? Anyway, whatever he was, he now had leverage to make Fred do whatever he wanted.

Second, Fred was not sure how he could set about setting up a date for him. For a start, he couldn't see scientist Fleur giving 'Marvin' the time of day, aside from purely professional interactions, with him masquerading as an oilman and she being totally opposed to drilling in the Arctic wilderness. Perhaps he should sound her out. Was she even single? Or heterosexual? Maybe Nel would know. But he didn't want to give her the wrong idea.

Maybe Marvin/Curt could come on the shore adventure with Fleur, and save her from falling out of the Zodiac? Or, even better, save her from being savaged by a polar bear? Fred thought of the polar bear that Polly had seen. Did it have to be a real polar bear? Maybe if he talked to Cyril, they could set it all up. He could see it now: Fleur is menaced by a polar bear. It's all in a rush, so she doesn't get a good look. Marvin saves her by going head-to-head with the polar bear. Polar bear disappears. Fleur is so grateful to Marvin that she agrees to go on a date with him. Almost ridiculously foolproof.

Better still, thought Fred, they take refuge from the bear in a snow hole, and in those circumstances, thrown together by fate in an icy refuge, they form a bond. Brilliant. Except this scenario was less Agatha Christie, and more Mills & Boon. He could see the film rolling now.

However, there was no reason for Cyril to co-operate in the first place, assuming he was indeed the possessor of the polar bear outfit. Unless… Unless it was the price for Lu cooperating with him in the Oil Emergency demonstration! That was the answer, surely: we'll get your sidekick to hold her end of the banner, Cyril, if you let 'Marvin' tumble you over in the snow. Brilliant.

Admittedly, there was a risk that he'd be shot by the person with the rifle guarding them against polar bears. That could come into the category of occupational hazard, although it couldn't be the first time for Oil Rebellion. The circumstances were rather different from their usual protests. Did the rifles hold bullets or tranquilliser darts? It was not a trivial difference. Fred thought he'd better chat to Fleur or one of the Science Centre people. But first, he had to talk to Lu. He wasn't looking forward to it. Why was it always him who had to do the negotiating? Feeling like the UN Secretary General facing a particularly difficult imbroglio, he drifted off into a troubled sleep.

Chapter 27

It was not yet 7:30 a.m., and Fred had wheeled himself to the sauna, where he had met with Polly. He'd woken early with worries. Now he felt hungry and grumpy, as well. Polly had taken his chair away, which he hated, but which was better than overheated metal in the sauna. She had promised to come back in half an hour so that he could go to breakfast. They'd explained about the sauna to Nel, but not about Lu. As far as Nel knew, Fred and Polly were having an hour together. It was a white lie. Fred didn't feel she needed to know about nubile young women in towels. For that matter, he didn't want to know about nubile young women in towels. But he was not sure he had much choice in the matter.

Fred was lying on the top bench, which involved a workout, in his boxer shorts, swathed in a towel. It was dark, and strangely relaxing. Fred didn't usually associate sweat with relaxation, but there was always a first time. Fred felt a bit less stressed after his bad night. He breathed deeply, lay completely motionless in the heat and very nearly fell asleep.

He was woken up by the door opening and closing, and sensed rather than saw a figure clad in a towel coming in, sousing the hot coals and lying on the middle bench. He felt he should keep his eyes closed, although the salty sweat smarted as it dripped off his forehead, and he urgently wanted to wipe them.

'Hi there!' said a young woman's voice. 'I hope you're naked too.'

'I don't think you do,' said Fred's deeper voice. 'That's why I'm keeping my eyes closed.'

'Oh, hell!' said Lu, shuffling away from him.

'It's OK,' said Fred. 'I promise I'm not a predator.' He realised that was exactly what he would say if he were a predator. He could hear her getting up.

'Please don't go. Polly sent me to talk to you.'

The silhouette sat down again, but in reach of the door.

'I didn't lay a hand on her!' said Lu. 'It was all completely consensual.'

'I am rather afraid it was,' said Fred. 'But I don't want to talk about Polly.'

'You don't?' said Lu, her voice revealing her relief.

'No, I want to talk about Cyril.'

'Oh, him,' she said dismissively.

'I think you were going to do a demonstration with him?'

'Yes, something like that.'

'He may be an arse, but I hope that won't put you off.'

'It *does* put me off.'

'Please do whatever you've planned. It's very important.'

'Why do you care?'

'Well, I'm a supporter of Oil Emergency.'

'I've never seen you at meetings.'

'Mostly passively. I give money,' said Fred. 'In fact, I'm one of your financial backers, with my standing order.'

'I feel guilty about them, not about him,' admitted Lu.

'So you should,' said Fred. 'After you've done it, you never have to have anything more to do with him.'

'Good. Because he's a bossy old fart.'

It somehow pleased Fred greatly that she, who presumably knew Cyril best, did not think much of him.

'He is rather. But I beg you, do it anyway. You owe it to your supporters.'

'No.'

'What?' said Fred. It had all been going so well.

'No. I won't. I'm sick of him.' Lu sounded defiant. Fred wasn't sure what he could offer. Was there a carrot? Or a stick? He was thinking metaphorically, but it wasn't helping.

'I don't know what I'll do next.'

'Well, nobody in the environmental movement will want to have much to do with you,' said Fred, and he could understand exactly how they would feel. That was definitely the last time he contributed to Oil Emergency.

'I might go back to dance,' said Lu, ruminatively.

'The action might give you a springboard,' said Fred. 'Think of the international coverage.'

'All they'll see is someone dressed up as a polar bear. Not the real me.'

Although delighted to have confirmed that it was indeed Lu that Polly had seen in the polar bear suit, Fred thought she had a point. People were unlikely to invite a polar bear on to *Strictly*.

'What if,' he said tentatively, 'I got my journalist friend Heather Crisp to do a human-interest story afterwards. As well as her news piece on the demo?'

'That would be great!' She sounded completely pumped up.

'You'll have some wonderful footage,' said Fred.

'And then they will see the real Lu!'

'I think I could put in a word.'

'Could you? I wonder what I would wear? For the interview?'

'Not fur fabric, for sure. Your normal outfit? Or whatever you wear for dance?'

'That's it. Something sustainable: bamboo takes much less water than cotton. Lululemon perhaps. That's on trend.'

Fred felt what his nephews would have meant when they said, 'Whatevs.' Instead, he said a neutral: 'Great!'

'I want to position myself as a dancer. Not a furry,' said Lu firmly.

Once again, Fred wasn't entirely sure what she meant by a furry, and felt it was better if he didn't find out. He grunted in agreement.

'Thanks! It's a deal. I'll do the action, as long as you talk to Heather.'

Fred leaned over and put out a hand. Keeping one hand holding up her towel, she shook his hand with the other.

'See you later,' said Lu, as she left the sauna. Fred raised a thumb, and possibly fell asleep. He was still snoozing when Polly came back for him.

He decided to go straight to breakfast and have a shower later. Polly poured a ladle of water over her hair and borrowed Fred's towel to dry most of it off.

'It's no lie to say I've been in the sauna, and this way it looks like it,' she said.

'I don't want Hugh to get the wrong end of the stick.'

'Certainly not!' said his friend.

*

There were wheels within wheels, Fred decided. Which was actually a wheelie thing to think, he realised. After all, he was unlikely to talk about making strides, when he couldn't. But he was certainly going to have to talk to Heather. He thought he could sell it to her. After all, he was her brother-in-law. Now he had to suss out Fleur. And then he had to sell it to Cyril. After which, all he had to do was sell his plot to Marvin/Curt. While avoiding his aunts. Always making sure that Hugh didn't get the wrong idea about Polly.

And they call this a holiday, he thought bitterly.

Chapter 28

Fred had a constitutional cuppa on the observation deck with Nel. It was a cloudy day, and there was nothing to see, but they thought they had better keep quiet because Hugh was there, trying to spot some interesting birds. Hugh went in after ten minutes, disappointed, because none were visible.

'Have you found out who Marvin is?' said Nel.

'Well, not Marvin, for a start,' said Fred.

'What's his real name?'

'Curt. Definitely Curt.'

'Did you find out what Curt was doing? Why he has a gun?'

'Still not sure. Perhaps CIA?'

'Surely, Cyril isn't a big enough player to get shadowed by his own CIA man?'

'Maybe he's on holiday? Even CIA men have to have holidays sometime.'

'Just like TV reporters have to have holidays? No, it all sounds too good to be true, all these coincidences. I am suspicious of Curt and I am also suspicious of Heather.' When Nel put it like that, Fred had to agree it sounded fishy.

'Who else are you suspicious of?' said Fred.

'Hugh, for a start. He's behaving very oddly.'

'Well, he is a bit odd, to be honest,' said Fred, feeling disloyal.

'Odder than usual,' said Nel.

Fred wanted to discuss this a bit more, but first he had to solve at least one of the current imbroglios. Which meant discussing Fleur.

'Do you know if Fleur has a partner?' asked Fred.

'Not sure about her…' said Nel, raising her eyebrows at him.

'I wasn't asking for me!' said Fred in horror. 'I was asking for a friend.'

'Was it Hugh?' said Nel. 'Don't worry, you can tell me.'

'No, it's not about him,' said Fred, firmly.

'I know you men, you stick together like dance bands on the Titanic.'

'Perhaps not the most apt metaphor on a cruise.'

Nel nodded.

'As far as I know, Fleur's single. But I don't think that means you should start matchmaking.'

'I promise I'll explain why it's important later.'

Polly came along, her eyes gleaming. She'd evidently been spending the interim reading about nutrition.

'I'm going to give up alcohol!' she said.

'Why?' asked Fred suspiciously. 'You're not exactly a problem drinker.'

'No, I'm not,' said Polly. 'But it's wasted calories! Did you know, each glass of wine is the equivalent of a doughnut!'

'If only it was!' said Fred, fervently. He liked doughnuts. Both women stared at him, pointedly.

'All right, all right,' he said. 'I'll go on a diet!'

He felt if he gave way on this, Polly would be less likely to give him a hard time about his drinking. Which was almost within his unit allowance, he said to himself. He was allowed six doughnuts, or rather glasses of wine, a week. So, what if he usually had seven? Some people had that much a day!

*

Fred left Nel doing her Nordic walking and went below to find Fleur in the Science Centre.

'Hello, Fleur!' said Fred. 'Hello, Ingrid!' The cat was dozing on the desk.

'Morning,' she said, looking up from her notes. 'Have you noticed how this cat always lies down where he's not wanted?'

'Is he in your way?' asked Fred.

'No, he's all right. But he does lie down exactly where he chooses. Now, how can I help? Would you like to take part in an experiment?'

'Possibly,' said Fred, who thought he probably already was. 'But can I ask you something?'

'Of course!' said Fleur. 'I am here to answer all your questions!'

I doubt you are, thought Fred, and took a deep breath.

'A friend of mine…'

'Yes?'

'A friend of mine wondered if you were seeing anyone?'

Fred wasn't looking at her, so he didn't see Fleur blushing.

'I can tell you, that wasn't the sort of question I was expecting!'

'I am very sorry,' said Fred. 'This is a bit embarrassing for me too!'

'I am sure it is,' said Fleur.

'He's a very nice friend. I think you might like him. You may think he can't possibly be your type, but he might be.'

'If I got over my initial impressions?' said Fleur.

'Exactly!' said Fred. This was going better than he had feared.

'Well, you can tell your "friend" that no, I am not seeing anyone. And I am not a bit prejudiced.'

'And if you were to see someone, would you rather they were male or female?'

'I don't really mind, it depends on the person. As I said, I am not prejudiced. Male probably. But there is one important qualification…'

'Yes?' said Fred.

'They have to be single,' she said firmly, looking him in the eye.

'Oh, I don't think that is a big problem,' said Fred, shrugging his shoulders.

Fleur looked at him strangely.

He suddenly realised that she thought he was the admirer. Her friend's partner. Oh no! How could he put her right somehow? But at least he'd satisfactorily ticked off his first task. Fred ploughed on.

'Can I ask you another question?' he said. 'About something entirely different.'

'I wish you would,' she said.

'What are the chances of the shore party encountering a polar bear?'

Fleur seemed enormously relieved. This was not the first time she had been asked this question.

'At the last count, there were about 2,650 bears in the Barents Sea region. Maybe a tenth of those are on Spitsbergen itself, according to the census. So, if they're lucky they might see one. People usually do see one. Bears are generally found on the shore, because they feed on seals, or out on the ice. But they keep their distance as a rule.'

'And if the bear comes near you, what happens?'

'Well, in the unlikely event of the bear coming really close, we would shoot it.'

'Shoot it dead?' said Fred, who had more than an academic interest in this topic.

'No, we'd use tranquilliser darts, not bullets. We don't want to kill a bear.'

Fred breathed a sigh of relief. This was exactly what he wanted to hear. But Fleur hadn't finished.

'In fact, we want to take its measurements and a sample of its blood, to understand more about it. Probably some sperm, if it's male. Although, they are hunted in other regions, like Russia for example, and there's a worry about their long-term future.'

'Are they endangered, then?' Fred didn't know whether you could take a sample from a man in a polar bear costume. But it would be very cold and they'd be in a hurry.

Anyway, he hoped that by then Fleur and Curt would be getting on like the proverbial house on fire. Where did that simile come from? He'd never thought arson particularly romantic. Maybe Hugh would know. He was good on etymology. He was probably good at arson, come to think of it.

'Not at present. But they are considered vulnerable. Which is the next category to endangered. The ice which they live on is shrinking. Particularly around here. Fewer seals. Less algae. Plus, the hunting.'

'Why are algae important? Do the seals eat it?'

'No, the polar bears do. Their diet has become more and more varied. They even eat grass sometimes. And the shrinking ice is important, because it means the subpopulations of bears become isolated from each other – the Norwegians, the Russians, the Canadians, the Americans.'

'It's a long way to swim!'

'Exactly. That's why we have a programme to increase genetic diversity.'

'What? How? Are they cloning polar bears now?'

'No, no, none of that. But we do artificial insemination for polar bears. Hence the sperm collection.'

Fred whistled in astonishment. Rather them than me, he thought.

Fleur seemed happy that Fred now appeared more interested in polar bears than her. But he thought he should show her where his true feelings lay.

'Thank you, Fleur. Any friend of Nel's is a friend of mine.'

'I am sure the feeling is mutual,' said Fleur.

'Because Nel is absolutely the love of my life,' said Fred emphatically.

'Er... good,' said Fleur, a bit flustered. Norwegians were even less likely to go for personal disclosure than Brits.

'See you later, Fleur,' said Fred, glad he had now made things clear, plus found out several important facts. He was beginning to think he had a talent for this. And he'd done it all so subtly.

'Any time, Fred.'

She was glad of any curiosity about the natural world. But he was deeply odd. He asked very strange questions. Norwegians would think him rather rude. But Nel seemed happy, which was the main thing. The Brits had different standards, after all.

*

Fred thought that the morning was going very well. After all, Lu seemed to be onside. Fleur's answers had been like BBC 6 Music to his ears. Now he just had to persuade Cyril, and then Heather. Spitsbergen was looming in the distance. Which meant that tomorrow was the big day, when they disembarked, and it all started to happen. Whatever *it* was. Yes, two more discussions to go before that. He felt like a hostage negotiator. And then it would be time for lunch.

First, he went in search of Cyril Earther. He hoped he wouldn't be in the Science Centre. He wasn't ready to go back there. Maybe he'd be upstairs, on the observation deck. He'd just have to search the whole ship until he found him. There were things he had to say. He wondered what might be most persuasive for Cyril. He certainly didn't want to explain that Marvin was Curt. Or that he had committed burglary. Or that Curt wanted time alone with Fleur.

When he finally found Cyril, in the forward lounge, the great environmentalist was surrounded by acolytes: mostly young females, but there were some older people too. They had probably read him weekly in the *Guardian*, thought Fred.

Well, he wasn't as impressive in the flesh; even an Assyrian would baulk at that beard. Cyril looked like W. G. Grace on a bad day. Although, it didn't seem to stop the fans asking him to autograph their papers. Cyril was in his element. He was the sort of prophet who enjoyed having followers. Most prophets probably did, thought Fred. If you told people how bad things were likely to get, they just venerated you even more. Jeremiah probably got all sorts of groupies. After all, you got credit for giving the unvarnished truth. It wasn't as if anyone changed their behaviour. But they certainly worried more about the world and the future.

'Cyril!' said Fred, when he got the chance. The fans obviously needed to go to the gym or something.

'Frank!'

'It's Fred, actually.'

'Yes of course, *Fred*. You're Nel's partner.'

'That's right,' said Fred, unaccountably chuffed to be remembered. Obviously, this fangirling thing was infectious. 'We talked about rewilding.'

'Got it. Now, how can I help you?'

'It's about Lu.'

'Oh.' Cyril's face fell. 'Do you think I've said something to upset her, again? She seems very touchy.'

'I have no idea what went wrong,' said Fred, diplomatically. Although he wished someone would have a word about that beard. 'Anyway, I just saw her, and I think I've put things right.'

'Excellent,' said Cyril. 'Thank you. We're depending on her.'

'So I understand,' said Fred. 'Not that she's explained what you're up to!' he added quickly.

'Best not to know,' said Cyril, seriously. Fred nodded.

'So you can rest assured that Lu's onside,' he said. 'And in return there's something I'd like you to do for me...'

And he explained his scheme for Marvin rescuing Fleur from a marauding polar bear and hiding in a snow cave.

'I am not sure I can do this...' said Cyril, concerned.

'Well, of course, there may not be a passing polar bear. But if there was, then it would be great if Marvin saved Fleur...'

'Certainly better than Fleur being savaged to death... She's a lovely person.'

'She is,' said Fred.

'I really like her,' said Cyril. 'Though I am not sure she likes me.'

'Of course she does!' said Fred.

'She seems a bit cold when I talk to her,' admitted Cyril.

'She's a great admirer of your work,' said Fred. 'She's said so!'

'Has she?!' said Cyril, brightening up. 'That makes me feel a lot better.'

'I'm glad I've put you straight on a few things,' said Fred. 'But don't forget what I said about Marvin, in case there's a passing polar bear.'

He looked meaningfully at Cyril. He thought he'd got his point across.

'See you later,' he said to Cyril. 'Good luck tomorrow!'

Cyril raised both his fists in a thumbs-up sign. Fred made an emphatic thumbs-up gesture in response. Now he just needed to talk to Heather.

Chapter 29

Fred was working away at his laptop, when he became aware of a presence. He looked up to find Heather smiling at him. While this was timely, it felt a bit uncomfortable.

'Writing your next?' she said, sitting down a bit too close for comfort.

'Trying,' he admitted. 'Ideas aren't very easy, but I have lots of anecdotes about rehab.'

'I bet you do,' said Heather. 'I remember sending you a box of fruit.'

Fred decided not to mention that by the time he was ready to eat fruit again, it had mostly gone off. It was the thought that counted.

'Just steer clear of memoirs!' she said. He nodded. However proud he had been of his first attempt at writing, he realised now that telling stories of his friends was not the way to go. Certainly, if you didn't want your manuscript nicked. Or worse, to lose your friends.

Heather took his hand in hers. He looked at it, and looked at her. Was she trying to take his pulse? And was there any call to look into his eyes like that? It was strangely compelling, as if he were gazing straight at a cobra. She squeezed his hand meaningfully. He was not at all sure he liked where this was going. But she wasn't deterred.

'I know you've always loved me.'

He spluttered.

'There's no need to protest,' said Heather gently. 'No doubt you will deny it, but I know you really do, whatever you say. Well, here I am! I have decided. I will be yours,' she announced.

'Mine?' said Fred in stupefaction. What if he did not want her anymore? Did he have a say in the matter?

'Yours,' said Heather, with an air of finality.

'But what about Nel?' he protested. 'I'm with Nel!'

'Nel?' said Heather, dismissively. 'I wouldn't worry about Nel. I am sure she can find someone else.'

'And Roderick! He is my brother, you know.'

'Don't I know it! But he isn't the real thing.'

'He isn't?' said Fred, who had certainly found his elder brother a bit trying over the years.

'He enjoys the Shadow Cabinet, and the Parliamentary Labour Party, and I have to say I don't. Not my scene. I have always seen myself as the consort of an author, not a politician,' said Heather, who had read English at college, and now seemed to long for a life of hosting soirées and chairing talks at literary festivals. In her hands, she was thinking, he could be the next big thing. A Booker Prize winner one day? Certainly a Book Club nomination. Perhaps not Oprah Winfrey or Reese Witherspoon. Maybe Richard & Judy.

'You have?' Fred felt it was much less glamorous than she appeared to think.

'Yes. Which is where you come in…'

'But Roderick…'

'He's just too clumsy,' complained Heather. 'If he can't knock it over, he'll drop it. Everything gets broken eventually.'

'He does have two left feet…' admitted Fred. 'He always has.'

'Two left feet and butterfingers,' said Heather. 'There's no point in me buying anything nice.'

'And this is enough to condemn him?' said Fred, who felt that the awkwardness was not really Roderick's fault. It was probably genetic. His father had been rather clumsy, he remembered.

'This, and the fact that he's having an affair with his researcher.'

'No!' Fred was shocked, but not entirely surprised. Roderick had always been a Lothario, he thought, with a tiny twinge of envy.

'Yes. I'm sure of it. Of course, I don't have time to accompany him to Stoke, and nor do the boys. Well, she certainly does. All fur coat and no knickers.'

'Gosh!'

'Well, she may have worn some knickers once, but not after she mislaid them on the back seat of our car. Really, the indignity of shagging my husband in a lay-by on the A500. In a hybrid!'

Fred was speechless. For once, he'd rather stick to a thousand words than one image. He did not want to imagine his brother in a clinch with a young woman. Heather was continuing: 'I think the fur coat was even bought by Roddy. And seeing as you have always loved me…'

'Always loved you?' Fred was so stunned by her declaration that he was reduced to echoing her every word.

'Yes, you have. For all those years after your accident... It's really quite romantic,' said Heather, thinking that it would make a good story in the *Mail on Sunday*, particularly if she was dumping a member of the Shadow Cabinet. She was not about to tell them that her husband was the Labour Lothario. Or maybe she would? It would be good to look like the victim, not the vixen.

'Well, that's certainly true,' said Fred, who had nursed a crush on Heather for most of his twenties. And indeed thirties. He couldn't deny it.

'Exactly. And now here I am,' said Heather, triumphantly, flinging her arms wide. 'Yours!'

He looked at her and felt only horror at the prospect. Perhaps he'd been having delusions throughout his twenties and thirties? She still attracted as well as frightened him, but her expensively coiffed auburn hair and smart clothes could not disguise the shallowness which had become entirely obvious to him. And if she imagined he would simply cast aside Nel, she was certainly bonkers. But he would need to back away gently. Heather was crucial to his plans with Lu and Cyril and Fleur. He also didn't want to appear either insulting or ungrateful. The poor woman had been treated abominably by one brother. He would not do the same.

'In the meantime,' he said. 'Let me tell you about my thoughts.'

'I am all ears,' said Heather, beaming at him.

Chapter 30

Later that night, as Fred was finally in bed alongside Nel, he told her what had been happening, Well, some of it at least.

'Marvin, or Curt rather, is threatening me. Because he knows I burgled his room.'

'I could have told you that was a terrible idea. It could get you struck off.'

'Blame my aunts.'

'Although it was you who stole his money.'

'In a manner of speaking.'

'In the manner of taking his Scrabble winnings from his room. No wonder he's threatening you.'

'Did you know Paul, that nice Englishman, is a policeman?'

'Better watch your step, then.'

'No, Paul told me in the bar that he does not have jurisdiction here in Norway. The real difficulty is Curt – he wants me to help him get together with Fleur.'

'Fleur?' Nel was astonished.

'Yes, he seems keen on her.'

'So, always assuming that's a good plan, how are you going to engineer that?'

'Not sure,' he said.

'Fred, dear heart, you are a terrible liar. No secrets, remember?'

He had to admit she was right. They had agreed that their relationship was to be built on total honesty. Even when it was embarrassing or painful. Especially when it was embarrassing or painful. That's why he felt so guilty about his Nando's habit.

Consequently, Fred put his cards on the table. He laid out his entire scheme for Marvin and Fleur to end up in a snow hole, hiding from the polar bear – played, in this scenario, by Cyril, although he supposed it could equally well be Lu.

There was a pause in the dark. He could almost hear the cogs turning. Nobody could accuse Nel of having a screw loose. She was more capable of logical thought than anybody he knew. Had she been in charge, ChatGPT would have been a non-starter.

'A few problems occur to me, in connection with this sequence of events,' said his beloved.

'Really?' said Fred. 'It seemed pretty watertight to me...'

'Well, have you considered that Fleur may not suddenly fall in love with Marvin, or rather Curt? You seem to think that proximity is all it takes!'

'At least he hasn't got an awful beard!'

'As I said, matchmaking is a risky business.'

'Not my problem. I just said to Marvin that I would get them together,' said Fred in triumph.

'Does she have any choice in the matter?'

Fred remembered how Fleur had reacted after his aunt's lecture. Marvin was far from flavour of the month with the science communicator.

'And remember, we have no idea what Curt is up to,' said Nel. 'He could be with the CIA or the Mafia or the Triads, for all we know.'

'True,' said Fred. Light was beginning to dawn.

'And isn't it our collective opinion that he is here to stop Cyril doing a newsworthy protest?'

'Correct,' said Fred, spotting the Diptera in the unguent. Now it occurred to him that Curt may have used him to get closer to the action. He only had his (drunken) word that Curt was in love with Fleur at all. But surely the word of a drunk was genuine? Fred realised how many drunk people of his acquaintance had spoken utter tripe when over-lubricated in a state of exuberance or misery. It was a bit like smoking dope: despite talking a lot of nonsense, you thought you had been brilliantly original and deserved the close attention of the Nobel Prize committee.

But maybe he was only pretending to be drunk? Fred was a very sincere and honest man, which he was beginning to realise was a handicap.

'So he won't want Cyril's schemes to succeed,' finished Nel.

'No, probably not,' conceded Fred.

'And another thing,' said Nel, who was getting her steam up now. Much as she loved Fred, she did not fully trust his judgement. He was great at constructing elaborate scenarios, but many of them came into the category of those best-laid schemes which were likely to *gang aft agley*. Better on the page than in real life. No better for men than for mice.

'Yes?' said Fred, increasingly dismayed.

'I am sure you're correct in thinking that Fleur wants to be a nature presenter on TV. We both trained as science communicators after all. Not even David Attenborough is immortal. And now Chris Packham seems to have vacated the stage. Fleur's wasted here. She could do so much more with her talents.'

'Exactly,' said Fred, heartened. 'There must be a BBC vacancy any day now.'

'But so far, your scenario has her fleeing from the polar bear and diving into a snow hole with Marvin?'

'Yes.'

'Not impressive.'

'No?'

'No pieces to camera. No befriending charismatic megafauna. No chance of winning her that coveted TV spot.'

Fred knew immediately that Nel was right. She had put her unerring finger on the fatal flaw in his plan. He had wanted to give Marvin his best shot at winning the heart of Fleur. But he hadn't considered that Fleur would want to come out of the situation well, which meant standing up to the apex predator, not diving into a snow drift in an undignified manner. Even if that did benefit Marvin, which he was beginning to realise it probably wouldn't.

'I don't suppose you have got a better plan?' said Fred, throwing himself on Nel's unerring wisdom, not for the first time.

'Wait here,' she said. She pulled on a sweater over her pyjamas and went to find their friends. A few minutes later, Fred was joined by Hugh. The women were nowhere to be seen.

'I think they're hatching plots in the other cabin,' said Hugh, sitting on Fred's wheelchair. 'You don't mind, do you?'

'No, go ahead.'

'I'm only dimly aware of what this is all about,' said Hugh, yawning. 'I imagine you tried to pitch Nel some shallow scheme you had afoot, which she saw through immediately.'

Fred filled him in, explaining who was who, and what he imagined their motivations to be, touching briefly on his ingenious plot. He didn't mention Lu. No need for Hugh to dwell on her.

'Your plan is a bit absurd, I hope you don't mind me saying,' said Hugh. Over several decades, he had rarely been shy about pouring cold water on Fred's schemes.

'If you think it's such piffle, then why don't you try and do better?' retorted his friend. There was silence for a few moments. Then Hugh started talking: 'You need Fleur and Curt to spend time together?'

'Yes.'

'And because you are a supporter of Oil Emergency, you don't want Curt to stop Cyril's demo about drilling?'

'Exactly.'

'Then lure them each to your room, lock them in and leave them together.'

'While we go ashore?' said Fred.

'My very thought!' said his friend. 'Nothing to stop the demo, nothing to stop them both getting better acquainted.'

'After they've got over being really cross at being locked in,' said Fred, thinking. 'But I like it. This might just be a goer.'

'Plus, they won't get cold and they can have a cuppa, or a wee, at any time,' pointed out Hugh, ever the practical thinker.

'Would you like a hot drink now? Or a whisky?' said Fred, remembering Hugh was his guest and he had offered him nothing, apart from a plan which had more holes than a piece of Swiss cheese.

'Cocoa with a tot?' asked Hugh.

'Coming up!' said Fred.

Which is how their partners found them, ten minutes later, each with their head on a pillow, cradling a mug.

'You could be Morecambe and Wise,' said Polly, who had watched repeats of the Christmas Specials with her nan as a child. They looked blankly at her.

'Have you come up with a better solution?' asked Nel. 'You go first.'

'Hugh might have done,' said Fred, and Hugh outlined his idea. There was briefly a pause. The two women looked at each other. Then Polly shook her head.

'I don't like locking a woman in with a man she hardly knows.'

'Especially as he might be armed, for all we know,' said Nel. 'Not one of your most cunning plans, Hugh.'

'None of us really know Marvin, let alone Curt,' said Hugh. 'But I take your point.'

'OK, we've established that neither of us can construct a cunning plan,' said Fred. 'What have you come up with?'

'The problem is,' said Polly, who was used to these sorts of conflicts, 'we think that they might all want different things… Curt wants to get cosy with Fleur… Fleur wants to get on TV… Cyril wants to protest something, probably Big Oil… Heather wants to film a protest… Curt wants to stop Cyril.'

'Not to mention Heather wants Marvin to get her an interview with the US president,' said Fred.

'Does she? Does Marvin even know the US president?' asked Hugh.

'He says he does,' said Fred.

'Huh!' said Polly scornfully. 'He says a lot of things.'

'Can we just decide on whether it's Marvin or Curt?' asked Hugh. 'I'm in danger of getting confused by all these machinations.'

'From now on, we refer to him as Murt. Although possibly not to his face. Is he a nice guy?' asked Polly.

'Well, he says he is,' said Fred.

'Of course he does,' said Hugh. 'But then he would, wouldn't he?'

'Plus, he has a gun,' said Fred. 'We saw it.'

'Also, do we know whose side we are on?' asked Hugh. 'That seems important.'

'We want the demonstration to succeed,' said Nel, firmly. 'Because we are against drilling…'

'Right-ho,' said Fred, and the others seemed to be of like mind.

'We want Cyril to protest. We want Fleur to get what she wants. We don't really care about Heather or… Murt,' concluded Nel.

'Although we don't want Murt to get me arrested or struck off,' said Fred.

'Good point,' said Nel. 'I hadn't thought about that.'

'Do we think Murt has a chance with Fleur?' asked Hugh.

'Oilman Marvin certainly doesn't. There's a chance that CIA officer Curt might. But frankly, I'm inclined to doubt it,' said Nel. 'I wouldn't fancy him, myself.'

'Me neither,' said Polly.

'Well, that's a relief,' said Fred. They all pondered in silence for a moment.

'Let's go to bed,' said Hugh. 'We might come up with the Leibniz solution by the morning.'

'Leibniz solution?' asked Polly.

'The best of all possible worlds,' explained her husband. 'Everyone happy.'

And on that good note, the birthday party turned in. Unfortunately, as Voltaire pointed out in *Candide*, all is not for the best in all possible worlds. Things happen, like the Lisbon earthquake. Or the pandemic. Or the climate crisis. Or, more banally, as Hugh thought to himself, society's apparent collective amnesia on the matter of the correct use of the apostrophe, a topic about which he felt so strongly that he was quite unable to visit the local greengrocer.

Chapter 31

It was the morning of their submarine adventure amid the Arctic waters off Spitsbergen. In the afternoon, they were going to actually land on the island. It was bright and sunny and 10°C. Hardly how one imagined the Arctic in April, although there were a few clouds further off that threatened showers, presumably of rain rather than snow. Photographers on the voyage longed for a rainbow, with agreeably pointy mountains and glaciers in the distance.

Fred wasn't sure if he could climb into the mini-submarine or bathyscaphe or whatever it was. Nor was he sure that he wanted to. A few of the other passengers were muttering about the submersible that had imploded exploring the Titanic. It was reassuring to know that in this case they were only going down a few metres rather than thousands, but many passengers had doomscrolled enough to be anxious, and it had certainly poured cold water on the enterprise. Even a few metres were piling on the pressure. Even the metaphors were ganging up against them. Therefore, rather fewer than 100 passengers were patiently waiting for the promised ten minutes beneath the waves.

Because the sub had been advertised as being, well, mini, only four at a time could join the operator and Fleur for the adventure. The birthday party group and their new friends had to wait their turn on deck. Nel had explained the physics, they'd inspected the steel of the sub and they had been reassured, so they were as excited to explore the undersea world as Jacques Cousteau or indeed Wes Anderson's Steve Zissou.

Each party successively was taken across the bay and back. There were no disasters. Indeed, queueing for a submarine began to feel as quotidian as queuing for a bus, only with less graffiti.

When they had finally worked their way up to the head of the queue, Hugh climbed into the submarine. With his head still poking out, he reported back to Fred, 'How are you on ladders? Because you have to climb in and out of the submarine!'

'I'm OK going down, at least a short way,' said Fred, thinking that gravity would at least help getting in. 'But not climbing back out.'

'It's too narrow for me to give you a bunk-up,' said his friend. 'But we can try.'

'I think I will have to give this one a miss,' said Fred. He had expected it would be impossible, but had wanted to check. Being a wheelchair user meant missing out on a lot, he found. 'Make sure you take photographs!'

'My turn,' said Marvin, moving politely in front of him, once Fred had declined the opportunity. He then climbed in the submersible with surprising agility. So did Cyril, and another passenger.

'Quite a lot of testosterone on that sub,' remarked Lu, who was waiting in line. 'I hope Fleur can manage them all!'

'My husband won't give her any problems,' said Polly. 'Unless she confuses "fewer" with "less".'

'Or says "going forward" – he hates that,' said Fred. 'In his case, it's suboptimal grammar, not excess testosterone that causes the problems.'

The submarine was winched into the sea, which remained thankfully calm. The crane was unshackled, and the submersible disappeared with a burst of bubbles. The watchers could track its progress by the snorkel, as the sub slowly crossed the bay. The waiting explorers occupied themselves by stroking Ingrid, who seemed in a good mood that morning. Or perhaps he just preferred women to men. He certainly didn't seem to like Fred, but that may have been fear of the wheelchair.

'Rather glad we're going on the next trip,' said Polly, who was holding her daughter by the hand, with Nel beside her.

'Do you think we can all squeeze in?' said Bella, who was waiting with Donna by her side.

'I would think so,' said Polly, 'they did.'

'Although I am coming too,' said Freya. 'Which makes five.'

'We'll manage,' said Nel. 'If necessary, you can sit on a lap.'

'Not sure you know how much nine-year-olds weigh,' said Polly. 'I am sure there will be space.'

When the tower of the submersible popped up ten minutes later, her theory was put to the test. One by one, four adults and one child squeezed in alongside Fleur, and the submersible went for its next dive.

Hugh came over to Fred, as the women of the party disappeared.

'It was amazing to see the bottom of the ocean,' he said. 'Apparently, the fish aren't as colourful as you might see in the Tropics, but it's still very impressive.' He handed Fred his phone so he could scroll through the images.

Fred flipped politely through the photographs. He handed back the phone.

'Tell me about the dynamics on that dive,' said Fred.

'Both Murt and Cyril wanted to sit next to Fleur,' said Hugh. 'I felt a bit like a gooseberry. I think the other guy did too.'

'Gooseberries on a submarine? That sounds like the beginning of a joke,' said Fred. 'Who was the other guy? Please tell me he wasn't interested in Fleur.'

'Another Brit,' said Hugh. 'I think his name was Paul. No, he wasn't after Fleur either. Certainly knew a lot about submersibles. Someone I'd like to talk to a bit more. But the main action was around Fleur!'

'I've met Paul. But what action? Did anything happen?' said Fred, in excitement. 'If you felt like gooseberries, does that mean there was flirting?'

'I am not a flirting expert, but no, not that I noticed. Although the views were great, the atmosphere was a bit lacking,' said Hugh.

'But who won the contest? Who do you think Fleur preferred?' said Fred. He was hoping against hope that Curt had connected with the scientist. All their schemes depended on there being chemistry between them. But if Fleur believed Curt to be Marvin the oilman, of course she'd be hostile, and so would Cyril.

'Probably VAR is required to settle that,' said Hugh. 'Cyril did tend to go on a bit. The rest of us just wanted to be guided by Fleur – she has actually done a degree in marine biology – but Cyril wanted us to know about ocean temperatures and microplastics. Mostly, we all just wanted to spot fish, which was the reason we were down there after all. The fish-spotters were finally satisfied when she managed to point out an Arctic char, which is basically a survivor from prehistoric times. They live for ages.'

'Presumably not millions of years?'

'I think you're thinking of coelacanths. But Arctic char live for twenty to thirty years. Which is a pretty good lifespan for a fish.'

'Enough time to get thoroughly bored, I would imagine,' said Fred. 'No doubt you'd want to avoid polar bears, not to mention seals.'

'Anyway, Cyril couldn't enlighten us on char, and Curt made all the appropriate noises, so he may have come out just ahead on points,' said Hugh.

When Polly and Nel, with Freya in tow, came up a few minutes later, they were chattering away like children let out of school early. They had seen a whale swimming through the offshore waters.

'How much do you know about krill?' said Nel to Fred, glowing with her new-found zeal. He found it difficult to be enthusiastic about plankton, and said so. This was the cue for a lecture about biodiversity, and the feeding habits of whales. Freya said that krill was a bit rubbish, but whales were amazing. Nel explained about the creatures they had seen.

'We were very excited about the hagfish,' said Polly.

'I bet you were!' said Fred, wondering what a hagfish was. It sounded far from appealing. He would have liked to have seen a whale up close. He'd seen a bit of a whale. From the moored ship, you could see the occasional fin or a tail fluke, out in deeper water. Though not the whole thing. They'd already seen seals swimming around the coast. Someone had said they had seen a sea otter. But no one had yet seen a narwhal, however patiently they watched the seas. They were mostly around Greenland, apparently.

There was a narwhal tusk hanging up in the saloon, which Freya insisted was from a unicorn. Fred was keen to disabuse her by pointing out the sight of a whale in the sea with its single tusk intact, but he'd had no luck so far. Those tusks were very rare and valuable, Hugh explained. So much so that in past centuries, they were given to monarchs as diplomatic gifts. They had mystic properties, like purifying water.

'Do they really?' Freya had asked, her mouth agape. 'It's probably because unicorns are so rare.'

'That's what people thought,' Hugh had said. 'We don't believe that now. But the tusk is solid ivory so it's very valuable. Sailors used to carve ivory and bone and make models or trinkets. They called it scrimshaw.'

'Tell me more about hagfish,' asked Fred of the submariners.

'Hagfish are the only animal with a skull but no spine,' said Nel enthusiastically, as if he was as interested in marine biology as she was. 'They secrete a defensive slime to help them escape. But in normal circumstances they are scavengers. They eat dead fish from the inside.'

'No doubt where the ideas for some of *Doctor Who*'s enemies originate,' said Polly. 'Hagfish, as the name implies, are not just spineless, but also extremely ugly.'

'They're disgusting!' said Freya. 'We saw them!'

'I think that's enough information! Did Fleur have to deploy defensive slime?' said Fred aside to Hugh. 'Bet she wished she had some!'

'Unfortunately, we didn't see hagfish or whale on our trip,' said Hugh. 'But she was definitely trapped. As we all were, come to that, although she was the only one with Marvin to one side and Cyril to the other.'

At lunch, Fleur was conspicuous by her absence, to the chagrin of the man they now knew as Murt, and also, Fred was fairly sure, Cyril. Both men avoided each other, sitting at different ends of the restaurant, glowering at their neighbours. This was quite helpful, as it meant that Fred and the others could eat their sandwiches, salvaged from breakfast, more quietly in the bar.

Meanwhile, the ship was pushing through the ice in the fjord to get up close to the island of Spitsbergen. With its reinforced hull, powerful engine and sharp prow, it was designed to make light work of Arctic landscapes and was eating up ice just as efficiently as its passengers were gobbling up gravadlax. The plan was to go ashore, which meant avoiding the ice floes and connecting with solid ground, and not be so full of lunch that you couldn't fit into your waterproofs.

One of the Norwegian sailors had told Freya about the Norse goddess Freya, who was apparently the goddess of love and had a chariot drawn by cats. Freya (the nine-year-old) was not very interested in weddings, but she was interested in whether she could sit in Fred's wheelchair and get Ingrid to be the propulsion. Ingrid had other ideas, and frankly so did Fred, although he dutifully sat on a sofa while Freya conducted unsuccessful experiments.

'Maybe the real Vikings had different sorts of cats,' said Freya.

'Did Ingrid not want to be your motor?' said Polly.

'He wasn't having any of it! He hates the wheelchair, hates being tied to it, and now hates most of us!' said Hugh, who had been trying unsuccessfully to help his stepdaughter.

'He quite likes me after all!' called Fred, from where he was lounging on a sofa. 'Now I don't have wheels, I am a far more attractive prospect. Particularly for sleeping on.'

'As Freud said, "Time spent with a cat is never wasted,"' said Aunt Donna, passing at that moment.

'I doubt very much he ever said that,' said Hugh. 'There is a whole industry involved in making famous people say unlikely things.'

'I think I prefer dogs,' said Freya, thinking of how willing Fenner always was to oblige.

'Ingrid has disappeared at the mere sight of you,' said Fred. 'I hope that teaches you never to tie down a cat. They're not the right species.'

Having finished her lunch, Heather wandered over to have a word with Fred. She wasn't sure it was wise for him to come ashore.

'There'll be loads of snow,' she said. 'You're going to get very cold.'

'Don't worry, Heather,' he said through gritted teeth. 'I've thought all this through. I have thermal underwear, padded coat and trousers. I even have a pad to keep me warm, it's got some chemicals that react and emanate heat.'

'You know we can't leave anything on Spitsbergen?'

'Yes. I've read the instructions just like you, and it will be fine,' he said, smiling at her. It was kind of her to be concerned, he thought, but he hated being treated like a vulnerable adult. So many people saw the wheelchair but not the adult guy, who had done all this before, and could take care of himself. Well, as long as others helped push him over the ice. With Nel, Polly, Hugh and now Heather onside, he thought he'd probably be OK. Plus, all the regular crew.

Fred wanted to test himself going ashore. He had little skis to fix on his wheels, to turn his chair into a sled. He wanted to start with a peaceful visit, and then the following day make sure he was in a good position for the drama. Which meant level ground. He wanted to be there to see if the demo happened, not sliding off into the middle distance. He certainly wanted Cyril and Lu to get across their message, but if one or both of them got shot full of tranquilliser in the process, that would be pretty dramatic also. He thought a comatose Cyril might be worth seeing and easier to bear. As long as it didn't make him attractive to Fleur. Really, it would be better to deflate Cyril than to boost him. How do you deflate a man in a polar bear suit? What would Murt do? Would he manage to end up in a snow hole with Fleur? There was a lot to play for, and Fred was determined not to miss it.

Chapter 32

After lunch, they were due to dock at a small settlement and go ashore on Spitsbergen for the first time. Everyone was very excited. This first stop was only for a few hours at the former mining site of Sveagruva, so that the ship's passengers could see for themselves how rewilding had happened. As Fleur explained, this was the vastly expensive process of removing all the buildings and equipment from the mining era, rather than leaving it behind derelict. The mine closed in 2017, prior to the rewilding programme. Now it was back to pristine wilderness.

The shore visit today was the first of their two landings on Spitsbergen. The next day, they were due to visit Ny-Ålesund in Kongsfjord, where the ship's passengers would disembark to look at the glacier and the distant mountains. It was there that Fred and Nel thought that the Oil Rebellion stunt would take place. It was a more photogenic spot, overflowing with wild and unspoiled nature. Today was just the dry run for the main event.

In their matching orange waterproof jackets and trousers, each wearing the expedition's branded wellington boots, the tourists brought colour to the landscape, like giant orange crabs crawling all over the land. Or maggots, suggested Nel, who was very ambivalent about tourism, even though she had to admit she was a tourist herself. People were stretching their legs, jogging around the shore or taking a moment to be quiet and look out over Spitsbergen and the sea. It was certainly nice not to have the constant chugging engine of the ship, but to be truly quiet. Paul, the Englishman from the submersible, gave them a cheery wave as he tried to find the best angle to take photographs.

Looking at the unspoiled slopes that met the ship, and the mountains beyond, Nel said, 'This is how everything should be: nobody would know anyone had been here. If only humans tidied up after themselves like this all the time, instead of scarring nature with their rubbish. We are such a rapacious species.'

'It's also a pretty good sales pitch for the Norwegian state,' said Hugh, 'which I'd remind you is rich because of oil and gas, which is about a quarter of their GDP.'

Cyril was taking photographs, and Heather and the cameraman were hovering near him, ready to do his piece about rewilding.

Fred had seen what there was to see, which was not very much. The whole point of the place was that there was nothing to see. They were here to see an absence. Now he was rather cold, although he was not going to admit that to Heather. The sun was behind clouds, and there was a bitter wind. Fred did his best to shield himself behind other people. He had proved his point by landing successfully on Spitsbergen and wanted to go now.

Freya was bored. There was nothing to see, and there were no shops, let alone whales. The water looked inviting, but she had been warned that it was still far too cold to swim, certainly without a wetsuit. There were birds overhead, but the animals were keeping themselves to themselves, no doubt because 100 visitors make far too much noise.

'What is so exciting about a bird?' she asked her stepfather.

'Between ourselves, Freya, those little brown jobs, or LBJs, all look the same,' said her mother. Her husband tutted, and kept on looking through his binoculars and ticking off different species.

'Think of it as a kind of birder bingo,' Polly said to Freya. 'But make sure you are as quiet as possible, or else Steppy will get cross.' Now he was nodding in agreement.

Hugh and Fred enticed Freya into a competition to build snowmen, which kept her occupied for a while. But by then Fred was feeling increasingly cold, so he decided to head back up the gangplank into the ship with Aunty Bella, before his legs turned to icicles. Hugh was busy looking up for birds. Freya had decided that this occupation was completely boring (lots of things were boring, including school, adult conversation and even her youthful obsession, the recorder – or at least, practising it). But Nel was still there, listening to Cyril talk about rewilding. Polly and Fleur were on hand too, watching Cyril do his piece to camera. In fact, Fleur was about to be in dialogue with him, as a genuine Norwegian who knew about Sveagruva and rewilding. Watching also came into the 'boring' category, so Freya was delighted when Nel suggested climbing the small hill above the mine in order to take some pictures of how it had been restored to pristine beauty.

They made their way away and up. It was cold, but luckily the wind had dropped. After a brisk ten minutes' walk, they were a lot warmer and they could look back. The figures down below looked very small. Nel took her pictures and was trying to get a long shot with mountains across the water, when Freya pulled her arm.

'Look,' she said. 'They are boarding the ship! We'd better go!'

Sure enough, parties of tourists were gathering at the bottom of the gangplank and taking it in turn to re-enter the ship. They didn't seem in a particular hurry. Nel put her camera carefully into its case and then into her bag, and looked at Freya, who was poised ready to go and anxious about getting back in time.

'Race you down the hill,' Nel said, and Freya hared off.

More slowly, Nel jogged after her. Life may well begin at forty, she thought, but only at walking pace. She saw Freya in the distance, ahead of her, and thought she'd better get on with it. She didn't want them to miss the ship. As she ran down the hill, her stride lengthening, her left foot slipped on the hillside that was barely covered by April's snow, and she took a tumble, full length on the shale. Seeing her sprawled on the ground, Freya rushed back to her.

'Are you hurt, Nel?' she asked solicitously, putting an arm around her friend's neck.

'No,' said Nel. 'I was just going too fast and came a cropper.'

But as she got to her feet, she winced. She had turned her left ankle, and it was hurting. She stopped and felt the joint. It was swelling rapidly and it hurt to poke it.

'Damn!' said Nel. 'That's all we need.'

'Is it broken?'

'No, I think it's only sprained. Just twisted badly.'

She limped on.

'Would you like to lean on me?' suggested Freya.

'I just might,' said Nel. 'At least, as far as the ship.'

It was not far to the quay, where their transport awaited.

'Ouch!' squealed Nel as they made it down the hill. 'Ouch!'

'Maybe you'll need a wheelchair like Fred?' suggested Freya.

'Not yet,' said Nel, in alarm. 'It's only a minor prang. Only temporary. I must have wrenched my tendon in the fall, that's all.'

'You are limping a bit,' said Freya.

'At least there's plenty of ice if I need an ice pack,' said Nel. 'That's some consolation.' She limped on towards the ship, one arm resting around Freya's neck, trying not to slip on the snow. 'Let's keep going!'

As they emerged from behind the hill, the shoreline looked white but empty. There was no activity. Certainly no mining and no coal heap. But also no ship. As Nel looked around in alarm, she saw their ship just offshore. It was turning to go back out to sea.

'Yo!' yelled Nel at the top of her voice.

'Wait for us!' shouted Freya, equally loud.

But it was too late. Nobody on the MV *Queen Ingegerd* was looking their way. There was no possibility of two voices being heard above the huffing and puffing of the ship turning. Whoever had done the headcount must not have taken account of them. Perhaps they'd assumed that they had boarded and disappeared with Fred and Bella. As Nel and Freya limped down to the quay, they could see the MV *Ingegerd* was heading out to sea.

Chapter 33

Back on the ship and de-cagouled, Fred and Polly were having a coffee together. Bella was reading her Official Word List, and her wife was doing her anagram practice. Nel and Freya had not been missed. As far as everyone was concerned, they were somewhere on the ship. In fact, it was quite convenient that they weren't there, because it meant that Fred and Polly could discuss what was really on their minds, having ensured no one was there to overhear. They were about to start talking, but then a crew member came by, looking for Ingrid, and they had to say they hadn't seen him. Finally, the coast was clear.

'So, what's the problem?' asked Fred.

'It's Lu. She thinks I'm marvellous,' said Polly.

'Well, you are, of course,' said Fred to his friend.

'But I don't want her to think I am,' said Polly.

You probably should have thought of that before having naked saunas with her, thought Fred, but instead he said, 'I certainly don't think Hugh suspects she thinks you are.'

'Oh god, no! Anyway, you said you had a problem too?'

'Yes,' said Fred.

'So what's your problem?'

'It's Heather.'

'What about Heather? Is she still married to your brother?'

'For now,' said Fred, gloomily.

'That sounds ominous.'

'As well it might…' said Fred. 'You know how I thought she was wonderful for a while?'

'As if I could forget!' said Polly. 'Why, I can't imagine…'

'Anyway, of course now I am very happy with Nel—'

'A lucky escape,' said Polly.

'Except that Heather has decided that she made a mistake.'

'What?' asked Polly. 'What's she done now?'

'She says she's got the wrong brother!'

'Much like the Labour Party.'

'Sorry?' said Fred.

'Only joking,' said Polly.

'It's no joke,' said Fred earnestly. 'Heather has now decided she wants to be with me, not Roderick.'

'Really?' said Polly in astonishment.

'Yes. That's the real reason why she came on this cruise.'

'And do you want to be with her?'

'Certainly not!'

If two people could shudder in unison, they did.

'But we need her to do the interview with Lu,' said Fred.

'So you've got to keep her happy?' said Polly. Her friend nodded.

'I wonder if it would work if Lu fell in love with Heather instead?' suggested Fred.

'Solve both our problems in one fell swoop. But highly unlikely,' replied Polly.

'Shame,' said Fred.

'It's certainly a shame we're both so darned desirable,' said Polly, laughing. Fred stared at her for a moment, and then joined in. After all, they just had to say a polite 'thanks but no thanks', and they would be fine. Wouldn't they?

'Where's Freya?' said Polly, suddenly.

'With Nel, I think,' said Fred. 'But I've no idea where.'

Chapter 34

Meanwhile, Nel and Freya were standing on the quay at Sveagruva, watching the departing ship. The MV *Ingegerd* was at that moment about to circle West around Spitsbergen to Longyearbyen, the island's major town, where it would moor and stay for the night, at this rate without them. Nel did a quick calculation. It was now early afternoon and the sun was about to set. She had read that there had once been a regular flight between Longyearbyen and Sveagruva. But she did not know when it went, or indeed, if it still went. Maybe there was no further use for it, now the mine was gone. And there were no roads. The only reliable way to get to Longyearbyen was by boat. Which had just left.

What should they do? Throw themselves on the mercy of some local, and get a message to the ship at Longyearbyen? At the worst, they would have to stay there until the end of the cruise, and see the others at the airport. Or maybe they could catch it up somewhere. Were there even places to stay around here? And they had no extra clothes or things! Prices at Tromsø had been bad enough; if there was even a shop in Sveagruva, it would be astronomical.

Nel was so frustrated with herself: not only had she fallen, but then she had missed her ride. It would have been bad enough if it had just been her. Worse that she had been responsible for Freya being stranded too.

The thought of Polly suddenly struck her. She would probably be doing her nut. She had had enough dramas with Freya for one cruise. She wouldn't have any idea where she was. Social workers probably always feared the worst. Nel suddenly thought of her phone and searched through her bag until she found it. She turned it on. Thankfully, even on this part of Spitsbergen, one of the most barren places on the planet, there was signal. She messaged Polly that all was well, and the two of them had missed the ship but would catch them up. She kept her tone calm, and optimistic. She did not want to alarm Polly. But would they? she thought. Or rather, how would they? Or when would they? Her ankle was throbbing and she could barely walk.

Freya, at least, didn't seem bothered by the setback. She was throwing bits of concrete into the water from the quay and watching them splash. No doubt putting the wind up any seals in the vicinity. Or Arctic char, or whatever fish lurked down there. It was all an adventure to her. Nel looked about.

In the gathering darkness of a polar afternoon, there was a hooded woman, like an apparition, standing by a Skidoo about 50 metres away. Holding out her hand, Nel grabbed Freya and leaned on her to hobble over to the woman. She was counting out a stack of notes to herself, in a language which Nel did not understand. Satisfied, she folded the notes into a wallet, and then shoved the wallet inside her jacket. She was very well padded, no doubt for the cold.

'Hello!' said Nel, hoping she spoke some English.

'Hi!' said the woman cheerfully. 'How can I help you?'

'We missed our ship!' she said, pointing at the MV *Ingegerd*, now getting smaller in the distance.

'So I see,' she replied gravely. 'No more ships.'

'We need to get to Longyearbyen.'

'No bus,' said the woman.

'Plane?' said Nel hopefully.

'No more,' said the woman sadly. 'No ship, no bus, no plane, no train.'

'Ah,' said Nel despondently. Not very constructive. They would have to find somewhere to stay for at least one night, maybe more. She hoped she could find someone. Preferably someone cheery, or if that was too much to be hoped for, at least someone who could speak in words of more than one syllable.

'Skidoo?' said the woman. That was two syllables and hopeful.

'Skidoo?' repeated Nel. The woman pointed at her machine. It seemed to be a cross between a lawnmower and a motorbike, only with skis instead of wheels. Nel thought it was probably terrible for the environment.

'We go to Longyearbyen,' said the woman. 'By Skidoo?'

'Really?' said Nel, suddenly hopeful. 'I could pay for petrol.'

'Petrol money good,' said the woman. 'It's 40 kilometres. A tank of petrol there and back.'

'How long would it take?'

'We get there by dark.'

'Perfect,' said Nel, thinking that 'dark' meant late afternoon here. It was gloomy already.

'You are two?' said the woman.

'Yes, just the two of us,' said Nel.

'Plus me is three,' said the woman. 'We need two Skidoo, maybe three.'

'Three?' said Nel.

'She drive her own Skidoo,' said the woman, pointing at Freya.

'But she's only nine!' said Nel in alarm.

'Nine is fine,' said the woman, calmly. Freya looked very excited. This adventure was getting better and better.

'Well, OK,' said Nel. 'But where are we going to get more Skidoos?'

'Where indeed?' said the woman, looking about. 'No place to hire. But is all right. We borrow my kid sister's Skidoo!'

'She is near?'

'Not far,' said the woman, pulling out her mobile. She spoke to someone, presumably her sister. Was she really a kid? Freya's age? What language was she speaking?

'Is that Nynorsk?'

'No.'

'Bokmål, then?'

'No!'

Nel considered. Perhaps it was Finnish. She thought she had a good ear for languages, seeing as she had heard so many in London.

'What then?'

'Russian!'

'Oooo!' said Nel. 'No wonder I didn't recognise it! I had forgotten that there were Russians on Spitsbergen.'

'Only few,' explained the woman. 'But there used to be miners... Still a base there, some of us stayed. Spitsbergen is no colder than Siberia,' she explained.

'It would be very kind if you could help us catch up with the ship,' said Nel, who couldn't help being English.

'Ship go West and then only North. Then East back to Longyearbyen,' explained the woman. 'We go more quick North, straight to Longyearbyen.'

'Across the glacier?'

'Yes. But not over mountain!' The woman laughed, a deep laugh that seemed to shake her whole body. Nel and Freya looked at each other, and laughed too. Nel felt that had broken the ice. Did they say that here? She must check with Hugh, he'd know.

'I am Nel, and this is Freya,' said Nel.

'Freya? Good name!' said the Russian woman. 'Norse god!'

Freya beamed. She had never been somewhere where so many were pleased by her name.

'Me Natalya Peterovska,' said the woman.

Further conversation seemed unnecessary, so they waited in silence. Did people around here talk about the weather? Freya was getting proficient at throwing bits of rock in the water. Natalya seemed happy to wait all day. Nel sat down and rested her ankle. She was relieved when another Skidoo roared up to them and skidded to a halt. The woman driving the second Skidoo was far from a kid: she seemed at least twenty. The Russian sisters conferred. They gesticulated, stopped and looked at the two English women doubtfully. Not good. Nel saw the second woman shrug and then nod.

'This is Nina, my kid sister,' said Natalya, introducing her. 'My parents prefer sons, I think. But not lucky!'

Nina nodded in their general direction.

'Nina feels we cannot leave driving to you,' said Natalya.

The younger woman nodded again.

'She will come too. She will take the girl,' she said to Freya, who clapped with delight. This was exciting. She'd never been a passenger on a Skidoo before. Nina handed her a balaclava and a helmet. Natalya said to Freya: 'We think it is safer, warmer, if you wear this. Also, the visor will protect your eyes from the glare.' She took out a little jar of what looked like Vaseline and smeared it on Freya's lips and exposed skin. She looked over at Nel. 'Do you have goggles? Dark glasses? Wear them if you can!'

Nel fired off a text to Polly to say that they had been rescued and that they'd see them in Longyearbyen, and then smeared on the paraffin wax.

Nel and Freya climbed up behind the two Russian women, who pulled on their goggles, gunned the engines and whisked them off on the Skidoos. Well, more bumping than whisking, truth be told. They rode like they were born to be bounced about, and took no notice of the thundering din of the engines. But all the movement made Nel's twisted ankle hurt more. She tried to think of it as no worse than a massage. Nel noted that they were seated aboard a petrol engine, scarcely more advanced than a lawnmower. But she put her climate-change scruples aside and thought, please don't let us crash into a reindeer or something. At least they should get to Longyearbyen.

After about two minutes, Nel realised how thankful she was to Natalya for driving them. It was extremely cold, she could barely see the track, and the handlebars seemed hard to cling on to. This way, she could shelter from the worst of the wind behind Natalya, a woman with the circumference of a young walrus. Nel looked across. Freya was holding on to Nina for dear life, with the dogged smile of someone who was determined to enjoy the experience. Thanks to the helmet, balaclava and Vaseline – as well as the thick ski gloves they'd already been wearing – they should escape frostbite, skin burns and snow blindness, not to mention head injury. Those would be hard to explain to Polly.

Were the sisters here to herd reindeer or catch fish? Surely not to mine? Both their new Russian friends had red faces, as if they spent all their time outside. It was too noisy to have a conversation about what they got up to here. All Nel could see was the expanse of snow, mountains and some stunted trees, as well as the occasional reindeer, who had shorter legs, paler colour, and looked more like sheep than the ones who pulled Santa's sleigh. And then endless stretches of white snow again, marked with earlier Skidoo tracks. This was clearly a well-used route, skirting the lower slopes of the mountains – nicely pointy, thought Nel – and keeping mainly to the valleys below.

As they bounced (the Skidoos), screamed (the motors), squeaked (the British) and grunted (the Russians) their way to Longyearbyen, at a speed which felt like 100mph but was probably no more than 20mph, Nel was thinking, and rethinking. She had never met Nina nor Natalya before, and knew nothing about them. They could well be taking them in the wrong direction entirely. She sighed. It wasn't as if there'd been a lot of choice, though she was aware that Polly might see things differently. At least they were women, which reduced the safeguarding issues.

When, after several hours of bouncing over snow, they finally entered the outskirts of Longyearbyen and discovered it was not one of the world's busier metropolises, Nel at least felt a huge sense of relief, even though she was frozen through and her ankle throbbed ominously. To Freya's disappointment, there was a shop or two, but no mall. They had been warned on the ship that although they would be allowed ashore at Longyearbyen, the settlement had no nightlife, and only a few thousand residents. However, a university, schools and a church were more than enough to entitle it to be called a 'town'.

They skirted the church, followed by something which looked like a school, and ended up at the quay. Municipal architecture seemed mainly to consist of concrete, corrugated iron and shipping containers painted cheerful colours. Nel scanned the sea. In the distance she could see a ship. Was it coming or going? As it got bigger, she thought the former. She sighed with relief. Natalya pointed it out and smiled reassuringly.

'Ship,' she said.

Maybe when it was cold, you saved your breath by only making these laconic statements of the obvious. Nel felt in her bag for her wallet. They had passed a garage on the way, so she could work out the price of fuel.

'Is this enough petrol money?' she said, holding out some notes.

Natalya nodded and took the cash. Freya demanded that Nel take a photograph of her sitting behind Nina. Then, while they waited for their ship to arrive beside the quay, they went into a convenient café, which had the considerable advantage of being warm, and Nel bought everyone hot chocolate. While she took advantage of the Wi-Fi to send another message to Polly, and doomscroll the news, the Russian sisters were chatting to Freya.

'A-deen, dva, tree, chye-tir-ye, pyat,' said Nina.

'Shest, syem, vo-syem, dyev-yat, dyes-yat,' said Natalya. 'Think you remember that?'

'It's pretty hard,' admitted Freya. 'I think I might forget.'

'I bet there are some Russian sailors on the ship,' said Nel.

'Sure so,' said Natalya. 'And many Russians in London!'

'I hear a lot of Russian being spoken on the streets,' said Nel.

'Oligarchs,' growled Nina.

Nel was so shocked to hear Nina speak so angrily that she burst out laughing.

Natalya and Nina smiled knowingly.

'I bet Steppy won't know what these words mean!' said Freya.

'He does know a surprising amount, but you might have him there,' said Nel. 'I don't think he is fluent in Russian.'

When she wiped away the fug from the glass, she could keep an eye on the quay through the window. She didn't want to miss the ship again.

'It was so great that we found you!' said Nel, turning to the Russian sisters. Their new friends nodded.

'Not much to do in Sveagruva,' said Natalya.

'Or Longyearbyen,' said her sister.

'Were you there for the ship?' asked Nel curiously. 'Or just passing? Either way, it was very lucky for us.'

They didn't answer straight away. Natalya looked at her sister. Either her English was exhausted, or she wanted to be discreet.

'She was selling to someone on the ship,' said Nina.

'Selling?' said Nel. Was this drugs? What might they produce here? Reindeer? Fur? Crystal meth?

'Selling,' said Natalya, nodding in agreement. She didn't seem about to elaborate. Nel thought this was a mystery which she probably did not want to explore. But who was buying?

'Ship's here!' Nina said to Freya, as she saw the crew members anchoring and roping the quay bollards. Freya jumped up and hugged Natalya and Nina goodbye. They all went outside to the quayside. Freya waved at her friends on board. Her mum, Hugh and Fred were waiting at the top of the gangplank.

'Dog sled next time!' said Nina. 'We'll have to wrap you in furs!'

'I'd be careful what you promise,' said Nel. 'She won't forget! Thank you!'

The Russian sisters acknowledged her with a wave. As Freya went up the gangway to find the others, they could hear her counting as she went: 'A-deen, dva, tree, chye-tir-ye, pyat…'

'See!' said Nel with a laugh. 'Thank you for rescuing us!'

'It was fun!' said Natalya. 'Now we are going to clear off, we don't want to be spotted.'

With that, the Russian sisters hopped aboard their Skidoos, and they disappeared in a cloud of blue smoke. Nel coughed and limped up the gangplank.

'Am I glad to see you!' said Fred, as he greeted her at the top. 'Both of you safe, if not totally sound! Looks like you need a wheelchair right now!'

'Apparently,' said Nel, 'electric Skidoos are available.'

'If the Gulf Stream reverses, we might need one in Kennington,' said Fred.

'I wonder who they didn't want to be spotted by?' Nel was thinking aloud.

'Who?' asked Polly. 'Those women on the Skidoos? I want the whole story!'

'I wonder if you can get an accessible version,' said Fred. 'Have you noticed the kicksleds that the old folk have here? They've obviously thought of everything.'

Polly, Hugh and Fred were very pleased to see Nel and Freya back on board. It had been a tense few hours once their disappearance was noticed. The texts from Nel were as mysterious as they were reassuring. Nel seemed to have caught the going-missing habit from Freya. To see them back in the flesh was a relief. Nel explained to Polly that none of it had been Freya's fault. In fact, she couldn't have been a better support for her.

'The Russian sisters gave us a ride!' said Freya.

'Wow! All this way!' said Polly.

'It was very bumpy,' said Freya proudly.

'If they were Russian, I hope they didn't get all your secrets!' said Hugh.

'Secrets?' said Freya.

'Only joking,' said Hugh.

'No secrets,' said Nel. 'But we did bounce a lot.'

'Next time, they said dog sleds,' said Freya, who liked the idea of being pulled along by woofers.

'Whip crack away, whip crack away!' said Polly. 'Though it must get pretty cold.'

'They promised furs,' said Nel. 'I don't want to know where from.'

'Sounds rather good…' said Polly.

'But for now, I am going to lie down,' said Nel.

'Not quite yet,' said Fred. 'Let us show you something first – see if you can spot the difference.'

'Do I have to?' said his partner. 'I feel terribly old and weary.'

'Nonsense,' said Fred. 'Forty is the new thirty. This will only take a few minutes. Come along.'

Chapter 35

Everyone marched along the corridor and took the lift down one floor. Fred was taking them to the saloon. He used his chair to burst through the double doors.

'Now, are you ready for a mystery?' asked Fred.

'I may have had enough drama for one day,' said his partner, wearily. But Freya was very excited to find out what had been happening on the boat. She had also played this game before. She had compared lots of pairs of drawings to spot the difference between them.

'So, something's missing?' said Nel, looking around the saloon. 'It looks just like it did this morning. Exactly the same.'

There was a moment of silence.

'The unicorn!' cried Freya, after a few minutes.

'What?' asked Nel, not unreasonably.

'The unicorn's horn!' she said, in distress. 'What's happened to it?'

'Could that be your mystery?' asked Nel. 'Might it just have fallen on the floor?'

Typical, thought Fred. Blaming carelessness rather than crookery. No doubt that was why he was a writer, and she was a scientist. Novels depended on conspiracy, whereas cock-up ruled the world.

'No,' said Hugh. 'We thought of that, and we looked carefully, everywhere.'

'Though we haven't talked to the cleaner,' admitted Fred.

'But who'd want it?' said Polly, mystified 'A *Harry Potter* fan?'

'It's ivory,' said Nel, slowly. 'And rare, and legendary!'

'As I said, a unicorn's horn can purify water,' said Hugh. 'It has healing powers. According to alchemists. People used them for sceptres.'

'More to the point,' said Fred, 'narwhal horns are rather rare, very valuable, and people collect them. Which is why I think it's been nicked!'

'Well, who might have nicked it?' said Polly.

'Seriously, can we wait until the morning?' begged Nel. 'This is a mystery that requires rested minds.'

'Fair enough,' said Fred. 'Let's reconvene at 7:30 a.m. for breakfast.'

'It's the big day tomorrow,' pointed out Hugh.

'Fine, then let's make it seven a.m.,' said his friend. The others groaned their assent.

Chapter 36

Meanwhile, elsewhere on the ship, Cyril was scowling at a heap of fur. He'd never wanted to dress up in the first place. It was against his dignity, as a leading environmental commentator, to robe himself in fur fabric, as if he was some children's entertainer. They were both in their cabin, and Lu was standing next to the closed door. She also had a polar-bear suit. Their costumes were piled up next to the bunks. She knew they fitted, because they had tried them out in London. She had even tried out hers on the boat (to Polly's nocturnal alarm). But now there was a problem. Or rather two.

Asleep inside Cyril's polar bear costume was a cat, known to his admirers as Ingrid. He hadn't been seen since Freya's wheelchair experiment, and now the reason was obvious. A pile of cosy fur fabric was the ideal place for anyone who liked sleeping as much as he did.

'Well, that's put the cat among the polar bears,' said Lu.

'Not a joking matter,' replied Cyril, through the respirator mask he whipped on whenever the cat was nearby. 'How on earth did he get in?'

'I suppose I must have left the door ajar when I went to the sauna,' admitted Lu. 'It wasn't my intention. But you know cats. They instinctively go to the person who doesn't like them. It's fascinating behaviour.'

'Not fascinating,' said Cyril, sneezing. 'Deviant. And no, I don't "know" cats. I despise cats. One of the great advantages of Spitsbergen is that it is entirely free of cats.'

'OK, we've got the message. You're not a cat fancier. But so what?' asked Lu. 'Just turf him out and get on in.'

'The *what* is the cat,' sniffed Cyril. 'As I've told you repeatedly.'

'He's the ship's cat. You must by friends by now. He's a big softie, really.'

'Don't you remember? I am allergic to all cats,' said Cyril, and sneezed again. His eyes were now streaming.

'Oh, yes, you did mention it, once or twice,' said Lu. 'And of course, you wear that mask. So, what happens when you come into contact with one?'

'As you can see, I sneeze a lot,' said Cyril, stiffly. 'Sometimes I come out in a rash. If it gets really bad, I stop breathing. Nothing serious.' He had perfected the martyr look over the years, and he used it now.

'Haven't you got medication or something? This must happen all the time.'

'I do have some antihistamine,' admitted Cyril. 'It tends to make me fall asleep, though…'

'Will it work if…' Lu prodded the cat, until he rose haughtily to his feet, decided he no longer wanted to spend any time there and stalked out of the door, which she opened for him. 'After a cat was actually in your costume?'

'That's high-dose feline. Allergy overload to the power of ten,' said Cyril. 'Quite honestly, I would prefer not to risk it.' The fur-fabric suit was now rather hairy on the wrong side, as the recent occupier seemed to have left ample evidence of his presence. 'There is a danger of death.'

'That would not be a good way to go. "Environmental protestor, 41, dies of a cat allergy during an attempted Oil Rebellion protest",' said Lu, with a giggle. 'Not exactly heroic.'

She was met by a silent stare of disapproval from her bearded comrade.

'Well, we have no hoover, and since I am not allergic to cats, let me try,' said Lu, and climbed into the suit. As she was smaller than Cyril, it was slightly baggy, but she felt it would do. She zipped it up and put on the head. She did a twirl.

'There you are. Itchy but acceptable,' she said triumphantly. 'Now, it's your turn. My suit has definitely not been a cat bed.'

Cyril took Lu's smaller costume, and stripping down to his long johns and vest, he pulled it on. With a bit of huffing and puffing, it very nearly fitted. It was as tight as a second skin. He was in no position to frolic, but as long as he proceeded in a stately manner, it might not split. Cyril thought he could manage that.

'Now try on the head,' said Lu, approvingly. 'You'll just have to "grin and bear it",' she said, and chuckled. Not only did Cyril not get the joke, but also the head did not fit. He tried. Then Lu tried to squeeze it on him, accompanied by gasps and gurgles as he struggled to fit in.

A headless polar bear was no good at all. But the other head had been slept in, or on, by the cat. So Cyril's only choice was the slightly smaller head, which seemed too much of a squeeze for him.

'You're going to have to cut off your beard,' said Lu.

'Impossible!' thundered Cyril. 'I swore I wouldn't shave until we had reached net zero. I've worn it like this since the Brexit vote. I stroke it for inspiration!'

He was almost in tears now.

'Nobody cares. It doesn't say anything. It's just a beard,' said Lu, impatiently. 'We need to get dressed for the action. The beard will have to go.'

'That's easy for you to say,' moaned Cyril. He gave a thunderous sneeze and glared at his co-conspirator. She took out her nail scissors and went for his chin, like Delilah after Samson.

'*No!*' Cyril shouted, fending off his attacker with his hands, or rather paws. 'I have a beard trimmer.'

Which was why, a few minutes later, a man dressed to the waist as a bear was shaving off one Assyrian beard, tears in his eyes. He felt shaving was best done with hands, not paws. The beard itself was dislodged in its entirety, like a fox's brush. Cyril gazed at it, choked up for a moment, and placed it reverently on the bed. He could already picture the scene in his memoirs. Perhaps he would frame the beard, or even auction it in aid of an environmental charity. Then the clippers went to work again, as he ran the trimmer around his face. He put the clippers on the side of the basin and felt his bare face. He looked in the mirror and stroked his chin. It wasn't the same. But he felt he could still be majestic when he had to.

Lu looked on. Men! They were all the same. Babies really, beard or no beard.

'Now try on the head,' she commanded. 'It's why we're here after all!'

Cyril took the polar-bear head and placed it on his shoulders. Without his beard, it fitted. Finally, he was complete. And he could breathe. While nobody could accuse him of being a member of an endangered species, he did look surprisingly bear-like. Well, at least bearish, from a distance.

'It does fit,' he said in a muffled voice. 'But I'm not sure I can see where I am going.'

'Nor can I,' said his companion. 'And no idea if I can hold anything in these paws. Let alone walk in these legs.' She thought Cyril sounded a lot better when you couldn't actually hear him properly.

'They'll get the idea,' mumbled Cyril faintly. 'And I do feel noble.'

'Come on, Samson,' said Lu. 'Anything for the cause! Let's take off the outfits and be ready in the morning.'

'If I can get it off at all,' came the muffled voice, as the wriggling started. If only a Nobel Prize was awarded for environmentalism, he thought, he would be in with a good chance. But did people appreciate what he did for the cause?

'I might go for a sauna,' said Lu. She had discovered an allergy to celebrated environmentalists, and now she needed to calm down. As she left, she carefully closed the cabin door behind her. Turning around, she nearly bumped into Paul. He said nothing, but gave her a mock salute and continued down the corridor. He seemed to be hanging around a lot, thought Lu. Perhaps he fancied her. Or maybe Cyril. That would be funny. He was a lovely man. But he really wasn't her type.

Chapter 37

At seven a.m. sharp, Fred, Nel, Hugh, Polly and Freya met in Fred and Nel's cabin to discuss the missing narwhal horn. The bedroom was rather crowded, but at least they were in no danger of being overheard. Four of them were active participants in the meeting, and one was taking advantage of their distraction to sit in the en suite and read her Jack London book. As a stowaway, she had only brought essentials.

'I think I may be able to cast light on the mystery,' said Nel. 'It's about the women on Skidoos—'

'Surely they can't have taken the tusk?' said Hugh.

'Shut up and let her talk,' said Polly. 'Go on,' she said to her friend.

'Natalya wasn't there by chance,' said Nel. 'She was selling something to someone on board—'

'I don't really care why she was there,' said Polly. 'I am just glad that she and her sister got you both back to us. Losing Freya twice on one holiday is more than careless.'

'But what have they got to sell here? Fish? Lumps of coal?' said Fred, thinking hard.

'I bet they have all sorts of things on Spitsbergen,' said Hugh. 'Rare minerals from those mines. Skins.'

'The sisters promised us furs,' said Nel. 'Where would they be from?'

'Arctic fox?' said Hugh. 'Is there a quota?'

'Reindeer?' said Fred. 'Plenty of them.'

'But none had red noses!' called Freya, who had heard the word 'reindeer' and was still feeling cheated that the Spitsbergen examples looked nothing like those she'd seen on Christmas cards.

'Could the crew be running a dodgy racket?' said Polly. 'Should we ask Fleur?'

Nel shook her head. She was thinking.

At this point, there was a knock on the door. They were joined by Fred's aunts, one of whom was far from slim, which meant that nobody could move in the accessible bedroom.

'We're just discussing what might have happened to the narwhal horn that was hanging up,' said Fred.

'Someone's got the horn,' said Aunty Bella to Aunt Donna.

'Have you got the horn?' said Aunt Donna to Aunty Bella.

'Is this an old Derek and Clive routine?' said Fred. 'Only, it might not be the best moment for a rerun.'

'At least we can remember the 1970s,' said Aunty Bella.

'I wasn't even born then!' said Fred.

'Exactly!' said Aunt Donna.

'You're both definitely in your anecdotage,' said Fred. 'But we've got a serious case on our hands, so unless you've lost another game of Scrabble to Marvin, now really isn't the right time.' He pointed to Nel, and his aunts fell quiet.

'You know, I reckon that's the missing piece in this puzzle,' said Nel, thoughtfully. 'Marvin, or Curt, or whatever his name is. Where did he come from, and what is he doing? Who even is he?'

'Well, I shouldn't really say but he's a CIA agent,' said Fred. 'He hinted as much to me. He had to explain the two passports and the gun that he had in his safe. He came across at first as a Texan oil millionaire, but he overdid it, really. Then he said he was not really an oil millionaire at all, but he was someone from the Secret Service on the trail of Cyril. He swore me to secrecy. I suspect he's lying low in his cabin.'

'Well, we knew he wasn't really an oilman,' said Aunty Bella. 'But Donna and I got the impression that he was a computer hacker. He assured us he was one of the good guys, trying to mess up the Russian databases. He made us agree not to tell anyone.'

'No, you are all completely wrong,' said Hugh. 'When I spoke to him, he told me that he had made his money in cryptocurrency. He was looking for a place where he could find cheap electricity and spare computing power, so he could make some more. Hydro or something. His next stop is Iceland. But it's all very hush-hush.'

At this point, at Fred's urging, they went to breakfast. He didn't want to miss it. Luckily, they arrived after the first rush had passed. Fred filled his plate with bizarrely matched breakfast items. Without saying a word, Hugh carried Fred's coffee and food to the table they had colonised. The others brought over their drinks and breakfasts. Fred looked at Freya's plate and realised that they'd both had the same idea.

Once they had caught up with eating, and Fred was just wondering whether to fill his lunchtime bun with pickled herring or Jarlsberg cheese, Heather walked past their table. She seemed to be wearing the outfit of a Russian tsarina, from fur-lined hood to diamanté-encrusted jacket and black leather boots. Or maybe she had come straight from the pages of *War and Peace*. Freya was immediately enchanted. Compared to the rest of them, in their orange nylon coats and rubber boots, Heather offered the chic approach to winter-wear. Bet it's nowhere near as warm, thought Polly grimly. She certainly hoped it wasn't.

'Heather,' Fred called her over. 'You're an investigative journalist, so what's your take on Marvin? We are debating whether he is a CIA agent, a hacker or a cryptocurrency miner.'

'Yeah, come on,' teased Polly. 'You're meant to be the expert here.'

'He's an oil millionaire, isn't he?' said Heather, who didn't much like Polly's tone. 'Hangs out with the American president, and people like that, in Florida.'

'But we've discovered that he's a con man,' said Polly, spelling it out slowly. 'He lied to everyone.'

Heather was horrified. The American had managed to pull the wool over her eyes, and she'd bared her soul to him. She thought desperately of what she had told him, and whether he could use it against her. Was she safe?

'The fact that he is operating at least four different cover stories is dodgy for a start,' said Polly, smugly. 'No wonder you were all sworn to secrecy. He can't have wanted you comparing notes. He tried to tell me he was on a witness protection programme, which sounded like nonsense. I don't believe he's any of these people. I always thought he was a confidence trickster. It was obvious the moment I met him. A very charming, but entirely untrustworthy man. I predict that when we reach Longyearbyen Airport, he's going to just disappear. With any luck, we'll never see him again.'

'How did he say he had made his money? What did he tell you he's doing here?' asked Fred.

'I never really talked to him one-to-one,' said Polly. 'But I suspected that he might be a big-time drug dealer. He has the same sort of brash confidence as they do, in my limited experience. Maybe the gangs are interested in running Asian heroin and cannabis across to North America and Northern Europe? Now there's less ice, I'd imagine the Arctic is opened up for fast boats to use those smuggling routes.'

'Then what's he doing on a cruise?' asked Fred.

'No idea,' said Polly.

'I think he was buying ivory and maybe furs and other things like that,' said Nel. 'That's why the sisters were at Sveagruva. They were selling things to Curt. And if a very valuable piece of ivory has suddenly gone missing, I reckon he is highly likely to be to blame. He's definitely a crook, and probably a smuggler, whatever his real name is.'

'Well, he cheats at Scrabble,' said Aunty Bella, grimly. 'That's all the information you need to know that he's a wrong 'un.'

'We thought we saw him in the cave, although we didn't get a good look,' said Aunt Donna

'So you think he's got the horn?' said Fred.

Aunt Donna collapsed into giggles. Fred frowned at her. She lapsed into suppressed giggles. Aunty Bella shrugged her shoulders and tried to shush her partner. The others ignored them.

'Maybe one of us should have a word with Marvin, or Curt, or whatever his real name is. Or should we just tell Paul?' said Fred. 'He's a British policeman,' he explained to the others.

'I am sure Paul already knows,' said Nel. 'I think he's only here because of the smuggling.'

'But he can't arrest him in Norwegian waters, can he? If he's a British copper, it's outside his jurisdiction,' said Fred.

Seeing the time, they all filed along to the lifts. At this point, Fleur came by and saw them.

'Aha! That's where you all are. You look very serious. Come on, Famous Five, it's time to land on Spitsbergen!'

'We're the Secret Seven, actually,' said Freya. 'Only, we don't have a dog.'

Fleur saluted, and hurried off to make sure her team were prepared.

'OK, here's what we're going to do,' said Fred, taking charge in the queue for the RIBs. 'Polly and Freya – you go on the first boat, if you can squeeze to the front. Aunty Bella and Aunt Donna, you're to keep Marvin busy, in any way you can, just make sure he misses the first boat.'

'How do you suppose we should do that?' Aunty Bella asked Fred.

'I don't know, challenge him to a game of Scrabble again? Just make sure he's out of his room because I am going to burgle Marvin's cabin again – after all, what have I got to lose? And if I find the hor— I mean, the narwhal tusk, I will signal to all of you that he's definitely the guilty party.'

'What about your trip to Ny-Ålesund?' asked Hugh. 'It's what you came for.'

'Don't worry, I am not missing that!' said Fred. 'If you and Nel can wait, let's all of us go in the third wave of boats.'

'Agreed,' said Nel. 'I think this outing has as much planning as an invasion.'

'At least there's nobody on shore waiting for us,' said Hugh.

'It's an expedition, not an invasion,' said Fred. He enjoyed turning his wheelchair into a toboggan, although he was glad he trusted his friends.

'Can I push you?' asked Freya. 'Because I have never seen a wheelchair slide before.'

'Nor have I,' said Fred. 'Once I get the hang of it again, you are welcome to be my assistant.'

With that, Polly led Freya off to the embarkation point, explaining to her the concept of innocent until proven guilty. Donna went off to see her friendly maid, asking about her ailment. Five minutes later, she slipped Fred the keycard to Marvin's room, and she and Bella went off to see if they could intercept him. They found him picking up the rules of a game called poker – which he seemed to have taken to like a duck to water – in the Adventurer's Lounge. He was with the same aggrieved group of Germans, who were trying unsuccessfully to win their money back. They were only too pleased to see Bella and Donna take him off their hands, so they could regroup in order to think of a game that they could beat him at.

'Beginner's luck!' he was saying modestly to anyone who wanted to know.

Chapter 38

At the embarkation point, there was great excitement among the passengers about the landing on the Spitsbergen ice. Except for Nel and Freya, most of them had only had the brief trip onshore at Sveagruva. The demonstrators appeared ready for the big moment. Fred noticed that both Cyril and Lu were now carrying similar bulging bags. He also could not help spotting that Marvin's waist was also bulging ominously. He didn't like that at all. He didn't want Marvin firing at the 'polar bear'. He nodded at Donna and Bella.

'We've still time to win back our money!' Bella said to the American, blocking his path to the boats. She had first checked that he wasn't wearing the watch which had helped him cheat.

'Win back?' said Marvin, rather rudely. 'It's a bit late in the day for that! I think you may have got what you need.' He turned and found Donna standing behind him. They looked unbudgeable, in matching purple woolly hats.

'Come on,' said Donna, taking his arm.

'What about the landing?' he protested.

'We can all go on the next boat,' said Bella, encouragingly. 'Plenty of time.'

Short of barging aside two British ladies of advanced years – which Fred thought would not have been good optics – Marvin had little choice.

'Ladies, I really have to get on that boat,' insisted Marvin.

'We can go together on the next boat,' said Bella again, firmly. Donna put the board on the table and gave each of them a rack. She handed Marvin the letter bag. He took it from her as if it contained poison.

'You go first,' she said. 'We'll give you a sporting chance.'

*

Once he could see that Marvin was immovably engaged in the Scrabble game, Fred returned to his suite. He had the keycard that Donna had purloined for him, plus her hairpin, and he quickly entered the cabin. He was no longer bothered about leaving tyre tracks in the carpet, because he guessed that Marvin would want to get onto the shore as soon as possible. He first looked at the safe, twirling the hairpin like an expert. With a swift movement, he lodged the pin into the safe and heard a click. This burgling malarky was becoming worrying easy, he thought. Fred swung the safe door open and found it empty. There was no sign of the narwhal horn. His heart sank with both disappointment and concern. No doubt Marvin had stowed his passports elsewhere after Fred found them there the last time, and the gun might be about his person. Fred shivered, thinking of his aunts, his friends, his fellow passengers. He did not want anyone to be shot by the American, and he had no doubt that, if their suspicions were correct, the impostor would stop at nothing.

Fred rolled over to the desk to continue the search. There was nothing in any of the drawers either. Again, he was not surprised. Perhaps they were wrong after all, he thought, but now that he was here, he might as well be thorough. He turned to Marvin's bags. Surely, he could not be carrying everything with him. Marvin had two bags: one, a normal suitcase, where he no doubt carried his suits and shirts and cold-weather gear. The other, a large Gladstone bag in what, Fred hoped, was fake crocodile skin. It stood upright in the corner. When Fred opened it; it seemed to only contain a few items of clothing, yet it weighed quite heavy in his hands. Perhaps that was the fake skin. He shook the bag. There was a rattle. He took out all the contents. It still rattled. Fred felt around the lining. It seemed intact. Then when he experimented with the fastener at the top, he felt something give. He felt around again. This time, the lining came away and uncovered another compartment, in the bottom of the bag.

Bingo, thought Fred to himself, and he was not referring to a seven-letter word in Scrabble. The compartment contained several intact narwhal tusks. Fred was not sure which was the one that had formerly hung up in the lounge, but he knew none of them were legal, given the laws protecting whales and other endangered species. You could buy skins in Longyearbyen, of fox, lynx and even polar bear. But you could not buy tusks, and for good reason. He took several photographs on his phone, including one which had enough background to prove to anyone that it was Marvin's cabin. Then he put everything back in the case, put the case where he had found it, turned and left the room by the same route he had entered: no point in leaving extra wheel marks if he could help it. As he left, he saw the maid working her way down the corridor.

'Could you make sure you hoover the suite at the end?' he said to her. That should cover his tracks. He went back to his cabin, where Nel and Hugh were waiting. They both stood eagerly and started immediately asking questions.

'Just let me text Polly, Bella and Donna,' he said, and fired off one of the photos he'd taken. They would know exactly what it meant, he thought.

'So?' asked Nel. 'Did you find the horn or what?'

He held out his phone so they all could see the photograph.

'Oh yes,' said Fred. 'No shortage of horns. The gun was missing from the safe too – we need to go and help the others.'

Nel and Hugh exchanged anxious glances and sprang into action.

Fred had always thought he'd be strutting on the ice. At a pinch, for example a building with poor access and an urgent need for the bathroom, he could walk around on crutches and stagger his way through.

But this time, he was packing skis. So he climbed carefully with the others onto the Rigid Inflatable Boats, which had just returned from depositing the first batch of passengers onto the shore. This meant getting the lift down to the lower-level embarkation point and edging out into them. It was ten passengers to a boat, or nine with a wheelchair aboard, so each boat would take at least three trips between the ship, moored in the sound, and the shore, 20 metres away. That way, all of the passengers would get on shore for a few hours. Heather and her camera operator seemed to have left earlier to take up their positions.

Hugh and Nel were wedging Fred upright, and he spotted Paul, so he said hello to him. Hugh was about to introduce him to the Englishman, who had been on the submersible, and was surprised to find that the two already knew each other.

'We had a drink in the bar a few nights ago, with Captain Andersson,' said Fred.

'There are no strangers here, only friends you haven't met yet,' said Paul.

'Don't tell me – Yeats?' said Fred.

'He had a second job selling Irish whiskey,' said Paul with a grin.

'You're a very well-read policeman,' said Nel.

'Spent far too long in bars,' replied Paul. 'And I have an English degree,' he added.

'Paul, I think you've met Nel?' said Fred. 'Between us, we've been spying on Marvin. Who is really called Curt,' he added.

'And we think Marvin, or Curt rather, nicked the tusk,' said Nel.

'Well, more than *think*,' said Fred, who stopped himself just in time from admitting that he had committed breaking and entering. Nel was glaring at him. Paul couldn't arrest him here, but would make a good witness if the Norwegians ever did.

'Thank you, but please don't put yourself in danger,' said Paul, looking across at the other boats. 'Although there's no sign of our American friend.'

'I think my aunts may have embroiled him in a Scrabble game,' said Fred.

'I am sure they will be along soon,' said Nel.

'Never underestimate my aunts,' said Fred.

'Look at that sea eagle,' said Hugh, who had been watching the skies as the boat neared the shore.

With them in the RIB, there was a crew member at the stern, ready to gun the outboard motor, and another crew member with an actual rifle at the bows. Having armed sailors aboard made it feel like a Bond movie. Fred hoped they really had been loaded with tranquilliser darts, as Fleur had promised. He guessed it would look bad if they killed any protected animals, so these reindeer, bears and wolves – real or humanoid – were safe.

Fred chuckled at the thought of Marvin being thwarted from joining them by Scrabble-playing aunts. He hoped he knew enough seven-letter words to keep his end up without his watch. At ten Norwegian kroner per point, someone could end up badly out of pocket. Would it be the first time Scrabble was used for a political demonstration? Probably not. But by delaying him, an advantage had been won for Oil Rebellion, and he just hoped they could capitalise on it.

The scene as they approached the land was astonishing. Around them there was the sea, flat and glinting, and ahead there was the low shore, rocky and grassy, a tweedy tundra of mud and springy moss and rocks, with no trees whatsoever. Beyond there was the glacier, a vast sea of rolling ice, through which the piebald mountains poked through. He could see why their pointy-ness had been remarked on, by whoever had christened the island 'Spitsbergen'. It was immensely quiet, once the ship's engines had been turned off – quieter than anyone had ever experienced. There was no traffic, no machinery, just the steady rolling of the sea against the shore.

The tourists spoke in hushed tones, adrift in the bare expanse of the Arctic worlds.

The glacier was like a wall, nearly as blue as the sky. It rolled on across the ground, inexorable, like a wave frozen before it could break. I've never seen anything like that, thought Fred. It must have been there since the last ice age. But hadn't Nel told him, or was it in one of Fleur's lectures, that Arctic temperatures were increasing at four times the rate of other regions? Which meant was this vast, immovable glacier could scarcely survive more than a few years before increasing temperatures destroyed it. Beautiful, then, but doomed. Not exactly timeless. Fred felt immensely glad and privileged to have seen it. The glacier ended at the shore, where it calved sheets of ice which sailed off Southwards, onwards to their watery doom. Humans could rewild all they liked, thought Fred, but it might be too late for nature. It was a gloomy prospect.

As they landed, they saw Fleur up ahead, ready for action on the tundra. Maybe she should put that on her CV: 'tundra interpreter'. Above them, it was as if the pointy mountains were glaring angrily down at the impertinence of the human dramas far below. Fred also spotted Heather and her cameraman capturing their disembarkation, which was clumsy, in Fred's case.

Nel and Hugh now watched as Fred fastened the two skis onto his chair. He pulled himself into the chair and tucked himself in. Now he was ready for them to push him. He did not like to rely on others, but he had no independent way of getting around. He was like a car on bricks.

With Hugh pushing, Fred glided silently to join the rest of the group. It was amazing! He could really get used to this.

Sadly, the skis were not going to be much use in Kennington. The tourists were gathering to hear Fleur talk to them about what they could see all around. Latitude notwithstanding, it was really just another rocky, cold beach, and Fred was familiar with them from his childhood. All they needed was a picnic provided by his mother and it would be a total throwback to his early days in Northumberland. Hugh and Nel stood beside Fred, while their new friend Paul wandered around the crowd, keeping his eye on their surroundings and looking out for Marvin.

Fleur was magnificent, as if she was truly auditioning for Attenborough's job. She spoke in lilting English, comfortably Nordic. She took them from the birds on the wing to the worms in the sand. In the distance, she pointed out for them walruses (or was that walri?) and the short-legged reindeer, paler than was familiar, finding something to eat amid the rocks and ice. She was even able to spot a grumpy polar bear, foraging in the shallows far-off. She had the camera home in on nearby algae around the shoreline. Fred could see how her word-perfect delivery, honed on audiences at the Science Centre and on expeditions such as this, would work perfectly on TV. Her jokes were appreciated, her explanations got a gasp. Her account of global warming and the end of polar ice elicited a collective sigh from her audience, which was very moving, thought Fred, and might play well when broadcast.

Dead on cue, just after Fleur had finished her piece to camera about melting pack-ice, two 'polar bears' appeared on the crest of the hill ahead of her. For a moment, everyone was both shocked and terrified. The tourists prepared to beat an undignified retreat to the inflatables – as advised in the briefing – and three crew members had their rifles to their shoulders, ready to fire. The others were conferring on walkie-talkies, no doubt planning the escape. Fred and his friends watched with interest, not fear.

As the two figures waddled closer, it became evident that these were not actual polar bears, but humans in fur-fabric suits. For a start, they were not walking on all fours. The immediate relief from the travellers was palpable. It was a false alarm. They relaxed and wondered what was about to happen. Any remaining doubt was dispelled when the polar bears, in the most un-naturalistic way possible, stood tall on their hind legs and whipped a banner into shot. As Heather's cameraman focused on the 'bears', their slogan became visible:

Oil Rebellion say: No Drilling in the Arctic

It was a perfect move, just what Cyril and Lu had planned and rehearsed for, and not at all what Fleur or the tourists had expected. Most were stunned. Several people clapped. A few looked furious to have their holiday hijacked. Fred kept an eye out for Heather. Sure enough, she sprang up in the foreground, ready to do her piece to camera.

At this point, the crew now reassured that it was safe, the boats landed the final batch of tourists onshore, Marvin among them. It did not look like he had won the Scrabble game. Bella's and Donna's body language was triumphant. They had not only delayed him, but they had also got their own back. They were wearing the same coats as everyone else, but their matching purple hats marked them out as different from the others: caterpillars among grubs perhaps, but caterpillars with mirror sunglasses.

Marvin saw the 'No Drilling' demonstration. It was not difficult to work out who was responsible. But there was not a snow hole in sight. Instead, Fleur appeared to be mesmerised by the antics of Cyril, Marvin's love rival. With a howl of rage, Marvin broke away from the others and ran towards the camera. This was one parade which he was definitely going to rain on.

The friends watched him coming as if in slow motion. Should they be impeding Marvin? They were frozen to the spot. Having missed the opportunity to trip him up, Fred felt there was little else he could do. He thought Marvin might be taking method acting too far, although it was probably a case of the green-eyed monster. As far as Nel was concerned, although she certainly wished success to Oil Rebellion, she normally eschewed direct action. Polly was just impressed by Marvin's turn of speed, given that he was a well-built man in his middle years. Ever oblivious, Hugh was looking at sea birds. Consequently, Marvin was unstoppable.

The mysterious man of action reached the cameraman, and with one great shove the camera fell to the ground. It must have landed on an outcrop of rock, because there followed the unmistakeable sound of expensive electronics breaking. The cameraman went as white as the snow that was beginning to fall. Heather turned around, saw what had happened and shook her head in exasperation. Did she have to do everything? On his knees now, the camera operator gathered up the pieces of his kit. After a brief examination, he looked over at Heather and shook his head despondently. She ground her teeth and thought quickly.

Meanwhile, Marvin was sprinting towards Cyril and Lu, looking as threatening as an American can look while wearing a cagoul. There came an alarming bellow from one of the crew: 'A bear! A bear!'

Everyone looked at the fur-fabric protestors, confused, and then looked around. Shambling over a nearby hill was the distinctive figure of a polar bear strolling along on its four paws. The bear stopped, and sniffed the wind, suddenly alert. Clearly having tired of its algae hors d'oeuvre, he, or she, felt that it was about time that he, or she, located the meat course. Whether it was a he or a she was a detail that nobody had the leisure to check. Sexing a wild polar bear is not easily done on the run. And if you have any sense, you will be on the run if you ever spot a wild polar bear wanting to get up close and personal.

Fleur and the other crew members were now issuing instructions, and the tourists were heading back to the boats as quickly and quietly as they could. This time it was an ordered retreat, not a sudden panic. Rifles pointed at the bear, prepared to shoot at any moment, the crew members looked ready for action.

Oblivious to nature red in tooth and claw, Marvin grabbed Cyril around the waist. What resulted was like sumo wrestling, only furrier. Finding tussling unsatisfactory, Marvin opted for punching Cyril's polar-bear head as the most eloquent expression of his frustrations. The smaller polar-bear protestor was now cartwheeling elegantly out of the way. Heather could not believe that such Arctic TV gold risked being unrecorded. If it wasn't on camera, was it even real? She was standing next to her cameraman, who was distractedly contemplating insurance claims.

'Don't miss that!' she said, crossly, and her camera operator picked up his small digital camera, which thankfully was still working. He had brought it to take some stills, but he used it now to capture the somersaulting polar bear. In the background was a real polar bear, on the tundra was an Oil Rebellion banner, and in the foreground was Marvin punching a polar bear (fake) on the head. As the cameraman got his shot, mist was falling, nature's fade-out, and events on land became increasingly obscure. Heather smiled in satisfaction. This was better.

Heather's lack of fear might have appeared to others as bravery, and indeed she had won awards for it. However, her attitude owed a lot more to stupidity than to courage. Ever the egotist, she assumed everyone knew who she was, and would not dream of hurting her, whether they were terrorists, civil war combatants, or even wild bears. She had once briefly been held hostage in Yemen, but had been handed back after forty-eight hours, less because of her reputation and more because she was driving her kidnappers mad with her hourly selfies and insistence on accessing Wi-Fi so she could file an award-winning column. She wondered whether anyone else had succeeded in getting pictured with a wild polar bear. It could be a world exclusive. Failing that, if she could discover who was cartwheeling in the polar bear suit, that could work for an interview. Assuming there was good footage to go with it.

All the action – with Oil Rebellion, armed and dangerous Marvin, two fake bears, one of whom was somersaulting into the distance, plus a real polar bear looking hungry in the fog – was missed by the stampeding tourists, who had decided as one that the boats were the best option. Everyone had been informed how fast a polar bear could move if they wanted to – 40 kilometres per hour over short distances – and how hungry they got these days, and nobody needed to waste time, given the personal injury implications. Lu was now safely in a snow hole, trying her best to look unappetising. Heather and her camera operator were trying to rebuild their TV camera, having given up on taking more shots with the smaller digital video camera. Marshalled by the armed crew members, the tourists waited onshore for their RIBs to arrive, trying to stay downwind of the polar bear. The passengers felt they needed to get no closer to the massive limbs and savage claws of the beast.

As each boat took on its complement of passengers, it quickly reversed away from the shore and returned them to the ship. Retreating smartly, Nel and Hugh pushed Fred on his skis across the snow. They eventually got to their boat. Hugh pushed and Nel pulled and Fred clambered. With that, he was across the bulwarks and sprawled in the base of the RIB. Nel and Hugh pulled Fred up and sat him on the bench seat. His wheelchair was folded and pulled aboard. As he often commented, he had said goodbye to dignity long ago. Everyone was panting, but alive.

Chapter 39

From his boat, Fred looked back at the foggy scene, trying to make out whether Marvin had managed to collar both protestors, and whether all three of them would be savaged by the real polar bear, which looked genuinely wild. In the falling snow, there seemed to be no sign of either protestor. When Hugh passed his binoculars to confirm, all Fred could see was the Oil Rebellion banner, which lay forlornly in the snow. It had landed opportunely, and Fred could see Heather's cameraman, using his small digital camera to capture a long shot of the banner and the deserted glaciers and mountains behind: 'No Drilling in the Arctic' indeed.

The polar bear was still very much in evidence, even though both protestors had fled. The bear had turned his attention to Marvin. He was hungry and Marvin was a big man, and the bear evidently thought that, with seals so scarce, a well-built American was just what he needed. Certainly more likely to put meat on his bones than berries. Marvin was trying to put some distance between them, jogging around the shore. The bear was effortlessly keeping up. This race was not going to end well for the human.

Marvin spotted an ice floe just offshore. With a flying leap, he managed to clear the intervening water, and land on the floe, winded and on all fours. He was obviously more athletic than he looked. He got to his feet and turned to face the bear. It was just about to slip into the water and go after him. Marvin's ice floe was drifting out very gently, having stranded the American in the bay, 3 or 4 metres from land. As Marvin should have remembered from Fleur's lecture, bears can swim for miles. The bear would not have called the situation shooting fish in a barrel, but only because bears are not good with metaphors.

Then, in the gloom, a shot rang out. Marvin had drawn his gun and was aiming at the polar bear back on land. He had obviously decided there was only room for one of them on his ice floe. Having the one weapon meant the game was not strictly fair, but Marvin was a winner, and winners got to win, he said to himself. He was certainly not about to become a take-out meal for bears.

'No!' screamed Fleur in horror.

'Don't shoot!' bellowed Heather, who was used to being obeyed.

At that moment, there was another shot, and the polar bear staggered for a moment, and then fell to the ground, as if poleaxed. Marvin was greatly relieved, and his Glock disappeared into his pocket.

Heather, urging her cameraman to capture the scene, was furious that the polar bear had been felled. She was even more cross when she discovered that he had been dropped by a scientist with a tranquilliser, not killed by an American tourist with a handgun. At least the shooting of a protected animal might have ended up being a good story in the media. She had plans for that polar bear, and him being unconscious would not work at all. She wondered whether he would wake up if someone poked him? Or flung a suitable rock? If only those meddling scientists would get out of the way.

Now that the polar bear was out cold, there was a limited amount of time. The team of scientists first checked that the bear was unconscious: sperm retrieval was easier when there was minimal chance of being killed. Fleur put out a latex-gloved hand and reached for the scrotum. IVF for polar bears was not a career option she had ever considered at school. Gently but firmly, she pushed the needle in. The polar bear groaned, as indeed any male was likely to. Fleur gently pulled the plunger back, so that the syringe filled up with liquid. She withdrew the needle, snapping it off into the sharps box. She placed the syringe into a small chiller bag and gave a thumbs-up sign. Now the team had to withdraw quickly and get back to their RIB. Polar bear sperm retrieval had only taken fifteen minutes from start to finish. The crew member at the helm gunned the engine. They were in a hurry to get the sperm into the freezer. Meanwhile, the polar bear still lay comatose in the snow. He would awake with a testicle which was as sore as his head.

Fleur's boatswain took the RIB at top speed in the direction of the ship and safety. She thought how heroic Cyril looked as he protested, and how valiant he had been, but where was he now? The last thing she'd seen was Marvin punching him in the head. But nevertheless, the protest seemed to have been successful. She assumed it had been caught on film. She had seen Marvin topple the camera, and she feared for her audition tape. But the most important thing was that everyone was safe, and nobody had been eaten by a hungry bear, not even Marvin, who probably deserved to be.

Heather's cameraman was using his small camera to take all the shots he possibly could of the unconscious polar bear. He wasn't sure what quality they would be, as it was so foggy. No doubt they would not be good enough to please Heather, but he was past caring about that.

The boats ferried passengers back to the ship and came back for more, but everyone was trying to catch a look of the comatose polar bear and reluctant to leave.

'Did you *see* him?' said a tourist, trying to catch a glimpse of what was happening onshore.

'He looked *savage*!' said another, whose day had been made by their escape.

'I would *not* have liked to have been clawed by him!' stated someone with a North American twang to their voice and a fondness for stating the obvious.

Cyril had slowly walked back to the boat, holding his bear head in one hand, as if he were an astronaut returning from a mission. He was rather cross to have been overshadowed by a real polar bear, plus his head was still spinning after Marvin had socked him, even through the bear costume. But Fleur had given him an admiring look and squeezed his hand, or rather his paw, as he went past. He thought she might be persuaded to have dinner with him, once he had had a shower and changed. But he missed his beard.

There was none of the adulation he had expected on the boat back to the ship. Instead, there was an uncomfortable silence, as people seemed to want to look at the sea or the shore, anywhere in fact but at Cyril. It turned out that his boat mostly contained Germans, who unaccountably avoided him. His bare chin was beginning to feel rather cold, and he was bruised from where Marvin had hit him. He thought he might have at least one black eye, but he would have to wait until he was in his cabin to survey the damage. He wasn't even sure if Heather's cameraman had captured the demo. She had pulled faces at him and pointed mournfully at her broken camera. All in all, a day which had started with lots of adrenalin had ended like a damp squib. Hopefully, enough people would have taken shots on camera phones for there to be some point in it all.

Lu had quietly reappeared, clambering through the mist, and took her seat in the prow of the last boat, dressed as an ordinary tourist once more. Somewhere back there, there was a snow hole containing a fur-fabric costume. Once they were back aboard their ship, Lu was so cheerful at having got away with it –both the protest and the potential wild animal onslaught – that she even skipped as she mingled with the crowd. Someone asked her if she had seen what happened. It was an older couple, with matching head warmers: a pair of retired teachers from Solihull.

'Not really,' she said, which was true. 'I didn't get a proper view of things.'

'It was some demo,' said the man. His wife nodded.

'Good for them,' said Lu, who was from Birmingham herself.

'Whatever happened to the third bear?' asked someone. 'I mean, the second person dressed as a bear? They just cartwheeled off.'

'Your guess is as good as mine,' said an American.

'I should imagine they escaped by the skin of their teeth,' said Lu.

'I reckon all those protestors should just be shot,' said the American, who sounded like a friend of Marvin's. 'Jail's too good for 'em.'

This was not a popular suggestion, with Lu or the rest of the group, and they all edged away from the American, who was as grumpy as a billionaire after losing a court case. The sun was low on the horizon, and apart from the voices of the tourists, it was quiet. The sea was calm. They could have been in church.

Meanwhile, back on the ship, Fred was saying, 'I'm too old for this!' to his friends, still recovering from their hurried departure. They were on the rear deck, looking out on the RIBs returning from the landing.

'Nonsense,' said Nel. 'Age is just a number.' It was a refrain she was trying to make her maxim, now that she had turned forty herself.

'I'm going to be ten soon,' remarked Freya smugly.

'Exactly! But you're a teenager, at heart,' said Nel.

'But without a teenager's bedtime,' said Polly quickly.

'Dressing as a polar bear was very popular in the 1920s and 1930s,' said Hugh, quietly, as he watched the others failing to surround Cyril with the praise that he was no doubt expecting.

'Why?' asked Fred, although the real question was surely how Hugh knew that.

'It was particularly the fashion in Germany,' continued Hugh.

'You're not saying dressing as a polar bear was basically Nazi?' said Fred, in disbelief.

'Why did the Nasties like dressing up as polar bears?' asked Freya.

'Not sure,' said Hugh.

'I wonder if Cyril knows that the Nazis set the precedent for the polar bear costume,' said Nel.

'I think he really should know,' said Hugh. 'I might drop it into the conversation.'

'Please don't,' said Polly.

'It would help him understand why the Germans on his RIB have given him the cold shoulder,' said Hugh.

'Marvin over there is about to get an even frostier reception,' said Fred. The friends looked over at the boat speeding towards the ship. Marvin had been rescued from his ice floe, and was now sitting alone in the bows, guarded by Paul.

On the boat ride from ship to shore, Fred had told Paul quietly what he had found in Marvin's bag. Paul was apparently an expert on the Convention on International Trade in Endangered Species of Wild Fauna and Flora, and his force had been monitoring Marvin for some time, which explained why he was on the ship in the first place.

In turn, Paul had got a message to Captain Andersson, who had prepared a warm welcome for Marvin back at the ship. He was no longer the honoured passenger, more like the thief and smuggler who would be locked in his cabin until the Norwegian police could come on board at Longyearbyen. Fred studied Marvin, who looked furious and was nursing his bloodied hand. Fred wondered if he felt lonely. He was certainly isolated. Nobody seemed willing to give him the time of day. That's what you got for punching national icons, he thought. Especially when most of the punters wanted the Arctic to stay, well, Arctic.

*

Fred's aunts Bella and Donna approached Lu once on deck.

'We think you were marvellous,' said Donna, giving her a congratulatory hug. 'Quite the celebrity!'

'You mean the cartwheeling polar bear?' said Lu with a wink. 'Yes, the girl done good.'

'Very much a bonus of our trip,' said Donna. 'That and the sweepstake we organised in the boat.'

'People were so exhilarated, they were ready to bet on when the real polar bear would wake up,' explained Bella. 'We did very well out of it, so drinks are on us.'

'Now I can enjoy the rest of the cruise,' said Lu. 'As if I am really on holiday.' She was still filled with the adrenaline buzz of the demonstration, and the escape from the real polar bear.

'You've cartwheeled your way into history,' said Bella.

'Well, it's fabulous to be in Svalbard, home of pointy mountains, odd-looking reindeer—'

'And a few passing polar bears,' said Donna.

'Has anybody seen an Arctic fox?' said Lu. 'Or Cyril, for that matter?'

'They're here somewhere,' said Donna. 'No idea about him. But it looked as if Marvin was having some strong words.'

'Cyril looks much better without the beard,' said Lu. 'But sadly, he sounds much the same.'

'I don't suppose you play Scrabble at all?' suggested Bella. 'Because if you are bored one evening, we could give you a game!'

'That's very kind,' said Lu. 'You know, there's only another night until we are back at Longyearbyen. Once I've had a sauna to unwind, that might be lovely.'

'Brilliant,' said Donna. 'We'd join you, only we're wrinkled enough already.'

'Speak for yourself,' said Bella.

Chapter 40

Back on the ship that night, there was a bubble of excitement around the dinner tables. By then, Fred and Nel had abandoned being strictly vegetarian and were making exceptions for fish. Tonight was bacalao, which Fred loved, and was relieved not to have missed. It was a thick stew, based on tomatoes and onions, and full of chunks of salt cod and potatoes. Everyone got stuck in, and bottles of red wine were passed around.

Everyone had experienced the drama of landing on Spitsbergen, which had been their goal after all. They'd seen a polar bear, which had been the icing on the fruit cake that was Svalbard. Several of them had been nearly savaged by that polar bear, according to them at least, although this was another tale that grew taller in the telling. Others had successfully protested against drilling in the Arctic. Missions were accomplished. Toasts were drunk. If bar prices had been more reasonable, boats would have been pushed out. As it was, the room, fuelled mostly by soft drinks, bubbled with more bonhomie than a dozen bottles of champagne could have produced. Marvin was imprisoned in his cabin. Neither his antics with Cyril nor his shot at the polar bear were likely to make him popular with anyone, least of all Fleur.

Amid the circulating passengers, Donna found herself next to Lu. She smiled at her warmly again. They'd talked earlier in the week, and Donna admired Lu's grace, as well as her pluck in protesting. Now she only wanted to know one thing.

'Was it lonely in your snow hole?' she asked.

'Not at all!' said Lu. 'Though it was only for about five minutes, not five months. There was too much adrenalin pumping for me to be frightened, let alone lonely!'

Donna nodded, sadly.

'From the boats, it looked rather dramatic!'

Fleur, who was sitting at the same table, turned round to face them.

'It was all kicking off!' she said. 'These trips are usually very tightly controlled. I was terrified that we'd either lose a passenger or, possibly worse, that we'd lose a bear. It could have been extremely nasty.'

'I suppose the bear was very hungry,' said Bella.

'Hangry!' said Fleur. 'Hungry and angry! Think how you'd feel! Scarce food, annoying humans waving things. It could hardly be worse.'

'Sorry,' said Lu.

'Everyone was very quick, taking the semen,' said Bella. 'I bet it looks very slick on film. I suppose it does focus your mind, when you realise your patient could savage you to death with one blow!'

'That's what you should be researching: the changing biochemistry of the flora and fauna,' said Fleur, nodding.

'Future-facing. More going on there than some nineteenth-century explorers.'

'Maybe you're right,' conceded Donna. 'Once I've written this book, maybe that's the next thing. I need something to do in my retirement! Of course, I'd need a vet or a zoologist.'

'If you wrote a book, it could be called *Balls to Polar Bears*!' said Lu.

'Not a bad idea,' said Fleur. She raised her glass to her, Donna and Bella, and moved on. All she really wanted to do was hang out with Cyril.

Fred noticed that Cyril was once more the centre of attention for his many admirers. Fred hardly recognised him now. It was not so much the lack of polar bear suit. It was the Assyrian beard that he had shorn off in the process. Cyril's eyes shone, and his face was almost noble, especially now he had a bandage around his head, thanks to the punch from Marvin. He could look safely heroic, after having been dragged and half-carried to safety by Paul. But there was nothing weak about Cyril's chin. Fred wondered why he had grown the facial fungus in the first place. Perhaps he was protesting the dominance of the five-bladed razor or shaving foam aerosols, or something.

Among Cyril's admirers was Fleur. She was now seated right next to him, and at one point Fred could have sworn that she took his hand. Hugh followed Fred's gaze and glanced over at Cyril and his fans.

'Interesting...' he said.

'If I didn't know her better, I would say that Fleur is star-struck!' said Fred.

'Hmmm, I'm not sure it's star-struck, as such,' said Hugh.

'Well, she's certainly cosying up to Cyril,' said Fred.

'She is rather, isn't she?' said Nel, seeing the two of them together across the dining room.

'She also got filmed by Heather and her cameraman,' said Polly. 'When she did her talk on the shore earlier.'

'Although apparently all that was lost when Heather's camera got smashed,' said Fred. 'Such a shame, because with it, she could surely have named her own price with the BBC or National Geographic or one of those channels.'

'I think Heather's cameraman shot her in action collecting the polar bear sperm,' said Nel. 'She's got enough footage. And I don't think it's fair to say that she's just attracted to Cyril because of his celebrity. She's not that shallow!'

'Are we talking about Fleur or Heather?' asked Polly.

'Maybe Fleur's pogonophobic?' suggested Hugh.

'What's that?' said Polly, rather regretting she had invited her husband to give the lecture that she suspected would follow.

'It's a phobia of beards,' said Hugh. '*Pogon* in Greek. Unlikely but true. I guess people think beards are threatening or unhygienic, or something.'

Polly nodded. Perhaps Hugh had finally realised that briefer was generally better. He smiled at Polly, who squeezed his hand. She was proud that he knew lots of stuff. Even prouder when he didn't feel the need to tell everybody.

'It *was* a pretty ghastly beard,' said Fred, who hated any facial hair. 'Although if she's changed her attitude purely on that basis, wouldn't that be shallow too?'

'I think she bravely fought against her prejudice,' said Nel. 'But the whole point of a phobia is that you can't help yourself. Aren't loads of people terrified of spiders, or even clowns? It must be a big relief to her that he's shaved it off.'

'A big relief to us all,' said Fred, with feeling. He thought the sooner the fashion for facial hair was behind them, the sooner the world would be a better place. The same went for tattoos. All the male staff at their NGO were bearded, and a new tattoo was frequently the subject of conversation over lunch. Fred couldn't fully get behind either trend, though he didn't say so. He hoped he wasn't discriminatory – each to their own – but he did have aesthetic preferences. He couldn't help shuddering every time the talk turned to 'tatts'. It was probably an age thing. Fred smiled at Nel. He was glad that her taste ran to middle-aged, arguably slightly overweight, men using wheelchairs.

Heather was also looking glum, but Fred did not make much of it. She glared at him as she passed, as if he was Public Enemy #1. He put it down to her problems with Roddy. It was preferable to her treating him like a sight for sore eyes. Perhaps his eagerness for offspring had managed to put her off. While thankfully not responsible for his brother's happiness, he didn't want to cause further problems in that department.

Heather's glumness made more sense when, a few minutes later, Fred also spotted Jason, her cameraman, looking downcast at the bar. For the price of a gin and tonic, he got the full story. Marvin's shove had broken the TV camera beyond repair. Although the cameraman managed to get part of the demo on his small camera, including the cartwheeling polar bear and Fleur's skilful sperm extraction, he had not got Heather's piece to camera. Her report did not make sense as a broadcast. They would just have to head back to base and hope the kit was insured.

'So the whole thing is lost?' asked Fred with mounting dismay.

'Yup. Heather's news item, Fleur's showreel, most of the Oil Rebellion demo – none of it can be used,' said Jason. 'Completely abortive.'

'But what about the bit on your smaller camera? Can't you use that?'

'No use to us now. Not without the other bits to top and tail it. In any case, it's not exactly broadcast quality... Good enough for the internet, maybe, but not for putting out on cable TV as our main piece. They are very paranoid about picture quality; the editor keeps saying this isn't some video diary.'

'What if we had a go at it? It might work on YouTube...'

'If you want it, it's yours,' said the cameraman.

'Leave it with me,' said Fred, rummaging in the bag slung under his chair to find his mobile. He knew that Cyril, Lu and the Oil Rebellion movement would hope for something to come out of their exploits. He guessed that they had not yet heard that their antics had been effectively a waste of time. But perhaps if the footage got to YouTube, at least some people would see it.

'Andy?' he said a few moments later. One of the many good things about Svalbard was that it had excellent phone reception. Because of all the scientists stationed there, a really good mast had been built at Longyearbyen. The line to England was almost as good as the reception he could get back in Kennington. It was afternoon, so Fred's nephew answered and listened to his uncle's suggestion.

'Yes, I think we could do that,' came his voice into Fred's ear. 'Sounds right up our street. If he can transfer it via Dropbox to me, Gerry and I will download it and get to work.'

There and then, Fred turned to the cameraman, gave him Andy's email address, and sent him scurrying off to his cabin to transfer the digital footage. Fred bought him another drink while he was waiting. He hoped the clips would turn out to be worth it. A double gin at these bar prices was quite the investment.

Chapter 41

Meanwhile, to say Heather was far from gruntled would have been an understatement. During the cruise, her irritation had mounted to fever pitch, as one thing after another had conspired to make her life difficult. And now she didn't even have an intro to the American president. Whether Hell had a fury to match hers was uncertain, but she was unmistakeably a woman scorned. Forgiving and forgetting was not on her to-do list.

First, there was only one explanation for Fred's behaviour, which was that he was a complete idiot. Wasn't he meant to have been in love with her for decades? And now, having been offered the woman quite literally of his dreams on a plate, he had quibbled, made pathetic excuses and generally not recognised the gift horse that he was being offered. Talk about #ungrateful! She was so far out of his league, it was unreal, as if the Harlem Globetrotters were playing Gateshead Town. Yet, unaccountably, Fred had favoured science over glamour, loyalty over loveliness. Rejection was a new experience for Heather, and she had no intention of getting used to it.

Second, to add insult to injury, her stupid fool of a cameraman had just dropped – dropped! – their camera on the ice and rock, with consequences which were entirely foreseeable. Heather didn't blame Marvin; she blamed her camera operator, who should have held on to his equipment. The timing had been so good right up to that point. Her outfit had said classy, but intrepid (no cagoule-nonsense for her). She had looked windswept, but noble. Her piece to camera had been word-perfect. And the footage of the Oil Rebellion protest, with the two fake polar bears and then the real one in the background, could not have been more BAFTA-worthy had it been scripted. All it had lacked was a tourist being savaged to death, and surely that could be arranged. They would have won awards for that piece, had it been broadcast as planned.

Well, she was going to take out her frustrations on someone, and she had a sneaking suspicion about exactly who was going to wish they had not been born. The whole excursion had been a complete waste of time. For a start, she hated getting cold.

Thank goodness nobody knew about it, or at least, nobody important.

A cabinet minister in the hand was worth holding on to for now, however clumsily unfaithful he might be. It wouldn't be difficult to get Roddy's researcher sacked. Roddy was as allergic to scandal as she was, and if she breathed a word to his Chief Whip, he would be dropped faster than you could say non-disclosure agreement. Since Covid-19, affairs with advisers were not what government was about. The sooner she was tucked up in her own bed with a stiff drink in one hand and the telly remote control in the other, the better for anyone in her immediate vicinity.

In the meantime, would it be possible to write a memoir of the whole Oil Rebellion/polar bear episode? She must have enough time; she spent hours hanging around in airports. Maybe, by turning the Spitsbergen debacle into taut prose, she could make herself into the heroine once more? Show how environmentally conscious she had always been? An interview with each of the protestors would be a good start. All she needed was someone to transcribe her thoughts. She would have no trouble coming up with something to say. She never did.

Chapter 42

On their final morning on the ship, as others were watching Longyearbyen approach, Polly beckoned to Nel and they both headed towards the sauna for a final time. Luckily, once they had undressed and tied their towels around themselves, they had the place to themselves. Except for a naked woman on the top bench. For a guilty heartbeat, Polly thought it was Lu, but it turned out to be Heather. She scowled at them both from behind her towel and stalked off when she realised exactly who it was that had joined her.

Both women were glad to see Heather leave. She seemed extremely put out, and it was certainly a lot more relaxing without her. It's not easy to slam a sauna door shut, but she certainly tried.

Polly and Nel looked at each other and giggled. They sat on the bottom bench, and Nel splashed water on the artificial coals. The sauna got perceptibly hotter within a few minutes, as the small room was filled with steam. They started to relax.

'I've decided on a career change,' said Polly after five minutes, wafting away the steam. 'I haven't even told Hugh yet!'

'I'm honoured you're telling me,' said Nel. 'What are you going to do next?'

'Hand in my resignation, retrain… Oh, you mean what job am I going to do?'

'Yes!'

'It's obvious, really,' said Polly. 'I realised when I was nagging Fred about being porky.'

'Please don't give him a hard time,' said Nel. 'It's so helpful to me that he has become vegetarian.'

'Cheese, pastries and alcohol are not the basis of a calorie-controlled diet,' said Polly, sternly. 'Have I ever told you that a glass of wine has as many calories as a doughnut?!'

'You have told me that before, several times. But he does eat things other than cheese,' said Nel, defensively. 'And he's far from a heavy drinker. I think he's at risk of becoming paranoid.'

'Sorry,' said Polly. 'He's not even very fat. I just care about his health.'

'Anyway, what about the Swiss and all that fondue they eat? There's nothing wrong with them.'

'Must be the mountains or cross-county skiing, or something,' said Polly. 'Hugh could probably tell us.'

The pair of them were silent for a moment, thinking about what Hugh could probably tell them.

'Anyway, enough about Hugh,' said Nel. 'What did you decide as a result of nagging Fred? Are you going to go off and regulate solicitors or something?'

'What?' said Polly. Her friend seemed to have got the wrong end of the stick. 'No, I'm going to leave social work and get qualified as a personal trainer!'

'Really?' said Nel. 'That seems like a big change. Why would you want to do that?'

'OK, it may be a big change. It may be less money. But it's also zero responsibility. I would be my own boss. My clients would have fewer problems too.'

'That's true,' said Nel. 'Who cares about unfit rich people?'

'Lots of people have personal trainers these days!' said Polly. 'You don't have to be rich!'

'Isn't it a bit, well, boring?' suggested Nel.

'No, not at all. I am very interested in the science of nutrition and in the different bodywork possibilities,' said Polly, rather pompously.

'You're already talking about bodywork,' said Nel. 'I can see that this is where it's all heading. I can see the advantages for you turning your hobby into a job.'

'Plus, what's the worst that can happen?' asked Polly. 'Someone forgets their exercises? Or doesn't find time to go for their walk? Or eats a slice of cake that's on the large side?'

'You would have to find some clients,' pointed out Nel. 'And do a training course.'

'I can build my business up slowly,' said Polly. 'I have savings. I can retrain. And it would mean still working with people, which is what I like best.'

'Plus, the *Daily Mail* are less interested in personal trainers than they are in social workers.'

'Exactly,' said Polly. 'Now I just have to break it to Hugh.'

'Why would he mind? If you're happier, it's better for the whole family, surely?'

'He doesn't think much of gyms, so I doubt he approves of personal trainers.'

'Well, he certainly approves of you, so he'll just have to accept it.'

'Plus, he could do with keeping fit. When you hit middle age, you're more vulnerable.'

'Point taken,' said Nel, with a smile.

They lapsed into silence in the sauna. The world might be going to hell in a handcart, but at least everyone would get there in good shape.

*

After Polly had found Hugh, somewhat exhausted after a few hours keeping Freya out of mischief, they decided to leave her with Fred and Nel, and go off for a morning coffee by themselves. Well, not exactly coffee: Hugh exercised his right to have builder's tea, or as close to that as was possible outside the British Isles. They passed on the cupcakes and Danish pastries. Hugh didn't want them, and while Polly certainly did, she thought it would look hypocritical for her to stuff her face, and so she stuffed her bag instead.

Once they had their drinks, they sat next to each other in the Explorer's Bar. They both had things they wanted to talk about.

'I've had a new idea,' they both said to each other at the same time.

'You go first,' said Hugh, when they had composed themselves.

'My idea was... I want to change my job. You know how stressed I have been about social work?' said Polly.

'Rushing around like a headless chicken?'

'That and my fingernails…'

'You hardly have any fingernails!'

'Exactly,' said Polly. 'Which is why I think I am going to pack in social work.'

'Wow,' said Hugh. 'That is something I wasn't expecting.'

'I am going to retrain. As a personal trainer…'

'Goodness,' said Hugh, taken aback. He didn't know what else to say, because he didn't quite know what a personal trainer did. Would she have to go to people's homes? Spend all her time in a tracksuit? It was quite a shock.

'I think I'd be good at it. I like people,' said Polly.

'You certainly like telling them what to do!'

'Hugh!'

'Only joking. Anyway, I agree, give it a go. But do you really think there's anybody who'd pay you?'

'Well, if there isn't a market in North London for a personal trainer, where is there?'

'Point taken,' said Hugh. 'Could you go back to being a social worker if it didn't work out?'

'They'd bite my hand off! Social workers are always in short supply.'

'Sounds like it's worth trying something different,' said Hugh. 'Seeing as you can always go back.'

'I just need a real change.'

'Then, go for it!' said Hugh.

'Anyway, what was your news?' she asked, squeezing his hand.

And Hugh explained to her about Fowl Play.

'Wooden chickens?' she said sceptically.

'Turkeys, guinea fowl, pheasants...' Hugh said. 'But not just birds. Anything. I could make a polar bear, if necessary.'

'That's a brilliant idea!' she said. 'It would really make the most of your carpentry skills.'

'And the whole reclaimed-wood thing,' he said, beaming.

'Plus, you have a natural affinity with young people,' Polly said.

'Have I?' said Hugh, rather pleased.

'You get on so well with Freya and her mates.'

'Fowl Play is a great name,' he said, embarrassed.

'Yes, fantastic!'

'Fred thought it up,' he admitted.

As they held hands in the Adventurer's Lounge, Hugh didn't want to speak too soon, but he thought that, between them, they might just have this marriage thing cracked. But right now, they had to rescue Fred and Nel from Freya, though looking at them, they didn't seem to want to be rescued.

Chapter 43

Gathering around for a last lunch, news of the broken camera had reached those concerned, who were badly disappointed. Now there was nothing to show from their antics, apart from a frozen vial of bear sperm. The demo had been a waste of time. Cyril and Lu were heroes, but only to the ship's passengers. Coffee seemed particularly bitter, and the cinnamon buns barely tasted sweet.

No wonder Fleur's last lecture was a scorching excoriation of all those failures to reverse the climate emergency with concerted government action, as had been promised in Paris. There had never been a fair COP since. Everyone talked about miracle fixes, of some magic new technology which would remove carbon from the atmosphere, but the miracle solution never arrived. Ingrid sat through the talk, staring at the audience as if to say, 'I told you so!' Cyril kept well away from the cat, and ostentatiously put on his FFP3 mask, with valve.

Fred and Nel went upstairs, where all the passengers were in a throng on deck. Above them, on the walkway outside the bridge, a crew member with a digital camera was trying to herd them into an orderly crowd for a photographic reminder of the voyage. Together with Captain Andersson, at the front of the scene, was Freya in her matching blue woolly hat, next to her mother and Hugh, with Fred and Nel arm-in-arm beside them.

Nel thought ruefully that the party now comprised her partner, his two friends, his god-daughter, his two aunts, her college friend and two Oil Rebellion protestors, plus Heather – it was nearly the same as Fred's birthday celebration at Threepwood Hall. So much for quiet birthdays. So much for 'gatherings' that turned out to be parties in the end.

Several digital photographs were taken. The crew member taking the snaps told everyone to '*Smil*!' and then, correcting herself, 'Say cheese!' Everyone obediently said, 'Cheese!' Hugh pointed out to Polly that you got a wider smile if you used the Norwegian word. Polly, who had a heavy nine-year-old on her shoulders, did not ask whether Nynorsk or Bokmål was better for group photos.

With the exchange of goodbyes, and sometimes phone numbers, the passengers dispersed. Many people gathered to shake Cyril's hand, but Marvin was nowhere to be seen, because he had been marched off the ship by the Norwegian Police. Donna, promising cakes, told Fred and Nel that it was about time they came to visit Grassington. At that moment, there was a shriek from downstairs. Fred and Nel looked at each other. They recognised the voice, and lung capacity, of Freya. She came running up to them, beaming.

'Guess what? The unicorn horn has come back! It's where it was, in the saloon. It must be magic. I think Captain Andersson will be very happy when I tell him.'

'That's fabulous! It might well be magic,' said Nel. 'I suspect that Captain Andersson may already know.' The nine-year-old raced off with her news to find her mum. Polly was not hugely surprised. Fred just raised his eyebrows at Nel. It was nice to see the two of them had bonded more on this trip. A few minutes later, Heather came up to the couple, as they stood at the rail watching Longyearbyen approach, and with it the end of the birthday cruise.

'Have you heard about the great narwhal mystery? It's quite exciting!'

'Nothing whatsoever,' said Fred innocently. 'Whatever can have happened?'

*

Heather's vague suspicions were soon quelled. It would always remain mysterious. She never put two and two together. It would have been quite a story had she done so.

Fred and Nel went below to their cabin; Nel was smiling her famous secret smile. At the beginning of their relationship, Fred had always asked her what she was thinking about. Now, he just enjoyed the fact that the woman he loved was happy. Fred was happy too. He was hugely relieved that there was no threat to his role as a solicitor. He couldn't afford to be struck off now, not when there was water pollution to fight at home and the climate emergency internationally. The campaigns needed a lawyer, not least to advise them when they were exercising their right to protest, and when they were breaking the law. Now everyone could breathe again.

'Do you want to join me in a tot of whisky?' said Fred, as they gathered their bags. 'I don't want to take the bottle with me, and there's only a little left!'

'I'd better give it a miss,' said Nel.

This wasn't like her, considered Fred, but thought no more of it. It was little hardship for him to finish the last of the malt before their departure. It would be a crime to leave anything in the bottle, and there had been quite enough crimes on this voyage already.

Chapter 44

That afternoon, the ship arrived back in the port at Longyearbyen, and the crew tied up. The buses were waiting, and there was even a fold-down ramp for Fred to wheel up. He thought how much he loved Norway. They accommodated him without making a fuss. It showed what was possible. All it took was money and the right attitude.

The crew, in their matching uniforms, lined up on the quayside to say goodbye. There was no sign of Helga Halvorsen, Freya's favourite crew member. Instead, proudly wearing her new woollen hat, Freya rushed up to her friend Captain Andersson and said farewell. He shook her hand formally. Fred waved at the captain too.

Fleur was due a few weeks' leave and, as a good environmentalist, she shunned the airport. She was accompanying the famous Cyril who, once in London, expected to be arrested for breach of the peace, or a public order offence, or whatever new crime the Government had dreamed up to prosecute environmental protesters. He was unlikely to be imprisoned, so the worst would be a fine, which his supporters were already queuing up to pay.

Nel had already said goodbye to her friend, with promises to meet in London. It was rather romantic, thought Fred – the journey, not the arrest – although it did mean Fleur would spend most of her leave on the train. Although, a twin bunk with her beloved might be rather fun. Fred thought he and Nel might like that sometime. With each other, of course, not Cyril. As long as it was accessible. He loved sleeper trains, despite rarely managing to sleep. Cary Grant had the right idea in *North by Northwest*.

When Fred and Nel and the rest of the birthday party got to the tiny airport, and checked in, they spotted a familiar figure in departures, and she wasn't alone. It was Lu, who waved them over. She was sitting on a stool at the bar. She looked much better in her own clothes than dressed as a polar bear or scantily clad in a towel. Beside her was someone who looked familiar, but Fred didn't recognise her. She was tall and blonde and Norwegian. She and Lu seemed to be together. Or at any rate, they were holding hands and laughing. Lu was smiling a lot.

'Are you drunk?' said Fred, suspiciously. It seemed unlikely. Not only was it the middle of the day, but it was also almost impossible to buy alcohol on Spitsbergen.

'I might be, slightly,' said Lu. 'Wouldn't you be?'

'After a successful demo against the odds?' said Fred, thinking that he probably would be.

'No, even better: imagine, I never have to see Cyril ever again! He's set off home by train already. He doesn't take flights, not Cyril,' said Lu.

'We knew that.'

'I gave my return ticket to Fleur. She says she wants to spend more time getting to know the great man. No chance of avoiding Cyril, with several days stuck on trains. She's welcome to him. And his bail conditions, once he gets back to the UK.'

'Is Paul going with them?' wondered Nel. 'Because that would certainly tend to cramp your style!'

'No, I think Paul was after Marvin, not Cyril. But the authorities will be waiting for Cyril when he gets off the train,' said Lu. 'They never did find the other polar-bear protestor, whoever they were,' she said, grinning widely.

'Funny, that,' said Nel, raising her eyebrows at her. Lu's companion giggled.

'Well, Fleur is obviously very keen on Cyril,' Lu said to Fred. 'I'm pleased for them.'

'His bare chin is certainly an improvement on his beard,' said Fred. 'Is Fleur staying in London?'

'I think she is. She said she has some meetings.'

'I think they're with broadcasters. I hope the footage is enough. Good luck to her,' said Nel. 'We need more diverse nature presenters.'

'My thoughts entirely,' said Lu. 'Sorry, have you met Helga already?'

'Morning!' said Helga, beaming at them.

'Morning, Helga,' said Fred, politely. 'I didn't recognise you out of uniform. Aren't you Freya's friend?'

'She's my friend now,' said Lu. 'Turns out she likes saunas.'

Helga blushed. Nel grinned at Lu. Fred smiled. He thought it was probably very much better if they did not know all the details. But it was good that Lu had met someone nice. Maybe she could go back to dancing. There were some great Norwegian dance theatres, weren't there? Or could Helga get a job on an English vessel? Fred always wanted relationships to last. But some connections were like ships in the night. It was early days to know about this one.

At that point, Hugh and Polly wandered over to say hello and goodbye. Filled with several tots of aquavit, and consequently all the amiability of a drunk, Lu flung her arms around Polly and kissed her smack on the lips. Fred could see Hugh flinching at the intimacy. It wasn't so much that he was jealous, rather that marriage had not dispelled his insecurities. He was constantly worried that Polly really wanted to be with someone else.

'Hello, Polly. It can't be far from my place to yours. I'd like to see more of you after we get back to London,' slurred Lu. But it was her final parting shot that Hugh was going to mull over for months: 'Not that I haven't seen all of you already.'

Fred winced and looked away. Hugh had definitely heard that, if his alarmed face was anything to go by. He looked like a man who's just realised he's gone away for a week and left the gas on. Thank goodness, Fred thought, he and Nel weren't sitting next to Hugh and Polly on the plane. He could hear the protestations beginning as Hugh and Polly queued ahead of them for the departure gate. Polly hadn't done anything wrong, and she was good at mediation. Fred had heard it confidently asserted that love conquered all, in which case, it had better get on and do some conquering, then. Fred sighed. No doubt one of them would tell him about it later.

Everywhere they went at the airport there were new friends – there was Aunty Bella and Aunt Donna, still clutching their Scrabble... There were their Norwegian friends, and the German group, and the elderly British Brexiteers, now suddenly friendly to the European passengers, and the Americans, and all the other faces that had become familiar over the last nine days – and Paul, waving at them.

Fred logged on to the airport Wi-Fi and checked his emails. Amid the junk there was a very welcome invitation to be part of a disability NGO delegation to the next COP, which delighted him. It was about time that the environmentalists got disability right. With any luck, the COP would be held down under or somewhere he knew people. He better start booking a ship now. And, of course, the Earth had higher temperatures last year than in all of human history. Not great at all. That polar bear they had seen was living on borrowed time. Or stepping on thin ice. It was certainly hotting up. For once, the metaphors mattered.

Nel and Freya joined Fred at the departure gate for boarding. They had been busy buying liquorice in the airport shop. Fred thought the flavour was how he imagined earwax to taste, but Freya and Nel shared a liking for it. So did most of the Nordic region, as far as he could see. There was no accounting for taste, and he supposed it was better than fermented little auk, or whatever they ate in Greenland. At least liquorice was not an endangered species.

And at least Freya was safe from domestic disagreement, with him and Nel, thought Fred. They might have different tastes, but they were the same at the level of bread and butter. And cheese, for that matter (in moderation). It was not so much that he was much more self-confident than Hugh, it was just that it was impossible to doubt someone so sincere and wholehearted as Nel. She would love him whatever shape he was.

He showed her the email inviting him to the next COP and she was delighted for him. She knew that disability and climate change was an area in which he could really make a difference. Plus, unlike her, he enjoyed working on the world stage. And this time, he had been to the Arctic to see for himself. Not many people could say they had watched the Oil Rebellion Spitsbergen action in person. Fred wondered if he could bear to be a friend of Cyril. He thought Nel would probably be quite pleased if they invited him to dinner in Kennington.

Once they had shown their passports and passed through to the gate, Freya saw Helga window-shopping the one outlet in the Departures area, and rushed over and put her arms around the sailor's middle. Helga lifted Freya into the air and put her on her shoulders. Helga was tall and strong, and Freya was enjoying her vantage point over the tiny airport. Rather her than me, thought Fred. He hated heights. Plus, although Freya was not the largest nine-year-old, he still wouldn't enjoy giving her a piggyback. Helga did not appear to mind. She seemed a genuine person, and sincere about her friendship with Freya, which Fred approved of.

Freya was flying back to London with Fred and Nel, because after Oslo they were headed for Gatwick – easy for South London – and Georgie, Freya's other mum, was going to meet them at Arrivals with Fenner, their dog, and probably one or two things she wanted to say to Freya. Georgie was also an old friend of Fred's from college days, though not quite as close a friend as Polly. Georgie spent as much time as she could in Brighton these days. Fred suspected that her new lady lived there. No doubt he'd find out the full story in due course.

In any case, Georgie had lived with the scare of Freya's disappearance, so she might be a bit cross: Freya had lied to her mum, after all. But, as everyone had found, it was impossible to be angry with Freya for long, and she was more than capable of looking after herself. It would not be in the least surprising if she later had a seagoing career. As long as it involved a woolly hat, she'd be happy. Adventures no doubt awaited.

Boarding a plane was always an adventure for Fred. Whereas others climbed steps, he was used to being put aboard via Ambilift, a sort of hydraulic van, or even by forklift, in some cases, after transferring to the narrow aisle chair which would be wheeled down to his seat. He never knew whether he would be first or last on the plane, but he knew he would always be last off. Although, there was one time on a budget airline when the Ambilift had arrived before the steps and he was first off – an unprecedented and never-repeated treat. He preferred not to remember the time in Berlin, also travelling on a budget airline, when he had been put on the wrong plane, and nearly ended up in Timisoara. If he hadn't worked out that all his neighbours were speaking Romanian and probably weren't destined for Stansted, he might be there now.

He felt lucky to be using a manual chair, and not just because it made his chest and arms so muscular. Although it was still possible for baggage handlers to break it – one time a badly attached clamp had even bent his wheel – it was far more robust than the power chairs which others had to rely on, and which were so frequently bashed about in transit. Every time he said goodbye to his chair, it was like losing a part of him. He always watched out for it, waiting on the tarmac to be loaded, and was always relieved when it was awaiting him at the Arrivals gate for a reunion. And it almost always was, thankfully.

Freya was delighted to board first with Fred and Nel, and felt very important. When everyone else joined the plane, she waved at all her new friends filing past. Lubna and Helga were going to stay in Oslo. Bella and Donna were evidently going to play Scrabble all the way home. Fred just hoped that Bella's practising paid off, and she got to the National Scrabble Championships that autumn. Fred thought that keeping quiet about the betting was probably advisable. He couldn't see the Scrabble world being very happy about crowning a Scrabble hustler as champion.

Once the rest had boarded the plane, and it had been de-iced, it then taxied and took off, en route for Oslo. Freya, who had the window seat, fell asleep against Nel. It had been an action-packed trip, and Fred and Nel were more excited about the aerial view of the Svalbard archipelago than she was. She muttered Russian numbers to herself as she drifted off.

'It's lovely to see how comfortable she is with you,' said Fred, smiling at Nel and indicating Freya curled up in the window seat. 'It feels like you've really got to know her this holiday.'

'It's been fun!' admitted Nel. 'And good preparation.'

'Preparation?' said Fred, puzzled. He tried to remember the calendar of events that awaited them back at The Big Green Campaigning Machine. Was Nel speaking at a school next week? Or was it another Parents for the Planet group?

Nel smiled at him.

'I'm pregnant,' she said.

Epilogue

Fred's nephews Andy and Gerry were as good as their word and edited the film footage of the Spitsbergen demo into a TikTok, which Fred certainly needed explaining to him. At a minute or so long, it didn't look like a beg, they explained, and it had a banging beat. They had thought of setting it to Drill music, but that would be too obvious. Now, with a poignant soundtrack, plus some clever reverse footage of the cartwheel, and a close-up of the banner reading 'No Drilling in the Arctic', it prompted, as hoped, greater awareness of the threat to the Arctic and global heating. Rarely can one shaven beard have launched such a chain of events.

The cartwheeling polar bear was on the front pages of every newspaper, and the TikTok was shown on every TV news for days. Heather's cable channel were furious that she hadn't got the scoop, and schemed how they could take the credit for the TikTok. Across the world, there was public revulsion at oil drilling in the Arctic, particularly among young people.

Regardless of hue of government, every country faced an aggrieved populace, and leaders, whatever they personally thought, were forced to speak out. As a side effect, everywhere, facial hair had never been more unpopular, and the polar bear costume returned to a prominence it had not enjoyed for nearly a century. Few student graduation photos in the decade that followed were free of a polar bear costume. Hugh chuckled to himself every time he saw one.

While the cartwheeling polar bear and the melting ice chilled the hearts of the whole world, the images were also responsible for a change in fortune for the protagonists. Although Heather never got her interview with the American president, on the back of the TikTok and her book about their excursion to the Arctic, she became a political interviewer to rival Christiane Amanpour or Stephen Sackur.

Cyril, who notoriously had come to prominence in his bearded state, was now a new St Paul in his fervour. His chin shone with righteousness and his eyes gleamed with zeal as he toured the TV studios excoriating Big Oil. His stunt became known as 'Cyril's razor'. Cyril's version of Ockham's razor was dependence on oil, as he challenged politicians to cut loose from hydrocarbons and adopt a net-zero economy. An ambitious marketing executive even sent a message asking if Cyril would advertise shaving foam, in return for a generous donation to Oil Rebellion.

Nor was Lu immune from the wave of support which followed the Spitsbergen protest. After her (North) pole antics, she received an offer from *Strictly*, and she duly won the show, dancing, of course, with a woman. A chat show followed: it was about time that there was a woman-led programme, and she was a natural, with personality and style to match. Her show began with a triumphant cartwheel into the studio.

Acknowledgements

Thanks are due to Robert Brown, Joanna Cox, Lissa Evans and Julia Redhead for invaluable suggestions. Fiona Ellis and Tom Wakeford each went to Svalbard, and survived to tell me all about it, from reindeer to Skidoo. I went to the Arctic with Joanna Cox and David Ruebain, who played Scrabble with me on a memorable Hurtigruten voyage. Kristjana Kristiansen arranged for us all to have a fantastic early breakfast in Trondheim. My neighbour Monica inspired me about being a personal trainer. Deidre Leaske told me about social work. My friends Lisa and Wildeve consented to my using their names.

Thanks to Jan Grue for Norwegian language advice. Appreciation to Suki and David Hubbard for providing a home from home where some of this was written. Thanks to Nick Watson for sharing neuropathic pains as well as P. G. Wodehouse joys. Gratitude to Lissa Evans, Hannah Kuper, Kate Beales and Katharine Quarmby for accompanying me through the highs and lows of writing. Huge thanks to my agent Emma Shercliff and my editor Daniela Ferrante and my copy editor Daniela Nava, who between them did everything possible to help make this sequel as good as the first book.

One final word. The Arctic contains 13 per cent of the world's undiscovered oil and 30 per cent of the world's undiscovered gas. Drilling in the Arctic is difficult and has a terrible environmental impact in itself. But there has already been exploratory drilling in the Arctic by Canada, Denmark, Norway, Russia and the United States (although Canada and Denmark have ceased drilling and imposed a moratorium). The United States has been responsible for exploratory drilling in the Arctic National Wildlife Refuge. Russia is currently using nuclear-powered ice-breakers to open up routes through the ice to its Northern ports, from where it plans to export oil and gas. In real life, there is no happy ending.

Preview
The Ha-Ha

Chapter 1

A small but exquisitely stately home, set amidst an emerald pond of parkland, Threepwood Hall was the ideal marriage plot. Through that pillared portico, Emma Woodhouse could have orchestrated the local gentry. Behind those blue window shutters, Bertie Wooster could have resolved the most challenging affair of the heart. In that kitchen garden, Lord Emsworth could have pottered to his heart's content. An adornment to the county of Suffolk, Threepwood Hall exuded bonhomie, from cellars to chimneys.

This balmy day in May showed off the Hall at its very best. The raked gravel waited expectantly, as if for the carriage wheels of the propertied classes. Beams of sunlight swept languidly over the rose garden and dappled a pond on which ducks dallied. Somewhere nearby, a pig groaned appreciatively as an underling scratched his back. The Heritage Trust had restored this Regency jewel with loving care. No wonder that more than one production manager had their phone number on speed dial, it was the type of location that demanded an epic love story.

The village beyond the Hall featured an appropriate supporting cast. In the church belfry, a trio of teachers were persistently venting their classroom frustrations on their bell ropes. Opposite the pub, a fund manager in red trousers was rolling the cricket pitch in preparation for the coming match and his own coronary. A mother pondering alimony in a puce puffer jacket was walking her labradoodle through the park. Everything appeared to offer visitors a return to an idyllic England before agribusiness and house price inflation had made the countryside a monoculture. But by Monday morning, each extra would have returned to London.

In the back kitchen of the Hall, a man of nigh on forty summers sat with his laptop open, stressing about his spreadsheet when he would have preferred to have imagined the woman of his dreams. Unfolded, as it were, Fred would have been a tall man. He had once played wing on the school rugby field, such was the length of his limbs and his fleetness of foot. Now, he could lay claim to 'long' but sadly no longer to 'tall'. Worse, twenty years of paralysis had left his legs like anaemic twiglets, as he had confessed to a sympathetic friend. Despite this, he still had the grace of the great rugby player, that ability to weave through obstacles and avoid the bruising encounters and crunching tackles which sadden most lives. Excepting the undodged disaster of the car crash, the life he led had been charmed, for the most part. As a result, he retained a youthful grace which endeared him to staff, clients and above all friends.

Ordinarily Fred was as sunny as a globally-warmed summer afternoon, with the genial disposition of a small-town solicitor. Today, however, despite the wheelchair-accessible stately home of which he was proprietor for the weekend, he was as tremulous as a climate activist beset by melting icecaps and extreme weather events. He peered at his notes, while fiddling with his wheelchair push rims in a manner that his psychologist pal would surely have slapped a label on. Dressed for the part in a rugby shirt and green corduroys, he was temporarily lord of all he surveyed, and he wasn't sure he liked it.

It had been so difficult juggling everyone's needs. He had filled the Hall with people who had almost nothing in common, except him. Most had been to one of his previous birthday parties, except Alberto, Robin's partner, who was a completely unknown quantity. Fred just hoped that the Costa Rican would get on with everyone, and vice versa. Another potential problem was Hugh, his oldest school friend, who would rather be taken for a misanthrope than admit to being shy, and who resisted every effort to be included. And since shortly after graduation, Fred's glimpses of Heather had mainly come via television screens or computer monitors, though she had always loomed large in his imagination.

Then was the big problem of divorce clustering. In his parents' day, divorce had been something that happened like a V2 rocket, a single hit that devastated entire neighbourhoods. Now it seemed to be like a chicken pox epidemic for forty-year-olds. First one couple succumbed, and then before you knew it the whole peer group had come down with a nasty case of decree nisi, which made it extraordinarily difficult to plan a get-together. You couldn't invite Person A and Person B together, even though you liked them both, because now they wouldn't exchange a friendly vowel. And then if Person C was the cause of the split of A and B, you couldn't invite him or her either... Person D and Person E would have had children together, and whoever had the ferals that weekend couldn't come. It had been a minefield. Which reminded Fred why he steered clear of Family Law as far as possible. He did a disconsolate wheelie in front of his laptop.

Take Freya, for example, only daughter of Polly, who was another college friend. Polly was bisexual and her ex, Fred's other friend, Georgina, was off with her new beau, or rather belle, that weekend so there was no alternative but to bring Freya along. Polly was one of his oldest friends and he loved her to bits. She was always going to attend; she had to, despite the seven-year-old in tow. It wasn't as if it was a problem for Freya to be hanging out with a bunch of adults. She'd seen everything and could swear in several languages. Thankfully there were enough twin rooms for her to share with Polly.

Thinking of Freya reminded Fred of catering, and he switched to another page of his spreadsheet. Freya must not have animal products of any kind, he'd noted. Not because of an allergy, more because Georgina would see red if her daughter were ever to sample cadavers (her words). In his experience, Freya seemed to follow her own unique dietary code, largely based around mashed potato, sweetcorn and vegan ice cream, a nutritional wasteland in which she apparently thrived. Fred glanced around the kitchen. He'd already allocated the left-hand fridge as vegan, and stocked the freezer compartment with Kinderglace, a wincingly expensive soya-based ice cream. If a birthday party was now impossible without a spreadsheet, did that say more about him, or about the modern age?

Also available by Tom Shakespeare

The Ha-Ha

Fred Twistleton is about to turn forty. Gathering with his friends to celebrate at a rented stately home, he finally hopes to get together with his college crush, the woman of his dreams, Heather. But Fred is also keen to publish his memoirs, and Heather realises the revelations they contain could threaten her career as a high-flying foreign correspondent.

When the treasured manuscript goes missing under mysterious circumstances, Fred's at a loss. Could someone have stolen it? Where has the resident pig gone? And will all the group remain friends by the end of the weekend? With burst pipes, sunken kayaks, and suspicious puddings, thank goodness Fred is only going to have one fortieth birthday.

Out now!